PENGUIN BOOKS

LOVING ATTITUDES

Rachel Billington was educated at a Catholic day school in London and later read English at university. She then worked for Associated Television as a researcher. In 1965 she moved to New York to work for ABC television on documentary programmes. New York provided the setting for her first novel, *All Things Nice*, published in 1967, which she wrote on her return to England. Her other novels include *The Big Dipper*, *Lilacs out of the Dead Land*, *Cock Robin*, *Beautiful*, *A Painted Devil*, *A Woman's Age*, *The Garish Day* and *Occasion of Sin*, many of which are published by Penguin. She has written the children's books *Rosanna and the Wizard-Robot*, *Star-Time*, *The First Christmas* and *The First Easter*. She has also had short stories and features published. She reviews for the *Financial Times* and for other publications. She has had four plays produced for radio and two for television, *Don't Be Silly* and *Life After Death*.

Rachel Billington is married to film and theatre director Kevin Billington and they have four children.

Loving Attitudes

Rachel Billington

Penguin Books

PENGUIN BOOKS

Published by the Penguin Group
27 Wrights Lane, London W8 5TZ, England
Viking Penguin Inc., 40 West 23rd Street, New York, New York 10010, USA
Penguin Books Australia Ltd, Ringwood, Victoria, Australia
Penguin Books Canada Ltd, 2801 John Street, Markham, Ontario, Canada L3R 1B4
Penguin Books (NZ) Ltd, 182–190 Wairau Road, Auckland 10, New Zealand

Penguin Books Ltd, Registered Offices: Harmondsworth, Middlesex, England

First published in Great Britain by Hamish Hamilton 1988
Published in Penguin Books 1989
1 3 5 7 9 10 8 6 4 2

Printed and bound in Great Britain by
Richard Clay Ltd, Bungay, Suffolk
Filmset in Palatino

To Charlotte and Eden,
loving friends

Contents

Part One

1

Part Two

53

Part Three

127

Part One

CHAPTER ONE

Mary was sucking cream off her right index finger. She dipped her finger into the carton and stuffed it into her mouth, sucking greedily. Her eyes were glazed, partly with pleasure, partly because she was looking past the kitchen into the garden. It was dark outside and a patch of snowdrops in the grass was lit dramatically from the window.

In the sitting-room her husband played building blocks with a fire. Now she could hear the roar as he blew and fanned. Mary Tempest sucked voraciously at her finger and the kettle began to boil.

From across the room the telephone rang with an old-fashioned resonance unlike its London warble. Mary dashed to the fridge as David appeared.

'The telephone's ringing.'

'It's so loud.' She gestured helplessly with the carton. The fridge, she indicated, had her in thrall; if not the fridge, the kettle. Inanimate objects were despotic, particularly this importunate telephone. Why should he not answer it? She wanted to wash her finger. David stared at her with fire-brightened eyes before turning away.

'Hello.'

She went to the sink.

'What? Who? Yes, she is.'

Mary let go of the tap with a sense of grievance for they were on holiday here.

'Hello?' She could feel the imprint of David's fingers on the receiver as she felt them on her flesh, a strong comforting grasp.

'Can I speak with Mrs Tempest?'

There was a girl on the telephone, her voice faint and oddly spaced, perhaps American.

'Yes, this is Mary Tempest.'

David took three strides across the room and drew the curtains. Mary saw the darkness fall across the snowdrops as if she were outside with them.

'Sorry. Who did you say you were?'

David was big in the room, not used to cottage intimacy. He put his arm round her and laid his evening-bristled cheek against hers. He had seen her sucking the cream.

She smiled, pushing her cheek upwards into his and he smiled too, moving away, pleased with himself, back to the sitting-room and the fire.

What was the girl saying? Her name was Elizabeth Crocker. She had come over from America especially to meet her.

It was ten o'clock and David's digital watch pinged from the table. He had discarded it there during supper, saying time was a predator, masticating minutes, months and years.

'It has taken a very long time to find you.' The intensity of the girl's voice forced itself into Mary's full consciousness.

Her own voice changed, becoming brisk and attentive, the voice of her unwanted working self.

'Can you give me an idea in what way I can help you? I shall be back in my office in four weeks.'

'I want to see what you're like. That's all.' There was a desperation in the girl's voice now. So unlike an American not to come to the point. Perhaps she was crazy. Perhaps . . . David had visited America last year.

'I'm seeing no one at the moment.'

David reappeared in the doorway. His face was red from the fire, his hair hung across his forehead, lending his normally pale and placid features a Bacchanalian air.

'I'm afraid I must go now.'

David mouthed: 'Whatever? Whoever?'

Mary shook her head, tears in her eyes. Outside the snowdrops were unlit, desolate.

David mimed putting the phone back on the hook but it was stuck to her fingers.

The girl cried out with redoubled energy, 'You see I'm your daughter!'

CHAPTER TWO

The sun shone on thin snow through which spiky grass pressed like hair on a bald head. Mary laid her cheek against the glass of the window and felt a wetness there that wasn't tears. Behind her David slept. I want to see what you're like, the girl had said. But did she have a right? Perhaps an academic question since there seemed no stopping her. I'm your daughter.

Mary turned round and looked at David, humped under the bedclothes. If the girl had been his lover, how would she be feeling now? The idea was a diversion, a red herring from her night thoughts or her inability to think. She could think about David's faithlessness, the possibility of him falling in love with someone else. It had a name and place in her consciousness. It happened to other people, her friends; it may have happened to her without her knowing it.

David heaved and groaned, spliced for a moment by a shaft of wintry sun. Mary drew back the curtains a little and remembered their arrival at this cottage and how it had seemed a refuge from the tight-drawn strings of London and people and work. Guilt and responsibility. She had expected to be stroked smooth by the slow quiet stoicism of the countryside, by David's loving attentions. Like a child. Did she want David to be her father?

I'm your daughter, the girl had insisted, perfectly within her rights. You're my mother, she could have added with echoes of crucifixion and divine presentation. Woman, this is your son. Son, this is your mother. And from that moment on, he took her into his home and looked after her.

Mary began to shake with the cold of wintry exhaustion and shock. She started up as if to climb back into the warmth of the bed and the heavy security of David's limbs, arms and legs folded over her like a clamp. But instead she went to the bathroom. Her face met her, managing to be both bleak and puffy, wrinkled crags of rock separated by puffed-up duvets of flesh. The early morning light bleached out her usually pink cheeks and dark blue eyes, turned her chestnut hair a greyish green.

Shivering, she splashed water on her face and neck. A flicker of hope gave her the energy to consider making two mugs of hot tea to drink in bed. The flicker burnt a little more brightly as she went downstairs. She would put off thinking till she had the tea in her hand.

David splayed his arms and legs to the edge of the bed. It was not as wide as their bed in London and he had been repressing an urge to stretch all night long. On occasions, marriage seemed one long repression to stretch. He had felt Mary sitting at the window but he could not move until she had left the room and gone downstairs. This was not the moment to display a luxurious revel in her absence, in freedom, in solitude. David stretched so hard that the bed creaked under him. Poor Mary. When she came up he would make her talk about it all.

The tea tray gave Mary satisfaction. Mugs of tea and heated brown rolls and butter. She had plucked a few snowdrops from the white garden coverlet and arranged them in a glass jar. But as she climbed the stairs, she caught sight of the stems hanging limply in the water with an uneasy sense of their vulnerability.

'Darling! I should have brought it to you.'

'I was awake. Up.'

'Yes.'

They sat side by side in bed, drinking their tea.

'Is it such a shock?' began David, tentatively.

'I don't want to see her!' She spoke wildly, as she had the night before when she had screamed, I don't want to see you! I don't want to see you! She had handed the receiver to David, whispering, I don't want to see her! I don't want to see her.

'I know. I know.' David patted her hand as he had patted her shoulder the night before. Ineffectual, but done with love. 'She exists. You always knew she existed.'

6

'Yes. Yes.' Tears filled her eyes so that the irises shimmered as if captured beneath glass. Mary seldom looked directly at those she loved or those who loved her. At work, she was straightforward, even aggressive but at home she was quiet, cheerful and secret. She did not cry wildly, I don't want to see her!

'Did she say how long she was in England?'

'I don't know.'

'At least she'll leave sometime.' David, speaking in calm and practical tones, looked at her kindly.

'Oh. Ah.' Mary felt as if her heart was being squeezed like a concertina, producing little ugly squawks. How could David speak as if this happening, this bolt out of the sky were something rational, open to logical thought?

'Did she tell Lucy who she was?'

'No. I don't know.'

'But Lucy had told her where we are?'

'Yes.' Now Mary could neither drink nor eat. Her mouth was filled with squeaks of distress.

The telephone rang. 'That's probably Lucy now.' David's brisk departure left a backwash of his relief to be gone.

The sun was hurting Mary's eyes so she turned over and put her head in the pillow.

Lucy lay on her stomach on the floor of her parents' London bedroom. She was drinking coffee and doing a fairly complicated back exercise at the same time as she talked to her father. This was unusual so early on a Saturday but she wanted to instill a sense of virtue in herself so she wouldn't feel such guilt about what she was about to say.

'I'm afraid I can't come down after all.'

'But we're expecting you. We're looking forward to it. Your mother's . . . ' David broke off in mid-sentence which was unusual for him but Lucy was too self-absorbed to notice.

'It's so far and I haven't the money and there's a party tonight!'

'Oh Lucy!' David felt more depressed now than he had all last night, all this morning. This was his daughter. 'But we haven't seen you since the beginning of term.'

'Sorry.' Lucy was forcing her legs against nature so the word came out in a gulp.

'Is there anything the matter?' She knew about that girl.

'Oh, Dad!'

7

She didn't know.

'Did you get a call last night from an American girl?'

He had been more like a man than Mary'd ever thought possible. He made it difficult for her to breathe even on their first meeting. She had never recovered from that feeling of suffocation which she had assumed was love but might have been terror or guilt. Or all three. He had been married, to a quiet woman about whom he talked affectionately and naturally but without any sense of what she had considered love. At that age, love had to be passion or it was nothing. He seemed to feel the same, although he was so much older, and he would never leave his wife. She knew that, although they didn't talk about it, just as she knew he had made love to many other women and girls before he had met her. And been in love with them too, most probably, although she didn't concentrate on that aspect. He was one of the most handsome men she'd ever seen.

'Lucy's not coming.' David touched her shoulder. His voice was irritable.

Mary rolled over. 'I'm sorry.' How could he be irritated by such an absolutely to be expected event? She made her eyes clear and wide.

David saw her calmness with relief. She was beginning to recover from the shock. Soon she would be able to see it was not the end of the world. People had all sorts of complications in their pasts, even in their presents. Something like a smile of self-irony, disguising a sliver of self-congratulation and a sliver of guilt forced him to turn away from Mary's open face. There were things that he had to remember to hide.

'I'm sorry about my, my hysteria.'

David sat down on the bed and gently stroked her forehead. She didn't have to apologise to him but all the same it was welcome as an indication of normal service. He respected her need for protective colouring.

'You had a perfectly natural reaction.' Her skin was young, desirable. He turned, with the idea of getting back into bed.

'The girl will come here because Lucy told her the way.'

8

He felt Mary's body become rigid. No. He would not touch her. 'But I shall be with you and I won't let her stay long.' He stood up now, brisk again. 'I'll go and shave.'

'Yes. I'll dress.'

'We can work out shopping and things like that.' The briskness of his motion, his organising intentions contrasted with her lassitude made him cruel for a second. He turned at the door. 'You must admit it's her right to see you.'

Anger contracted Mary's stomach and glazed her eyes further, none of which David noticed.

He shaved merrily, pleased there was piping hot water in this little cottage, way out in the country. He would be kind to Mary for these four weeks, help her through this crisis, take the opportunity to atone for the affection he felt for a girl, no woman, for she was not young, the affection he felt for a woman in the office. She was no threat to Mary but he would be glad to regulate the balance of good behaviour. He did not consider the possibility that the appearance of Mary's child by another man might affect him.

Lucy went back to the bed where her friend still lay, sprawled and naked. His black hair spread across the pillow and his eyes were shut but she knew he wasn't asleep.

'I did it.'

'Congratulations.'

He thought she was too close to her parents, particularly her father. He thought it was important at her age to break right away from her home and find her own attitudes.

'Would you like some coffee?'

'Yup.'

He still didn't open his eyes nor smile but Lucy was not offended. She knew that the manner which an objective observer might perceive as selfish or uncouth actually disguised love and tenderness. Otherwise why would he be with her? She was nothing special.

Mary dressed slowly, putting on a pink sweater, painting her lips and cheeks to match. Downstairs she could hear David opening and shutting cupboard doors. Usually his energy encouraged her at the beginning of the day but today it was distracting. She would take a walk on her own, in the snow. Elizabeth Crocker, the girl had given herself that name.

The hired car was red and shiny but the gears were stiff which made it feel unwilling like a horse which had been ridden by too many amateurs.

Elizabeth, who was impatient and efficient, looked sideways at the map and reckoned it would take her four or five hours to reach Skillington. The man at the garage had said the roads were very bad for the last fifty miles. They might even be snow-covered if the winds had caused drifting. It was a wild part of the South-West, he'd implied, not easily penetrated. When she'd suggested snow ploughs should have been out by now, he looked at her with such a lack of comprehension that she wondered if they had another word for snow plough here in England. Not for the first time she missed Bob.

Bob and she were to be married in the spring and he had wanted to come over with her. Of course he had wanted to be with her but she had insisted she must see this thing through on her own. Besides Bob was the one who had suggested that her mother might not be too thrilled at finding her popping up suddenly out of nowhere – well, out of Brooklyn, New York, to be exact. Bob, although not so clever as her, was always right.

Elizabeth sighed and changed gears noisily as she hit yet another traffic jam. Where was this motorway that was supposed to get her out of London? At least her mother's husband seemed a kind sort of man. And he might have been forgiven for doing a little quiet screaming himself. But then the English manner made it so difficult for her to know what people were thinking.

'I don't want to see you!' her mother had cried out. Well, at least that was clear.

And here she was, driving out to force a meeting. What else could she do? She should have called Bob, but the time difference had defeated her. He would have shared some of the heavy weight that was groping inside her. It wasn't healthy to feel so much tension. She tried to breathe deeply and slowly the way her yoga teacher had demonstrated but succeeded only in narrowly missing going through a red light.

'Fuck!' She slammed on her breaks. Tears tickled her eyes but she rubbed them away angrily. One thing she was not going to do was turn back.

*

A screen of heavy grey clouds was sliding across the sun. It happened so slowly that Mary didn't notice until she found she needed a light in the low-ceilinged living-room.

David had gone into town to do the shopping. He had left her with a look of understanding for her lethargy, as if it were only the legacy of a sleepless night, but she knew he was glad to go. He would probably have a beer in a nice old pub and read the local newspaper. He was good at escape, taking on the colour of his surroundings. When they went abroad, tourists asked him the way.

Now that the sun had gone in, Mary didn't feel like walking. The fields and hills looked cold and intimidating. Instead she would make a large fire and sit beside it, reading one of the books chosen for just such an occasion. The girl could not come yet, even if she had set out early with American-style efficiency.

My baby, an American woman, twenty-two years old, determined to come and see me. Mary hesitated over the fireplace with a page of screwed-up *Financial Times* in her hand. The baby had been born in an Oxford hospital. Although she had decided to have it adopted before the birth and the hospital had been suitably instructed, on the second morning a nurse had brought her along to be breast-fed.

The nurse, whom she could picture better than the baby, was young, red-eyed as if from too little sleep or crying. She thrust the baby forward saying briskly, 'Three minutes on each side for the first time. Do you need any help?'

'I'm . . . ' The nurse's efficiency was too intense for Mary.

'Bottle?'

'No. I'm . . . '

'Come on, then. I'll give you a hand.'

She found her nipple pushed into the baby's mouth before she could explain. Immediately a vice pulled at her, making her gasp.

'There you are. A great little sucker.' The nurse rushed out again with an approving expression.

Ten seconds later, she was back. In an even greater hurry. She pulled the baby from Mary's breast.

'Why didn't you tell me?'

'I . . . '

But this time her words were drowned by the angry baby's crying. The nurse shut the door firmly behind them but Mary listened to the baby's crying all the way down the corridor till it reached the nursery. That was the sum total of her relationship with this daughter who was coming to see me.

She hadn't seen him again either, Richard Beck, such an ordinary name now. The father as much as she was the mother which was not at all.

Snow with serrated edges like ravioli floated across the window. Mary went back to stuffing pink newspaper into the fireplace.

Elizabeth was recovering from a crash. Only a very small crash. More of a bang really, as she turned out of the forecourt of the cafe where she'd stopped for lunch. It was entirely her fault, caused by lack of sleep, strained nerves and unfamiliarity with the right-hand drive.

She explained this to the driver of the car who was angry in what she considered an unreasonable and very un-English way.

'You bloody women drivers! You're all the same.'

Elizabeth was astonished by the force of his anger.

'But I only just touched your bumper. Look, there's not a mark.' She was shaking, partly with cold and partly with shock. This was a perfectly reasonable way for her body to react, she told herself, while this man, with his loud-mouthed bullying, was well on the way to a nervous breakdown.

'There should be a law forbidding bloody women to have cars.'

Elizabeth felt sorry for the woman, presumably his wife, cradled in the front seat of his car. He must turn on her in just the same way every time she burnt the toast.

Elizabeth was a medical student but for the last year she had been majoring in psychoanalysis. At the root of all relationships is the relationship with the mother.

Lucy and her friend, Jo, sat in bed eating baked beans and burnt toast. This was Lucy's only concession to feminism. She hadn't burnt the toast deliberately but on the other hand she hadn't taken the trouble to throw it away and start again. It was a fine point, perhaps, but one that Jo would understand.

'This toast is burnt.'

'Yes.' A pause. Perhaps he didn't understand. 'Do you mind?'

'Not particularly. Do you?'

'If you cover it with beans it doesn't taste too bad.'

'No.'

A pause. 'Shall we go out somewhere?'

Jo looked at the window. 'It's snowing.'

'We could go to a film.'

'What about the party?'

'It doesn't start till late.'

Jo leant over to put his plate on the floor. 'I'm going for a pee.' He looked at her sideways, as if estimating. It was the sort of look that caused Lucy to hold her breath. She couldn't imagine what he was thinking but she knew it was something important about her. He reached out his hand to her breast which was demurely covered by a man's shirt – one of her father's as it happened, which Jo would not have appreciated.

'But first I want to squeeze your breast. Like this.' He squeezed until Lucy felt her nipple harden and scrape against the shirt. 'And then I want to open your shirt and pull it out.'

Lucy had big firm breasts, her best feature as she knew very well, as Jo had told her. She watched almost objectively as he held the round globe outside her shirt. If it wasn't that his touch made her soften all through, she could imagine that her breast had nothing to do with the rest of her body.

'And then I'm going to bend over and suck your nipple.'

'I thought you wanted to go for a pee,' mumbled Lucy, using the hand nearest her still-covered breast to put down her baked beans.

'I do. But the need got diverted into another channel.'

'Two channels for one licence,' giggled Lucy weakly. Was it only sex they had in common?

CHAPTER THREE

He had been her first lover, the first man she'd ever been in love with, the first man who had made love to her. Love, terror and guilt. The existence of his wife had cast a cloak of darkness and secrecy. But then passion likes darkness and secrecy. It grows red and strong like a fire when you enclose it with a sheet of newspaper.

Mary held up the remains of the *Financial Times* across the small fireplace.

David started on his second half of the local beer. The first had tasted strong, of hops and smokey fires and summer earth, but this second was nondescript, which was always the way. Nothing ever lived up to the first heady experience. David sighed contentedly for it was an old idea with no real power to depress.

He looked round the saloon bar and read a notice advertising home-made pies. Would it be an act of gross marital disloyalty to stay here and have the perfect lunch in his own company or the undemanding company of these other country beer drinkers? To his left was a young burly man in a tweed jacket who looked like the new race of prosperous farmer. He was drinking a large gin and tonic. To his right was a middle-aged couple, comfortably scruffy with a pint each of Guinness in front of them. He thought he'd seen the woman at an antique stall in the snow-blown centre of town which would explain why they needed a warming drink. Across the room sat a heavy old man with a drinker's red puckered nose, but sharp blue eyes and a strong West Country drawl. He was cracking jokes with the barlady who was pale and thin and pretty.

For that moment David felt more affection for these strangers than he did for his much-cherished wife.

The snow was sticking round the edge of the windscreen and it seemed to be coming down more heavily not less. Elizabeth looked at her watch irritably: 1.30. Not more than another couple of hours of daylight in this weather. Surely England was supposed to have a temperate climate? Rain she was prepared for. Her parents had talked of the English rain constantly as if it were the reason they'd emigrated to Canada, and then on down to America, and now all the way across to the West Coast. They'd end up in Japan at the rate they were going.

Elizabeth pressed down on the accelerator.

The telephone rang, making Mary drop her book. She wasn't reading it anyway, merely holding it as protection. After the telephone rang three times she went slowly to answer it. She decided to impersonate an unco-operative au pair since she did not wish to speak to that girl again, particularly when David was not here to breathe confidence over her shoulder.

"Ullo. No. She eez not hair noo.'

So taken was Mary by her impersonation that for a moment or two she failed to recognise her husband's voice.

'What are you playing at?' He sounded aggressive partly because he was trying to rise above the noise of the bar which had filled up dramatically and partly to disown his guilt.

'I didn't want to speak to her.'

'I hardly sound like an American girl.'

'I was silly.'

It did not seem the moment to give her a choice about his return. 'I'm grabbing a bite here. It will save you cooking.'

'Fine.' It was fine, Mary told herself. Her idiot impersonation had shamed her into a show of will. She saw it had stopped snowing. 'Now it's stopped snowing I'll go for a walk.'

'Good idea. I won't be long.'

Lucy and Jo argued about which film to go to. They both felt gripped by a youthful lassitude which made bickering the only possible course of action.

'Japanese films are so slow, I lose the thread of the story.'

'Thread of the story! This isn't *Gone with the Wind* you know.'

'Don't be such a snob.'

'You're a middle-class illiterate.'

Lucy entertained a fleeting image of how he'd held her lovingly wound inside his arms and legs barely half an hour ago. It lasted long enough for her to seek compromise.

'There's that old French film, *Clare's Knee*?'

Jo stroked her arm. 'Make us a cup of coffee, Luce. Maybe we shouldn't bother with a film at all.'

He loved her, of course.

The cottage that David and Mary had rented was part of a run-down estate on Exmoor. The big house was owned jointly by two sons, one in the Foreign Office and therefore usually abroad and the other working for Wimpey's, the construction company and therefore also usually abroad. They let the two little satellite cottages with the result they were more cheerful and in better condition that the main house. On their rare visits their wives often insisted on staying in one of these, rather than face the dust and mice droppings of neglected grandeur.

Mary walked past the second small house, her eyes on a low red sun which had suddenly appeared on the sky-line. It was the only colour in an otherwise black and white landscape, as if the great Weathermaker, Mary thought fancifully to herself, had started with an engraving and then decided it needed cheering up with a large dollop of vermilion. She imagined the giant paint box suspended above the clouds.

'Mrs Tempest! Mrs Tempest!'

Eventually Mary heard and saw a copper-coloured head leaning out of a window.

'I'm Ian's wife. Your landlady.' She laughed. 'How about a cup of coffee?'

Mary came up to the window. Ian's wife was younger than Mary and wore the energetic and restless expression she herself wore in London. She also wore elegantly inappropriate clothes and was clearly suffering from the cold blasting through the open window.

'I'm going for a walk,' cried Mary. 'Shut the window, do or you'll freeze.'

'You are brave,' replied Ian's wife who was called Sarah. Or perhaps Suzy? 'Come in on your way back. You'll need it more, then. Ian says we'll be snowed in if it starts again.'

If we're snowed in, thought Mary, staring at the window, she won't be able to come. The thought gave her a jolt because it showed her that Elizabeth Crocker was there in her mind all the time, even when she had appeared to be taking a determined walk while cogitating on that great Landscape Painter in the sky.

She began to walk more fiercely, kicking up the feathery snow around her legs. Ian's wife was certainly too young to have an illegitimate twenty-two-year-old daughter – and probably too efficient.

She would walk right up to the hills where the dead bracken bowed under the weight of snow.

It was ridiculous to feel drunk on a pint and a half of beer. It must be partly the knowledge that he was not going to the office for four weeks. He had brought work, of course; in fact he could only take so long away because he was preparing for a big fraud case that would come up soon after his return. He had planned to go on a diet, not liking the middle-aged look of his spreading stomach, but he already suspected that the pleasure of food and drink taken at leisure was going to be too tempting. That chicken, ham and mushroom pie had been extraordinary.

'Fuck once twice and three times!' The roads had started to freeze and it was only three o'clock. Surely it couldn't freeze and snow at the same time? Judging by the map, she had at least another half an hour to go. Why couldn't they lay sand like any self-respecting community? Elizabeth was fast becoming anti-British. It was the inefficiency that drove her crazy. It was her dislike of inefficiency and muddle which had led her into medicine, because there you had to do the right thing accurately or else someone might die. It amazed her how some people were prepared to live their lives in a constant state of muddle. For example her friend, Sal, was now on to her third affair with a married man. It was almost as if she liked being in a constant state of unknowing. It was beyond the realms of fantasy that she had fallen in love with all three, always presuming there was such a thing as 'love' in inverted commas of which Elizabeth herself had her doubts. Media hype most of it.

Real love was about duty, responsibility, sharing, all of which she and Bob had found together. It was about a future based on a proper understanding of the present. Elizabeth relaxed as she thought of her prospective husband, and stopped looking so conscientiously for icy patches on the road.

'But what time were we asked to the party?'

'We'll help get it ready.'

'But it's only just after three. It can't begin till six.'

'I said we'll help get it ready. Anyway it'll take us hours to get to Richmond.'

'But I hate arriving somewhere when I'm not expected.'

Jo didn't answer this. He was putting on a white dress shirt which he wore without its detachable collar. He took it out of the battered cricket bag which he carried with him everywhere. It was the first thing Lucy had noticed about him at the student bottle party where they'd met. He'd been so careful with it, setting it down tenderly when absolutely essential as if it contained, at least, a baby. She'd joked about it but he hadn't smiled. Now she understood that, in his nomadic way of life, it represented stability, containing all his worldly possessions. She hadn't tried to joke about it again.

Mary was climbing up the hill laboriously. The wind had blown the snow so that it lay in waves rather than in an even birthday-cake coating which made the going unpredictable. But, even with this excuse, it was annoying to find how out of breath she felt, how heavy her legs, how uncomfortably hard beat her heart. Youth, and fitness, well below her forty years, was part of her self-image, part off her success at her job.

In need of cheering, Mary contemplated herself, as she moved through the executive reaches at Broadcasting House. She had reached salary scale band five before her thirty-fifth birthday. She had made her way successfully in a man's world and now found herself sitting at long tables in the company of men only, herself not just the one woman but also the best-looking, the youngest, the fittest. It was the wind, she now decided, which was holding her back. She had hardly noticed it in the valley but on the hillside it blew strongly. Another step or two and she would allow herself the exhilaration of turning round to admire the view and the extent of her climb.

I am a strong, successful, woman, Mary told herself, as the wind blew icily against her cheeks where her hat didn't protect them and her nose ran gently. Moreover, I have a loving husband and a pretty, clever daughter. She turned round.

'We're on the wrong line.' Lucy peered at the underground guide glued on the wall. She was a little short-sighted which meant she had to leave her seat and stand close. This made her more irritable than usual at this further evidence of Jo's lack of interest in the practicalities of everyday life. He simply didn't mind things like being on the wrong line. That's why he allowed so much time for a journey and, if they did arrive early, he didn't mind that either.

Lucy suspected he modelled himself on one of Dostoevski's heroes, though she couldn't be sure whether prince or peasant. In uncharitable moods she told herself that the only characteristics he had in common with either were Russian black locks and passionately chiselled features. But then she was ashamed. At least he was honestly trying to break the bourgeois mould while she still had all the most conventional responses. How pathetic, for example, that she dreaded wearing glasses.

'You should wear glasses.'

'Oh, shut up!'

Jo smiled. He approved of anger, particularly in her.

'We should have changed to the District Line and we're on the Northern which will take us in absolutely the wrong direction.'

Jo continued to smile. Then he opened his bag and extracted a battered paperback. Jo bought all his books secondhand so that they were uniformly brown and smelly. He said he did it in order not to support the capitalist system but it was possible he was joking. She had noticed he didn't say things like that to anyone else.

The train stopped at Waterloo. What were they doing at Waterloo? The doors opened in polite invitation.

With sudden decision, Lucy grabbed her bag from beside Jo, enjoying for a second his gaping astonishment, and ran out of the doors which, less politely, only just allowed her to squeeze through before clamping fiercely shut.

Dancing triumphantly on the platform she waved a V sign at the departing train and shouted, for his maximum dissaproval, 'I'm going to catch a train to Exmoor and have a lovely cosy . . .'

But she couldn't fit the last words in before the blunt end to the tube had slid like an earthworm into the dark tunnel.

'Weekend,' she completed to herself. At least her father would be pleased to see her. The only pity was she hadn't brought her dirty washing from the house.

David put on his car lights. He was surprised to find he'd spent quite so long in the pub. It must be the result of not wearing his watch, although it was as much the darkness of a lowering sky, now starting to flicker with snow, as the approach of night. At least if it was snowing it couldn't be freezing too. He must watch carefully for the turning left with the long driveway to the cottage. In front of him a small red car making very slow progress obscured his vision. Deciding the left turning couldn't be quite yet, he prepared to press the accelerator and overtake.

At that moment the car in front put out its left flicker and stopped.

Slamming on his brakes, David felt the car slide from under him.

No. No. No, he thought to himself, it's just not fair. My very best hope is to land in a bank of snow, otherwise I'll hit the bloody moron who's caused the problem. Wrenching the wheel to the right, he slid diagonally across the road.

Elizabeth was completely unaware of the problem she'd caused until she saw a large silver car float by her window. Even then she was muddled enough by the left-hand, right-hand aspect of British roads to wonder if it was on a conventional course. Only when it hit the opposite bank fairly gently but in a fountain of snow did she fully understand.

Putting her head on the wheel, she began to hiccough tears.

No answer. Lucy tried and failed to see the time on the station clock. She'd just have to telephone when she arrived. She hung back the receiver which smelled unpleasantly of cigarettes and unwashed hands and went to catch her train.

There, Mary thought, standing atop her ridge, the truth is I can do anything I set my mind to. Now to get down before dark.

CHAPTER FOUR

David did not have an imaginative nature. He was not tempted to dwell on a near escape from death or injury, on the ways of fate which had led him into danger and led him out of it. When the police appeared in the shape of a patrol car fortuitously passing, he could not make up his mind whether it was good or bad luck. Perhaps that indecisiveness about something actually irrelevant was a sign of shock. He could have been killed. The police arranged to have him pulled out of the bank quickly and efficiently. On the other hand they insisted on calling out the breathalyser car which was a bit of a cheek considering the weather conditions and the brilliance with which he'd avoided a real crash. The girl was no help at all. Of course he should never have told them he was a barrister. Police, particularly country police, never like barristers.

'I guess it was all my fault,' said Elizabeth to the police officer.

'That's a hired car, is it, miss?' The man was big and fair and spoke in a West Country drawl, not unlike American which Elizabeth found reassuring.

'Yes, I only arrived in London yesterday.'

'And you set off from London in conditions like this?'

The man's wonderment verging on disapproval challenged Elizabeth.

'Where I come from we think nothing of driving hundreds of miles in a day.'

'I see.' The officer looked meaningfully at the large silver car now being hoisted out backwards from the snowdrift.

'We have properly gritted roads and snow ploughs too!' she cried defensively.

'Is that so?' The officer got out a notebook and a pen. When he first found her he'd thought her quite sweet, with her big blue eyes and her tear-stained face. Clearly you had to believe all you read about American women. 'While we're waiting for your friend to be breathalysed I'd better take a few details.'

'He's not my friend!'

'But he was turning down the drive, too. At least he should have if he hadn't overtaken you and hit the bank instead. Lucky for him he had a substantial car.' The officer allowed himself a small smile. There was definitely something pleasing about a barrister in a Mercedes diving head first into a snowdrift.

'Oh.' Elizabeth stared at the police car where David sat waiting with the second officer. It was dark now and they were silhouetted by the car's interior light. 'I didn't know.'

'He's rented a cottage there. Of course there are two cottages and the big house. You could be visiting someone else?'

'I don't know.' Elizabeth looked at her fingers with the expression which had appealed to the officer in the first place. 'What's his name?'

'David Tempest. Barrister at Law,' the man read from his notebook. 'Home address 37 Camden Park Road, London N.1.' He looked up. 'Confidential information but hardly a state secret. Throw any light?'

'Yes,' whispered Elizabeth staring again at David's profile. 'I was on my way to visit his wife.'

Mary came down the hill with her feeling of exhilaration intact. The darkness tempting her to speed, the wind pushing her from behind, made it possible. She arrived at the bottom, hot and breathless. This was why one came to the country, she thought, not to sit in pubs hearing dull country gossip.

The track turned right and gave her a view of the cottages. Immediately her spirits sank. Their cottage was dark. She realised, with unwelcome self-knowledge, that she'd only climbed the hill to impress David; more, to punish him for being so long away. And now he was not back to make a fuss of her and tell her how brilliant and crazy she was.

Mary reached the first cottage with legs weighing heavy and face stiff with cold.

'Wow! You certainly take long walks!' The same window was thrown open and the same coppery head revealed.

'I had to reach the top,' Mary was brief. The woman must be very bored to sit like a fly-catcher in the window.

'First signs of madness,' said Ian's wife, Katy or Suzy, cheerfully. 'Now come and have a cup of coffee or brandy or whatever you mountaineers have.'

'That'll be lovely,' said Mary, suddenly understanding that a bit of lively company was just what she needed. 'I don't think my husband's back yet.'

'Nor mine,' said Ian's wife but the explanation of his whereabouts was lost as she shut the window.

Mary was not a natural giver of confidences; apart from David, there was no one whom she could totally trust with herself. David heard everything, or almost everything. He was her friend, lover, confidant, husband. He had come at the beginning and rescued her. But as she sat in the cosy little sitting-room with Ian's wife (who turned out to be called Helen) vividly describing the horrors of being a Foreign Office camp follower – 'In Riyadh, I wasn't allowed to drive; in Poland, if I did drive I couldn't talk in case the car was bugged –' Mary found herself longing to explain about this 'daughter', this approaching alien who wanted to turn herself into a lost sheep.

The fact that she didn't know the woman and found her complaints self-indulgent made the idea more tempting. The long cold walk followed by the heat and the mug of tea laced with whisky that Helen had made for them both caused her head to buzz and swell. She felt extremely unlike herself and it was not unpleasant.

'I wanted to get away. That's why I went up the hill.'

'Oh dear. Is the cottage so awful?'

'No. No. It's perfect. It's just that now and again one has to escape. You see . . . ' She hesitated. She was talking like some silly sixteen-year-old, like Lucy.

'That's what Ian says. He loves it here. For the freedom. I get terribly fed up. Now the children have gone back to school there's absolutely nothing to do. Particularly in this weather.' She looked towards the window and gave a theatrical shudder.

Mary laughed. 'I wanted some peace. Nothing to do. In London I'm a non-stop nine to six, but then this girl rang.' Again she paused. As Helen's bright enquiring face wavered in front of her, she remembered she'd had no lunch which explained the potency of the whisky.

'Asking herself to stay?' prompted Helen.

'Yes. No. A visit. She wanted to see me.'

'In this weather you'll have to ask her to stay. What a nuisance. Couldn't you put her off?'

'I tried. But she insisted. She's American.'

'Oh well.'

'Yes.'

Now was the moment to explain. She's my illegitimate daughter. Born when I was just eighteen, adopted at birth. It didn't even sound very exciting in these days of single parents. Thirty per cent, was it now? Mary tried to remember a figure that had passed across her desk in connection with some worthy programme or other. The adoption was what would seem odd now, not the birth.

'Bring her over for a drink, if that helps.'

'What? Oh, thank you, you see I've never met her. She's the daughter of someone I knew, someone I was close to a long time ago.'

Mary stopped. She became still. Helen, about to give her another slug of whisky, stopped too, arrested by her expression.

That's it! thought Mary. That's what I've been trying to escape from. I loved him, I loved Richard; she pronounced the name to herself as she had done in the past with a feeling of magic – I loved Richard far more than I ever loved anyone before or since. I felt such passion for him that I could hardly breathe when he was near me. He was in my mind every second of the day. Every action I took was related to him or it was meaningless. My whole life only existed for him.

'Are you all right?' Helen leant forward anxiously.

'Yes. I was remembering . . . '

'What's that?' Helen looked towards the window.

'The only time I was ever in . . . ' began Mary. But Helen was at her post at the window, curtain drawn back, preparing to unhook the latch.

'Look!' she cried excitedly. 'Two or three cars, a whole procession of cars and a police car. What can have happened?'

David congratulated himself on his patience and good humour. Any small blot on his conscience caused by staying so long in the pub had been balanced by this later virtue. He had avoided hitting the silly girl which, in the event, had only caused him bruises but might have been far more damaging. He had shouted at no one. He had waited patiently for the breathalyser van and then he had been entirely vindicated by the results. He had not been over the limit, for which he must thank God for greed and home-made pies.

'I expect you get a fair amount of road accidents on these winding roads?' He now felt recovered enough to attempt a bit of patronage for the policeman driving him back. Another policeman had volunteered to bring back his own surprisingly uninjured car.

'Tractors coming slowly out of fields,' agreed the policeman. 'But motor-bikes are the worst. The young lads can't resist a turn of speed, particularly after a pint or two.'

'Silly idiots,' agreed David as if he wouldn't recognise a pint if he saw one.

Behind them the girl's headlights rose and fell as she bumped along the rutted drive. According to the policeman she had driven all the way from London which was a pretty extraordinary thing to do in these weather conditions. Escape from the twin threats of death and breathalyser was producing a kind of euphoria which made David magnanimous. She must have been terrified. He would speak to her consolingly when they arrived. Presumably she was a friend of Ian's.

Ian had joined them as they started off down the driveway. David had shouted an explanation at him, from car window to car window. Ian was a good sort who'd lived around the world and they would lift a glass together as soon as possible.

'I expect your wife will be in a bit of a state.' They were nearing the cottages now, crossing a low bridge, climbing upwards.

'Not unduly,' David replied, confidently expecting Mary's mood to match his own. 'My wife's not the worrying sort.' The existence of Elizabeth Crocker had become submerged under the drama of events.

Elizabeth's heart beat far too fast and, despite the cold, her hands were damp with sweat on the steering wheel. She realised these were the worst possible circumstances in which to confront her mother but there was nowhere else for her to go. If only she'd been able to talk to Mr Tempest, explain to him, but he'd been so taken up with the police. She didn't dare picture Bob, back home, thinking about her as he ate his pastrami on rye – he usually ate pastrami on rye for lunch – or she knew she'd begin to cry again. As it was she must look a dreadful mess. She'd make an attempt at repairing her face before she got out of the car.

'Jesus!' She exclaimed out loud as the car hit what felt like a boulder under the snow. Did they call this a road?

'There're no lights!' David looked with surprise at their darkened cottage. 'Perhaps she fell asleep . . . '

'Hardly likely, sir. With the curtains undrawn.'

Were it not for the 'sir' David would have been irritated by the man's knowingness. Why did policemen always feel they had to know everything?

'Shall I drive to the next one?' Without waiting for an answer, the policeman continued on the track.

David swivelled in his seat. 'But . . . '

'She's probably gone for a bit of company.'

David began to mumble something but was stopped by the sight of Mary standing behind Ian's wife – what was her name? – at the door of the second cottage.

'We're getting a welcome,' commented the policeman with satisfaction.

Despite being in the last car, Ian was the first to reach his doorstep. His energy, bounding across snowy wastes, surprised Mary who still wore the dazed look which had so impressed Helen. Mary was remembering Richard's energy which had seemed so attractive viewed from her youthful lassitude.

'Jolly good!' cried Ian. 'It looks like we've got a party.'

'But what happened?' Helen clasping her hands round her for warmth, stepped further out.

Mary, on the other hand, retreated inwards.

'An accident,' she heard Ian say. 'Poor old David had a narrow miss, though. I expect he's a bit shaken up.'

Mary had seen David sitting beside the policeman and even in the darkness could tell by his attitude that he was perfectly well. She wondered whether all long-married couples could read each other's moods as easily as she could David's.

Elizabeth crouched over the dash-board light trying to see her face in her little compact mirror. She had seen the two women in the doorway of the cottage and assumed the first woman, with the brilliant coppery curls and the eager manner, was her mother.

'There's nothing worse she can do to me than she did twenty-two years ago,' she muttered to herself.

Ian, Helen, David and the two burly policemen made the cottage seem very small. Mary retreated further.

'Well, darling, you nearly became a rich woman.' David kissed his wife on the cheek.

'What do you mean?'

'Life insurance.' He laughed cheerfully.

'So tell us what happened. And do sit down, if you can find room. Ian, get the chaps something to drink.' Helen seemed to feel she was giving a party.

'Not for us on duty.'

'Oh, come on, officer, the breathalyser's out on active duty, so you're quite safe.' Ian began to pour large whiskies even though the policemen were firm in their refusals.

Elizabeth realised the door to the cottage had closed and she had been forgotten. The breathing-space was welcome but it would make her entrance unavoidably dramatic.

An image of herself climbing quietly in through the window and pretending she'd been there all the time presented itself. No! She pursed her newly-lipsticked mouth. She must take a grip on herself. She looked at her watch – a going-away present from her father, guilt money as she'd thought at the time, although now she liked it well enough – and saw it was 3.15 p.m. in New York. The watch told the time round the world.

'So then this girl . . .' David stood in order to tell his story the better.

'What girl?' Helen stared at him.

'The girl who was driving the car.' He stopped, looked round the room and addressed the nearest policeman, 'Where is the girl?'

'Oh cripes! We've forgotten her.'

His schoolboy expression made Helen laugh and even Mary smiled.

Since she was standing at the far end of the room by the window, she drew back the curtains. 'There's someone in a car out there, I think. A red car.'

'That's it.' David frowned. 'I must say she does seem an odd fish. Why ever hasn't she come in?'

'I'll get her.' Mary crossed the room quickly before one of the men could intervene. She found the small room claustrophobic and her cheeks burned from the whisky after her icy walk.

'Who is she?' asked Helen as Mary left the room.

'Elizabeth Crocker, an American,' said the blond policeman stolidly.

Elizabeth saw the second woman advancing across the snow towards her and, in order not to look thoroughly ridiculous, she began to get out of the car.

'Just coming!' she called.

Mary heard the American accent and stopped. So this was the girl, her daughter who'd come to haunt her. She looked up to the night sky. It was completely clear now, an absolute blackness pierced by flickering stars. How long was it since she'd seen a sky as perfect as that?

'Just look at the sky!' she cried as the girl approached.

Obediently the girl raised her head and looked upwards.

'It's so clean it seems artificial.' Mary whispered now. This girl would have to take her as she was. It was her own decision to come and find her.

'It's beautiful.' The girl's voice was not too bad but Mary could see she was only being polite. Her face was very small, strained and pale, despite too much make-up, and she had begun to shake.

'You'd better come in.'

'Yes. I've come to see . . . '

'I know who you've come to see.'

The girl looked at her doubtfully as they walked towards the cottage. The snow was very loud under their feet. When they were nearly at the doorway, Mary stopped again. 'I'm Mary Tempest,' she said.

'Oh.' Elizabeth had imagined this meeting too often to be able to give the actual moment any reality. 'Oh, I'm sorry.' She didn't mean to apologise but her large blue eyes staring at Mary had the pathetic innocence of a child's.

Without planning it, Mary found she had put her arm round her shoulders. 'Yes. We'll be able to talk later.' As she said this, she registered a powerful sensation of relief. Here was the girl, her daughter, standing in front of her, and she had put her arm round her with no effort at all and even told her they would talk later. 'Yes,' she said firmly, going through the door, 'we'll rescue poor

David and then we'll go back to our cottage. You must be on the verge of collapse.'

Only David saw anything special in Mary arriving with her arm round the girl. Elizabeth Crocker. She had Mary's colouring, her chestnut hair and large blue eyes but her face was drawn on a meaner scale. Somewhere lurking there was an angular dark man with a hard chin, lizard mouth and pointed nose. David had seen a photograph of Richard soon after he'd first met Mary.

David, who was comfortably large and fair before he became grey, was unpleasantly aware of this other man's presence in the room. It gave him an actual physical pain somewhere near his heart. He put down his whisky and rubbed his hand over his eyes. Why had Mary put her arm round her? She was not usually a demonstrative person.

CHAPTER FIVE

The organisation and effort needed to effect a friendly separation from Ian and Helen, and the two policemen, served to cover any strong emotion. All the cars had to be moved to let the police car out and then Helen became violent in her demands that they stay for supper. If I was Ian, I'd be insulted, thought Mary dissapprovingly.

After the cars were moved, the groceries had to be carried in – all this under the magnificent starry sky that had so impressed Mary. Once inside and on their own, there were the groceries to be unpacked and stored, supper to be considered, a fire to be made and bedclothes found for Elizabeth.

Despite Mary's continual admonitions that she should rest, Elizabeth insisted on helping and, to David's disguised irritation, followed Mary around in a suppliant, almost pathetic manner.

Mary, on the other hand, was brisk and cheerful. David, looking up from the fire as she came in with a dish of nuts, could only describe her attitude as 'happy'.

'Are you all right?' he asked grumpily, having just looked to see the girl was safely in the kitchen.

'Oh yes!' exclaimed Mary.

But what was Oh yes about it, thought David, with that girl in the house. Or was this not the same woman who had screamed out: I don't want to see her! only the night before? Obviously not.

'I'm so glad you both arrived safely back,' she added, giving a warm smile as Elizabeth came into the room. 'You might have been killed.'

Too true, thought David, taking a handful of peanuts. The girl – David refused to think about her as Elizabeth, a name he particularly liked – would have to return to America.

Together Mary and Elizabeth prepared supper and laid the table. Elizabeth described her journey.

'And now you must go up to your room while supper's cooking,' said Mary. 'We'll have our talk later.'

The truth was she wanted to be on her own for a moment to savour that feeling of being in love that had come to her in Helen's cottage and then come again under the brilliant black sky. Even though it was only a memory, for she supposed that's what it was, it had been the strongest emotion she had felt for many years. David's car accident had, as a direct result, raised very little emotional response in her. The arrival of this girl had seemed of secondary importance – just as her conception had been secondary to her love affair with Richard and her birth to its break-up. Under these circumstances it was not difficult to be impersonally kind to her. She seemed a comfortless child.

Mary sat down at the kitchen table. Richard had always looked at her in a particular way when making love, an intent expression of concentration which she had never seen on anyone else's face. That was what she wanted to think about now.

David sat back and admired the fire he'd built. It roared and blazed and crackled, sending out puffs of sweet-smelling smoke and an occasional dart of bright blue flame. Fire-making was an art; he'd been taught by his father when he was a boy and never forgotten, although in London they had gas central heating. Which, he trusted, they'd left on in case of burst pipes.

Suddenly David felt amazingly tired. He lumbered into the armchair and immediately fell asleep.

Upstairs, Elizabeth also slept. She had put a photograph of Bob by her bed. He was wearing the tie she had given him for his birthday and a toothy smile.

The telephone rang. Mary went over slowly, unconcerned.

'At the station?' Lucy's unexpected arrival only partially dispelled Mary's languor. 'Oh darling, you'd better get a taxi. Daddy's had an accident and an American girl's arrived.'

*

Lucy's spirits, so high since she'd abandoned Jo, began to flag. She'd come all this way to be looked after by her parents and now she had to wander round an icy station trying to persuade a taxi driver to take her out to some God-forsaken hole. If Dad had answered her call he'd have come and picked her up – crash or no crash. And who was this American girl?

Only pride stopped her from regretting the evening of youth and jollity which she had thrown up for this unwelcoming desolation. Nor did Jo believe in fidelity. In fact he argued a strong case in favour of infidelity.

'Hey!' shouted Lucy to a taxi trying to head for home. 'I'll pay double rates if you'll take me.' That'd teach her mother to be selfish.

Mary sat down at the kitchen table again but the image of Richard's dark and narrow face was replaced by Lucy's smooth and youthful contours. She looked at the grain of the wood for a while and then went into the sitting-room and looked at David, fast asleep. His face, so well-known, the softness round the chin, the oval of his eyelids, the large and slightly crooked nose, the widow's peak of strong bushy hair, the half-open lips, fuller now in sleep, gave her a sense of warmth and comfort. They made her want to go to sleep too.

But when she sat down in the other armchair her mind began to run busily, reproducing over and over again his name, Beck, Richard Beck, Richard Beck. A name without an image.

As if wakened by her inward agitation, David opened his eyes. When he saw her, he gave a peculiarly sweet smile. Mary smiled back and felt the machine in her head die down.

'Lucy rang. She's at the station. Or on the way here by now.'

'Lucy?' David blinked. 'What about the girl? Where is she?' It would be too much to hope that she was part of his dream.

'Elizabeth's asleep.'

Upstairs, asleep. That was a relief for a moment. He heaved himself upright. 'You won't tell Lucy?'

'Of course not.' Mary crouched down and put another log on the fire. 'It's nothing to do with her.'

'No.' But as he agreed David was surprised by the realisation that the girl upstairs was his stepdaughter, Lucy's half-sister. You could hardly describe that as nothing to do with her. They didn't look very alike certainly, Lucy had inherited his large fair looks, but their veins ran with fifty per cent of the same blood. This idea was deeply repugnant to David. He flushed and looked away from Mary.

'They'll have to share a room,' Mary tried to catch the expression on David's face. She could feel he was upset.

David stood up and walked to the door in an agitated manner. He decided to be honest. 'I don't like the idea of them sharing a room.' It seemed to him obscene, in a complicated way linked with ideas of incest.

'I'll have to warn Elizabeth. But she seems a nice sensible girl.'

'Sensible!' David recalled how his car had flown sideways into the bank of snow. Was it shock that caused him to be so tired, so agitated? 'Hardly sensible.'

'Oh, yes. She's a medical student, you know. And engaged. She seems years older than Lucy.'

'She is years older.' David went through the door into the kitchen. The conversation had become too painful. Mary's words followed him, Only three years older. What had happened to her? Why was she so able to cope, so calm and cheerful? It was unnatural. David poured his second large whisky of the evening and briefly recalled the quiet, health-restoring time they'd planned for this holiday in the country.

Lucy couldn't believe her ears.

'I'm not going down that driveway if you pay me ten times over the odds.'

'But it's miles long. I can't even see the house!'

'I've got my suspension to consider.' The taxi driver banged his hand on the wheel. 'And that, my dear, is that.'

And that, my dear, is that! The insult of it. Flinging notes, Lucy scrambled angrily out of the car.

'It's a fine starlit night,' the driver called after her with the same infuriating patronage. 'You'll have no trouble finding your way. If I was ten years younger, I'd escort you myself.'

Ugh. Ugh. Ugh. Lucy stamped angrily through the snow which was a silly thing to do since she sank far deeper than necessary. I hate men. I hate men. I hate men. After a while she saw no reason not to shout it aloud: 'I HATE MEN!' At the same time losing her footing, she fell backwards into a snowdrift. It felt like puffed-up pillows behind her. Above her brilliant stars whirled dizzily round a pure black sky. Lucy staggered up on her feet again; she was smiling. Jo was right, she was an entirely superficial person, not even able to do anything as important as hating men for more than a few minutes.

Elizabeth woke up very slowly so she knew exactly where she was by the time she opened her eyes. It was a trick she'd learnt in childhood when her parents were always dragging her from house to house, from one school to another. She touched dear Bob, admiring not just him but the bright blue tie she had bought from Bloomingdales. Dear Bloomies!

She left her bed and went to the little square window with its pretty chintz curtains. She stared out, expecting to see a huge vista of nothing but instead she saw a girl's figure dancing her way down the track where the car tyres had packed it solid. She waved and dipped and floated her arms above her head.

Did no one behave sensibly in England? Now the girl was closer, and lit by a beam from the kitchen, Elizabeth could see that she was young and pretty with fair hair sticking up in that strange English way and that she wore a seraphic smile.

As she reached the door and disappeared from Elizabeth's curious gaze, she called out, 'I'm here! I'm back!' But then, obviously having a better idea, she reappeared in front of the window and began to dance again, spinning and jumping. After each jump, she faced the window and cried loudly: 'The spirit of winter is here! Come and pay homage! The spirit of winter is here! Come and rejoice!'

Who can she be? thought Elizabeth for no one had mentioned another occupant of the cottage.

David looked over the rim of his whisky glass and saw his daughter dancing out in the snow. Immediately his worries disappeared. Ever since she was a little girl she had produced this happy reaction in him. She was so full of life and joy and generosity. At this point a nasty image of Jo was quickly suppressed.

He went over to the window, clapping and smiling. 'Where's your taxi?'

'The spirit of winter needs no nasty, smelly car. She flies on the winds. The winds!' Arms open, Lucy bounced with long strides to the door.

David met her with open arms too. He had not seen her since her university term had ended. She was far more beautiful than he remembered, more womanly, more everything. 'It's wonderful to have you home!'

'Oh, Dad. Why are you always so appreciative!'

Elizabeth, descending the stairs with tentative steps, hesitated. Even now she did not link this girl to her mother. Mary had made no mention of children; there had been no sign of a child. Confused, Elizabeth failed to realise this was a rented house.

Lucy saw her over her father's shoulder. 'Oh, hello. You must be the American.' She felt friendly toward everyone. Even this dull-looking girl. How right she'd been to abandon Jo!

'Yes. I'm staying.' Confused, Elizabeth took another few steps down and found herself next to Mary who'd just come through the door from the living-room.

'This is Elizabeth Crocker,' Mary said, putting her arm on her shoulder. 'She's the daughter of an old friend of mine and she's come for a little visit.' Her arm dared Elizabeth to contradict the story. 'And this is my daughter Lucy.'

David, with his arm still round Lucy, tried not to stare. 'How about supper?' he said instead.

'Mummy said you had a terrifically narrow escape.'

Mary came now to give her daughter a kiss. 'Whatever made you come so late in the day?' Since Lucy didn't answer she began, 'A row with . . . ?' but, catching a fierce expression on her husband's face, instead turned to the stove. 'Supper should be ready. Elizabeth and I made a lasagne.'

They sat at the small table. Lucy was excited and talkative, her rapid words and flushed pink cheeks, her creamy English voluptuousness making a sharp contrast to Elizabeth's pinched sallowness, her neat clothing, her slow speech. They were so unalike that David began to wonder if there hadn't been a mistake. Records are notoriously inefficient. He promised himself that if he got the chance he would question her to find exactly how she'd tracked down Mary as her mother. Surely it was all supposed to be kept confidential anyway. Thinking such optimistic thoughts and seeing her at such clear disadvantage to his own beautiful, witty, ebullient daughter, he began to feel almost sorry for her. It did not seem quite so dreadful that they were to share a bedroom. Inappropriate, certainly – like stabling a riding school hack beside a racing horse – but not obscene.

'What's for seconds?' Mary stood up. 'If not thirds!' exclaimed

David, looking at his wife without painful emotions for the first time that evening. 'This is the best lasagne you've ever cooked.'

Mary smiled back. She was glad that he had decided to accept the situation and be happy again. After all, Lucy's return had turned out for the best. David loved Lucy so much, perhaps even more than he loved her. The thought was not new to her and gave her pleasure rather than pain. She did not feel deeply proprietary toward David anymore or perhaps she never had or at least not as she had toward Richard. Her thoughts drifted away from the kitchen table.

Lucy noticed her mother's expression and was irritated. It was rude of her so obviously to absent herself, particularly when there was a guest at the table – even if she was pretty much a bore. Elizabeth had launched into a detailed explanation of her life, the constant hard work to pass more and more exams, the scramble in the vacation to earn money, the borrowing at unfair rates of interest and her seriously considered engagement to Bob. Lucy ran her fingers through her hair so it stood up in points like whipped cream. Whatever would Jo make of someone like this girl? Perhaps he would approve of her seriousness. He certainly wouldn't want to kiss her breasts.

Catching her mother's vacant eye, Lucy reverted to her original theme. Her mother should pay more attention. Not so long ago she had visited her office and been impressed, even amazed, by her practical energy and concentration. It was as if she left that side of herself behind when she came home. Was this what marriage did to you?

'Well, I guess that's my life in a nutshell.' Elizabeth finished her monologue with a strained smile.

'But what about your parents?' asked David compulsively.

Even Mary reacted to this, looking at Elizabeth with sympathetic curiosity.

'Oh, they went to the West Coast, next stop Japan.' Elizabeth gave an unconvincing laugh. 'They're restless by nature, I guess. While I like to be rooted.'

'You're a long way from home for someone who likes to be rooted.' Lucy pushed her chair back and stood up. 'I'm flaked. Does this place boast hot water?'

Elizabeth looked up at this half-sister of hers. She saw a pretty, overweight, spoilt girl. Lucy was wearing a man's pin-stripped jacket over a tight black sweater with visible holes and a long black skirt whose hem was partially held up by three safety pins. She wore no make-up or jewelry except a stripe of green eye-shadow and three diamond earrings crammed onto one ear-lobe. Elizabeth failed to appreciate that Lucy was dressed for a party. She also found it difficult to believe she was a serious student. During all her chatter about university events, about people and parties and clubs and lecturers and essays, she had never mentioned what subject she was reading. Elizabeth would have understood this if she had been anarchistic in her views or preoccupied with politics but she gave the impression she was there purely for fun. Perhaps this was the English manner, the famous 'laconic wit' that she read about in reviews of English novels. She must not be judgemental until they knew each other better, which they presumably would after sharing a bedroom. It was odd that in her imaginings of a mother she had never suspected a sister.

'Just don't take all the water, Luce.' Mary began to clear the table.

Elizabeth stood quickly to help her.

'No. No. You go to the fire and then, if I were you, I'd jump into Lucy's water after her.'

Both David and Elizabeth flinched perceptibly at this suggestion, David on emotional grounds, Elizabeth on hygienic. Mary, scraping the lasagne dish, failed to notice.

She is kind to me, thought Elizabeth, treating me like another daughter. I might not have expected it after our telephone call. She's kind but a little remote. I wonder if I'll dare ask her my questions. Elizabeth thought of her questions, written out in her neat hand on a little pad in her handbag. She'd done it as a kind of therapy but then she'd realised she must put them to her mother. Why did you make no attempt to see me or even find out if I lived or died?

'I think I'll go upstairs now. I'm feeling pooped.'

'That's right, dear.' Mary didn't turn from the sink. Pooped. What a funny word. 'You can keep an eye on the bath water better up there.'

'Yes.' Elizabeth didn't say she only planned on a wash.

'I'll come and say goodnight to you two girls later.'

Elizabeth went. David, still sitting at the table, watched her go, stiff-backed, neat-figured, but graceless.

'Do you think we can get rid of her tommorrow?'

'Who?'

David was too irritated to reply. Discernably stamping, he mounted the stairs.

Mary had the kitchen to herself once more. Immediately Richard Beck began to surface. He used to lay her down on the bed and undress her very slowly, saying she was beautiful, like a princess, like a queen. He'd studied each detail of her, admiring everything, not allowing her to laugh and say that he was biased, that she was too fat, her thighs were awful. He would get quite cross, saying he loved her and she was beautiful and perfect and all she had to do was lie still and shut up. It made Mary smile to think of it, almost laugh.

She sat down at the table as she had earlier and remembered how he held her breasts, with such love and then kissed the nipples so tenderly. He had loved her so much. And she had loved him too. When he stroked her body she could hear herself giving little mews of contentment.

Lucy sat up in bed with a bright expression. Despite her bath, she still wore her earrings and green eye-shadow. Elizabeth, passing by with her sponge-bag, worried about the state of her pillow in the morning.

'I left the bath in.'

'Thank you.' Elizabeth sighed. She was no longer so confident that sharing a bedroom would bridge the Atlantic and produce understanding, or even whether she wanted it.

'You don't like her, do you?' Mary came upon David, her eyes unnaturally bright.

'Who?' David put his finger in the new Freddie Forsyth and leant back against his pillows.

Mary was not deflected. 'I didn't want her. Remember. But I can hardly throw her out into the snow.'

'She nearly killed me.' David's manner was mild. He did not object to her presence as much as Mary's affectionate – yes, affectionate – treatment of her.

Mary laughed. 'For someone nearly killed, you seem in remarkably good health.'

'It was a miracle. Personally, I don't think she's your daughter at all.' David opened his book again.

'Oh, well,' muttered Mary.

Clearly floundering, thought David, looking over the top of his book.

'Oh, well,' repeated Mary. 'If that's your attitude.' Let him think that if it made things easier for him. Perhaps he was right. It hardly mattered. The girl would go back to America and she would be left with . . .

39

'I mean, without wanting to be tactless, it hardly seems possible that you could produce someone so . . . I mean you only have to look at Lucy.'

'What about Lucy?' Mary sat on the other twin bed. She knew David was working himself up to saying something cruel and braced herself. He had a perfect right under the circumstances.

'A different father could hardly account for quite such a difference – even if he was the dullest man in the world.'

'Richard wasn't dull!' Mary's cheeks went scarlet and then pale. She stood up. 'I'm going to kiss the girls goodnight.' She hurried from the room. His name spoken out loud after so many years' silence had the power of an obscenity.

Elizabeth looked down with horror at Lucy. She was hunched over the bedclothes sobbing and heaving. Even groaning. Elizabeth had never seen such passion. Perhaps she had found out about their relationship.

'Lucy.' Tentatively she put out a hand.

Immediately Lucy rolled over, knocking the hand away. 'Oh aah! I want to die! I want to die!'

'Oh, please. It can't be so bad.' Elizabeth felt like crying herself. 'What is it?'

'You wouldn't understand.' Her voice was distorted and her face even worse. Elizabeth's fears for the pillow case were even more than realised. 'You've got your Bob and your work and a future . . . '

'What? What?' Elizabeth could hardly understand but this didn't seem to deter Lucy.

'And I've got nothing. Nothing! Jo doesn't care about me at all. Except as a body and if I didn't just happen to have big breasts he probably wouldn't even care about that. Or them. And he doesn't care about that or them much anyway. He'll be screwing someone else now. Now! This very minute. I know he will. He doesn't believe in love, you see. He thinks it's a bourgeois invention to entrap the workers into marriages so then they can't afford to strike. He thinks . . . '

Elizabeth wondered whether to sit on Lucy's bed with its dangerously turbulent occupant or sit on her own which might seem unfriendly. But she had to sit down or she might faint. She felt she was going deaf which was always a prelude to fainting. Deciding on a compromise she fetched a chair and sat down close to Lucy who was gulping out her misery.

'And I don't have any views about anything. And I was lying here and I suddenly thought that perhaps I don't even love him. And that I'm incapable of even that.'

'Of what?' said Elizabeth sypathetically, feeling it time she said something.

'Of LOVE!' wailed Lucy, coming to rest like an exhausted fish on her back.

'But I thought you were worried about your boyfriend . . . '

'Oh. You couldn't understand! I told you. You've got your Bob. Look at him with a tie on and smiling. Jo never wears a tie and absolutely never smiles.' The fish started to flap again, though more gently than before.

Elizabeth was reminded of her friend who had the affairs with the married men. And yet Lucy had everything.

'Did something happen between you and your boyfriend?'

'I ran away from him. I left him sitting on the tube. The subway. He was staggered.' Strangely to Elizabeth the idea seemed to cheer Lucy. She heaved herself up on one elbow. 'He's incredibly conceited. That's one of the reasons he's so wildly attractive. Most men at that age are so nervously pimply.'

Now that Lucy seemed better, Elizabeth began to feel self-conscious about their close proximity and couldn't resist a longing glance towards her bed. But Lucy took her hand. 'You know when I first saw you, I had no idea we'd get on like this. Tomorrow we'll go exploring. You've got a car.'

'Yes,' agreed Elizabeth weakly. 'I must get some sleep now.'

Mary listened at the door before opening it. She hoped to hear girlish confidences but there was silence. Inside, it was dark.

'Goodnight, girls.'

'Goodnight Mrs Tempest.' Since there was no response from Lucy she did not go over to kiss her. Mrs Tempest. She had been Mary Fellowes when Elizabeth was born.

'Your feet are cold,' David grumbled sleepily as Mary got into bed. It had been the same all through their marriage.

'You used to warm them.' But this wasn't true. It was Richard who had warmed them, with his tongue slipping between her toes until they felt all wet and slippery like mango slices.

41

CHAPTER SIX

The sun shone clear on the white landscape. After an hour or two it began to melt the snow on the roofs of the two cottages. Drips spread round the guttering, dropping like a bead curtain, thinly spaced.

From one cottage emerged Ian with a spade, gumboots and an enthusiastic expression. He began to shovel snow from the pathway. Behind him Helen stood in the doorway, drinking coffee with an air of lassitude.

'I don't know why I'm up so early.'

'It's after ten on a stunning day. That's why you're up.' Ian shovelled and puffed, his cheeks already reddening.

'They're not up.' Helen indicated the other cottage where every curtain stayed closely drawn.

'That's different.'

'What do you mean?' Helen's attitude brightened as if even talking about people lessened her sense of isolation.

'You know.' The snow was heavy and Ian gave a little grunt as his back took the weight. Christ! He wasn't even forty till next year. The end of this year now.

'I don't know.'

Ian stood upright and leant on his spade. 'Car accident for David who usually has everything so absolutely under control. Atlantic crossing time change, plus accident for that American girl. Late arrival after youthful high jinks for Lucy.'

Helen giggled. 'She did look an idiot dancing about in the snow. I couldn't believe my eyes at first. And Mary.'

'You tell me Mary's problem,' said Ian, throwing snow so it spread in an arc like a frilly-edged cloak. 'I can see you have a view.'

42

Helen did have a view but she didn't like it to be broached so directly. She frowned into her coffee dregs.

'You think she's too perfect, too balanced to be true,' encouraged Ian.

'Yesterday I had that tension feeling of a woman in her middle forties . . . '

'Early forties. If that.'

'It was the way she said "escape" – so violently, so unlike what you'd expect from her.'

'She's hitting a mid-life crisis, is that what you're saying?' Ian laughed. 'People usually are who rent these cottages. I sometimes think it's a bit of the kill or cure treatment.'

'Oh look,' said Helen. 'Someone's coming up the track. It might be a young man with long hair or a young girl with broad shoulders.'

'Probably the postman.' Ian went back to his shovelling.

Lucy and Elizabeth sat in a shelter they'd made for themselves out of snow. Protected from the wind and in the full light of the sun, they actually felt warm, particularly after the exertion of climbing the hill and building their little den.

Lucy pulled out a packet of biscuits from her pocket and Elizabeth produced a tartan thermos flask.

'This is the best breakfast I've ever had.' Lucy sighed luxuriantly.

'It's lunchtime for me.' The smell of the coffee made Elizabeth smile dizzily. She had woken at six. This trip into the rising sun had been her idea, her present from across the Atlantic. 'We have snow every winter in America and Bob and I have always felt at home in it.'

'At home in it. What a lovely expression. Now I feel at home in it too. Cheers!' Lucy raised the thermos while Elizabeth gulped from the lid.

Mary was trying very hard not to wake. This was perverse since she was having an unpleasant dream about a room full of snakes from which any normal person would have wanted to escape at the first possible opportunity. But Mary didn't want the day to start. Or at least the still sleeping part of herself didn't.

The waking part, which at times surfaced almost completely,

43

knew that David had left the bed and dressed, that he had set up his work on a table in the window and was even now contemplating his books. She had spent so much time with David in the confines of a bedroom that she felt his presence even though apparently quite deeply asleep. She had felt him kiss her, for example, even though the next instant she had been faced with six, admittedly smallish, snakes and the responsibility to chop off their heads.

Mary struggled to the surface again and saw David leaving the room with extreme caution. She smiled a little at this consideration and remembered, as she did so, their irritation with each other the night before. She would not let that happen today. Roused fully by her good intentions, Mary opened her eyes, pulled herself upright and was rewarded by the dazzling optimism of the sun.

'There's someone coming along the track.' Elizabeth shaded her eyes.

'So there is,' Lucy, mouth full of biscuit, didn't bother to look down. She was too short-sighted to see at that distance anyway.

'I think he's aiming for your cottage.'

'Probably the postman.'

'On a Sunday.' Elizabeth who had very good eyes, continued to peer down curiously. He was such a strange-looking man, boy, girl? 'I thinks it's the abominable snowman.'

'I thought medical school taught you the difference between man and beast.'

'That's the whole point of the abominable snowman, no one knows what he is.'

'Then why do you call him, he?'

Mary, blinking in bed, heard the door open downstairs and then heard voices. She imagined Ian coming over with plans. He was the sort of man who felt secure only when making plans.

David came in with two cups of tea. 'Oh you are a darling!' Mary exclaimed only a little guiltily. It would make him happy to make her happy and then it would be her turn to, happily, make him happy.

David sat down by the window. 'Jo's here.'

'What?'

'Jo.' Mary now saw David's face had a greenish look of supressed fury.

'Lucy's Jo, you mean.'

'If you must put it like that.'

'However did he get here?' This, she knew, was not an appropriate response. The day was gone now, hopeless. She and David always quarrelled about Jo.

'People like Jo get everywhere. He said he hitched a lorry. What does it matter how he got here?' David stood up forcefully. His tea formed into a wave and slopped over the edge of his cup to the floor.

Mary watched; he was right to be angry. Jo was dreadful and how dare he follow them out here? But Lucy loved him. Mary remembered her love. Her feelings of love. With an effort she forced her face into what she knew would be irritating sympathy. 'I suppose he'll take Lucy off.'

'He can't stay here. I told him. There's no room with that girl, apart from anything else.'

Mary suddenly felt a hysterical desire to laugh. It was too dreadful for poor David. First 'that girl' as he called her and then Jo. Perhaps it was as well to laugh while she could. 'Where are the girls?'

'Asleep, I suppose. They haven't appeared.'

'Elizabeth must be exhausted.' But this wasn't the right comment. 'What's Jo doing?'

'Making himself a huge breakfast. What else?'

Mary remembered that it was the extreme depth of irritation in his tone when talking about Jo which eventually led her to his defence.

'And to think,' David turned to the window, 'it's one of the most beautiful days of the winter.'

Mary got out of bed and put her arm round her husband. 'It'll be all right, darling. They'll all go and we'll be left on our own in peace, just as we were when we arrived.' But as she spoke she had a strong sense that she had just told a lie. She would not be as she'd been before.

Lucy and Elizabeth slid down the hill, arm in arm. When they reached the bottom, they ran, kicking the snow and laughing, past Ian's house. Flakes of white settled across his newly brushed pathway. He had moved inside, his attention diverted to plans for a rescue bid for some sheep he imagined trapped in a drift-filled copse.

'I never thought I'd have fun while I was here,' said Elizabeth more soberly as they reached their own cottage.

'And I never thought I'd have fun with you.' Lucy looked at her tangled hair, bright blue eyes and pink nose. 'You look quite different from last night.'

'And I guess you do too.' Elizabeth thought of the hump in the bedclothes, the smeared green eye-shadow, the wallowing whale of self-pity.

But Lucy only laughed. She had discounted that side of herself. Only the present existed and in the present she felt wonderful!

Lucy and Elizabeth burst through the door of the cottage.

Jo, who looked so confident as he found his way round an alien kitchen, was not quite what he seemed. It was not surprising he was hungry since he had spent the night after an unsatisfactory party and in adverse weather conditions, following Lucy. The truth was that Jo, the proud product of a loving and ambitious mother, needed a woman close at hand. Or, better still, under his hand.

When Lucy, breathing out snowy freshness, came banging into the kitchen, Jo, popping a last piece of fried bread into his mouth, watched her closely. She looked dazzling, cheeks flushed, hair tumbling about her heaving boobs. Last night he'd met a girl who'd felt like a washing board, producing a distinct image of the old-fashioned piece of corrugation thrown out by his mother. That was when, confusing the urge for maternal warmth with the urge for sex, he'd decided to follow Lucy. Lucy, in every way, was about as far from a washing board as you could possibly get.

'It's the abominable snowman having breakfast,' said Elizabeth as both girls spotted him at the same time.

Jo wiped his mouth on the back of his hand. 'Lucy never said she had a sister.'

Mary stood at the top of the stairs looking down. Jo's words – so absolutely typical that they should come from him – Lucy's laughing disclaimer, Elizabeth's face, hand raised to her cheek, – impressed as a scene from a film. This was her life, her creation, her responsibility. She must be strong.

'Hi girls! I didn't know you were even up! And Jo too. Where did you spring from?' She moved down the stairs, positive, good-natured, commanding. It was her work self, brought home under pressure.

"Morning Mum!' Lucy sprang across to kiss her. 'We had a tremendous walk at dawn and Jo's here like a mirage out of the snow. Liz thought he was an abominable snowman. Now we're all going to have a vast breakfast, although Jo's already had one. And if you just sit down, we'll do everything!'

She loves him, thought Mary. This selfish slob. This illiterate oaf – which was not fair since Jo was very well read. She loves him and she's transfigured by her love – which was not altogether true either since Lucy had been at least halfway along the road to transfiguration while at the top of the mountain and unable to recognise her beloved tramping along the track below.

Love is the most important thing in the world, thought Mary while she gave Elizabeth a peck on the cheek. When you don't love, you're dead.

David sat upstairs, staring at his books. Usually the prospect of hard thought put him in a good humour. But the noise now rising from below – mostly girls' excited voices for Jo affected an irritatingly low tone – made it impossible for him to concentrate.

Looking at the snow, now shimmering crystalline on the surface, he banged his books shut. Why come to the country if you sat crouched over your desk all day?

'We'll go in two teams,' said Ian, studying a 10:1 map, 'and meet up. Here.' He prodded it with his finger. 'How are you doing with those sandwiches?'

'Are you sure everyone will want to join in?'

'It's a well-known fact that without organised activity, Sundays are unadulterated hell!'

Mary didn't like the way David looked. He was wide at the hips and his face was flat like an uncooked pancake. This was untrue as he had a prominent nose but she was tramping behind him, wallowing in the snow and imagining him as she felt him, rather than as he was. She thought to herself that even when she'd most loved

47

him at the start of their marriage, she had not liked the way he looked. She had simply put up with it for the sake of their love and their marriage. But now she might as well admit the truth.

She even preferred the physical appearance of Ian who was the most terrific bore. How had he managed to get them on this expedition? But he was dark and wiry and physically energetic. David was so cerebral. Just look at the way his hips swayed as they walked up this horrible mountainside.

Mary stopped and looked back. 'Come on girls or Ian will take marks from our team.'

This was not a joke. Ian had divided them into two teams. He had chosen Helen and Jo, leaving David with Mary and the two girls. They were supposed to be racing each other towards the same objective which was to rescue some sheep thought to be trapped among snowdrifts. Whether they were real or notional sheep Mary wasn't clear. The expedition was code-named Pennington, also for uncertain reasons.

David was happy, striding ahead of his women. He could even manage to include Elizabeth under that heading, now that they were outside in a new bright day. Besides she compared well with Jo.

Ian wore a huge haversack on his back. He'd worn the same haversack to sally up the foothills of the Himalayas, to explore the ruins of Palmyra and the buried Buddhas of Southern Sri Lanka. Helen had fallen in love with him on the first of these expeditions and sometimes thought she could describe the haversack better than his face.

'Do slow down a bit, darling!'

'I want to be there before them so we can get the picnic laid out.'

'I thought it was supposed to be a race.'

'We had the shorter route.' Ian stopped to let Helen catch up. He pointed to the black figure of Jo beetling out ahead. 'Now he's really fast.'

'Young,' said Helen. 'And to think he looked so hopeless when we came upon him.'

'That's the point.' Helen realised she'd keyed a well-known lecture. 'The young need organising. They have the energy but no discipline. Look at Andie and Jim . . . '

Helen sighed and stopped listening. If it wasn't for the Foreign Office, Andie and Jim wouldn't have to go to boarding school and she could have them with her now.

The copse, etched black against white, was easy to find. It sprouted from a hollow, unusual so high in the hills. Jo stared and because he was more cultured and romantic than he allowed to show, tried to remember whether Samuel Palmer had ever painted snow. On the whole, he thought not. Moonlit pasture would be the nearest.

A fire blazed, red slashes against the white and black. Perhaps Ian had his uses. Mary admired the efficient way he produced mountains of sausages and potatoes. 'Got to wait till it dies down!' he shouted.

The children scurried about fetching twigs and pouring drinks. Even Jo had lost that unconvincing pale look which was so irritating.

Mary accepted a glass of mulled wine and balanced herself comfortably against a tree trunk. She had placed herself a few yards from the centre in the hopes she could be private. Ian, after all, had taken over the role of cheerful major-domo. But already she sensed a move towards her both from David and Elizabeth. She wondered which would reach her first.

How beautiful Mary is! David looked at his wife, standing wrapped in her long crimson cloak. How prettily shaped her face! How graceful her figure! How womanly and girlish and charming! It must be all the fresh air and exercise climbing through the snow, but he hadn't felt so attracted by her for a long time. Her air of remoteness too, caught at his heart, as if she was not altogether his. The idea of secretary Veronica bending over suspenders seemed infinitely vulgar and unappealing.

David moved towards his wife, wanting to stand by her, put his arm round her shoulders.

Elizabeth saw Mary as if she were indeed the mother of her dreams. Exhaustion and the extraordinary events of the last twenty-four hours had heightened her usually prosaic imagination. Her adopted mother, the mother she grew up with, had not been beautiful. She had been small, plain and gingery with a dissatisfied restlessness. Elizabeth had never seen a woman like Mary, who could stand still for so long but not in the block-like way which the stupid did, but with a kind of serenity. Yes, she looked serene. Elizabeth took another gulp of her mulled wine, although her head was already buzzing, and moved purposefully towards Mary.

She didn't notice David making tracks in the same direction. As she reached Mary and saw her skin now flushed with pink as Lucy's was, she wondered if it was her Englishness which made her seem different. But since she didn't want that to be the case, she dismissed the idea. Already Elizabeth was learning to paint events in her own colours.

'Hello, dear.' On the whole Mary was happier to welcome Elizabeth than David, who she now saw deflect his course and return to the fire. Elizabeth, she thought to herself wrongly, would not be so insistent.

'Tell me,' said Elizabeth, 'why you gave me away?'

'Gave you away?' What did she mean? She had told no one. 'I'm sorry, I don't understand.'

'When I was a baby. You gave me away.' Elizabeth's face went a dark red, making her eyes water and her nose tingle. 'You didn't want me. You gave me away.'

'Oh, I see.' Mary's voice remained totally calm, although she felt a terrified inward draining. So this was why this girl, this stranger, had crossed the Atlantic and tracked her down. It was to make an accusation. But as she thought this she noticed for the first time a resemblance between the intense face in front of her and the face of her lover, Richard Beck. It was his expression of concentration when he made love to her, the expression that had made her love him more than anything else, now turning a young girl's features into his.

Mary put her arm round Elizabeth. 'Don't say that.' She spoke gently. 'It wasn't like that.'

'It felt like that to me.' Her voice was defiant but her lips trembled and her eyes glistened with water.

'No, it didn't.' Mary spoke firmly, gripping the girl's shoulder. 'You had a perfectly good mother and father of your own.'

'Yes. But.' Elizabeth ducked her head down.

'You're a sensible girl. A rational girl. A medical student. I understand you wanted to see me, but you mustn't invent things. You were never mine. You're not mine now. I am your mother, it's true, but only because I gave birth to you. In no other way. You are what your real parents made you, what you made yourself. You have your career, your Bob. All this is far more important than I am or ever could be.'

Mary looked down and saw Elizabeth's face still agonised.

'In a way I'm a dream. You must think of me as that. I'm not going to enter your life in any other way. You must not try and make me the answer to whatever problems you have. Everyone has problems and they can't solve them by finding long-lost mothers. Nor can you.' She paused.

'A dream,' said Elizabeth softly.

Beyond the girl's head Mary saw Ian begin to serve sausages from the fire. She felt inappropriately hungry, as if this convincing of the girl was taking the strength out of her. She moved the hair back from Elizabeth's face. Without a coating of make-up, it looked like a child's face. Stop. She must not think like that.

'A dream,' repeated Elizabeth. The idea appealed to her. Standing against the dark tree trunk in her red cloak, Mary did look like a dream. Compared to Elizabeth's life in New York, this whole episode seemed like a dream. She didn't know how she'd be able to explain it to Bob. How her mother was both warm and understanding and yet utterly remote. In a way she had felt closer to her during that original telephone conversation when she had screamed in denial.

'Yes. A dream.' Mary moistened her lips. The smell of sausages carried strongly on the cold air. 'You'll forget about it when you get back home. Not entirely forget. But you won't want answers to questions which are unanswerable. When you're older you'll find there're all sorts of questions that have no answers.' Mary saw she was winning. There was an obedient look about the girl now.

'I think I see.'

'Yes. But I'm glad you came and found me.'

Elizabeth's face lightened and she looked at Mary properly for the first time since the start of their conversation. She didn't want to believe that Mary was lying.

'You are? Truly?'

'Yes. But I'm also ravenous.' Mary took her arm from Elizabeth's shoulders and gave her a little push in the back. 'Let's get something to eat or the others will scoff the lot.'

'Yes.' Elizabeth took a step forward. 'I guess I'm hungry too.' But her face was still bewildered, her unanswered question binding her to Mary.

'Of course you're hungry. It's only natural.' Why won't she go, thought Mary. Doesn't she understand the danger of resurrecting the past!

'Just tell me why you didn't love me!' cried Elizabeth, clutching onto Mary's sleeve.

'I didn't not love you. I didn't know you!' Mary too raised her voice in desperation. From the other side of the fire David watched and, seeing her emotion, moved as if to help, but the attitude of the two women put him off. They were so close, locked together as if in an embrace.

'I'm sorry,' whispered Mary, 'I can't tell you anything else. Please. Believe me.'

Slowly Elizabeth let go of her mother. She felt tired enough to lie down in the snow and go to sleep. Like a sleep-walker, she shuffled away towards the fire. She had crossed the Atlantic and received nothing more than an apology. She couldn't remember now what more she'd expected.

She'll be all right now, thought Mary, go back to America with a dream where before there'd been a vacuum. She'll write occasionally. I'll write occasionally, even send her a present when she marries, has a baby. What I did was wrong but there's no way I can put it right now, no amount of beating my breast will help her. She is not my child.

Mary looked up and saw David watching her from the other side of the fire. She turned away and bit into her sausage quickly. Why did he watch her like that? His pale face was grave but it did not wear that look of intensity that Richard's had worn.

Mary tried to swallow her lump of sausage and failed. Why should she feel like crying now?

I love her, thought David. I can't think how I ever looked at another woman. She's dealt with that girl, I can see that and soon we'll be alone together. And then I'll show her how I love her. How boring I've become, thinking of nothing but work and a little sex on the side. I'll change that now.

His eye was caught by Jo's black figure, coming forward to rake the potatoes out of the ashes. But even that did not dim his good intentions. Jo would not last.

Lucy had never thought of Jo as an ordinary human being before. But out here in the snow, obeying Ian's commands good-humouredly, he was revealed to be like everyone else. She did not yet know if this made her like him more or less. Certainly it made him less dangerously exciting. In fact, come to think of it, she had never really liked him anyway. He had never given her the opportunity with his constant demands, sexual and otherwise. Surely Ian stood for all the bourgeois establishment values he most despised, that he despised her for being a part of.

Lucy stared at him. With his face darkened by the fire and his hair fallen into an unfashionable parting and his occupation purely practical, he had never looked further from the Russian intellectual of his aspirations.

'Boy scout!' called Lucy suddenly, making Elizabeth, but not Jo, jump nervously. 'You look just like a boy scout!'

She expected at least a scowl. He had a brow-lowering variety which made his nose lengthen and his mouth curl into a thin red line. Instead, he smiled.

'Now you know my guilty secret!'

It was left for Lucy to produce the scowl.

Helen was telling Mary about her hopes for their next posting.

'We really deserve something decent, or at least nearer home, this time. But Ian's hopeless. I know he seems efficient and organising – on occasions like these he is – but he's a terrible coward when it comes to pushing himself forward in his career. And if he doesn't, other people will . . . '

Mary did not feel it necessary to give this monologue her full attention. Besides, her brain seemed to have become frozen since her conversation with Elizabeth. On the other hand her fingers tingled with the heat of a baked potato.

After she and Richard Beck had made love and were lying quietly in each other's arms, she used to run her fingers very lightly over his back. He had loved that and her fingers had seemed to become extra sensitive so she could feel every tiny roughness, mole, even the pores. After a while he would want to kiss her again and she would lie back smiling, waiting for him.

They would spend hours making love, long afternoons when he should have been at his office. His hair was greying at the edges and when he lay on top of her his face dropped into little wrinkles. But she liked it. She didn't think of him as old. In fact he wasn't old, younger than she was now. Mary gave a warm smile.

Helen saw the smile which came just at the moment when she had revealed her deep incompatibility with Ian. She stopped talking. Really, it was too rude. Mary clearly hadn't been listening to a thing. And when you considered how sympathetic Helen had been yesterday when she'd come into the cottage in such a state.

Mary heard the silence and saw Helen's frown.

'I'm sorry,' she began. But as she set herself to placate, she was suddenly struck by an extraordinary thought. Whyever shouldn't she go and find Richard Beck? Whyever not? He existed somewhere.

Helen, seeing the apology suddenly dispersed by something more complex, became, perversely, less irritated. She didn't mind Mary behaving rudely if the reason stemmed from her own neurotic problems. She understood that sort of behaviour which was standard among her friends.

Poor Mary, standing there with glazed eyes and flushed cheeks. She looked like someone drunk or doped.

I'll go and find him, thought Mary. I'll go and find Richard Beck.

Part Two

CHAPTER SEVEN

Richard Beck read the notice at the underground station with distaste. 'Lift out of service due to repairs.' That was the second time this week. It was not that he minded walking down the eighty-eight stairs, although coming up them was not a jolly prospect at the end of the day, but he was irritated by the inefficiency. Once a week was acceptable, twice inexcusable.

Richard showed his pass at the barrier with a disapproving frown. The London Transport official did not bother to look up. They were all the same these businessmen with their newpapers and brief cases, anxiously heading for retirement. When they took off their suits, there was nothing inside.

The snow disappeared as Mary travelled east. By the time she reached London, the world was quite ordinary again, grey, brown, black.

Because Mary had said she must go to the office, she went. Naturally no one wanted to see her there so she picked up her letters and went away again immediately. Their disapproval had made her feel invisible which was not altogether unpleasant. She wanted to be invisible for a while. She wanted to be a spy on her own life without it being dominated by her presence.

Cold now and longing for a coffee, she went back to the house, where she was relieved to find many signs of Lucy but no Lucy. Not that she would have shown any curiosity at her mother's unexpected arrival. Children of her age have no interest in events outside themselves and even those events are seen from too close a perspective to have any reality. She had been in love with Richard like that – love through a telescope, distorted, magnified.

'Hello.' Richard doodled on his pad. The company had a new operator who was very slow with her plugs. The office joker said she needed hole aversion therapy.

'There's a Mrs Tempest for you, Mr Beck.'

'Put her through . . . before she rings off.' He added this for the benefit of his secretary who smiled politely over the cup of coffee she was bringing in. He had always got on well with his secretaries as long as they were reasonably pretty.

'Yes. Richard Beck speaking. How can I help you?'

Did he know her, this Mrs Tempest? The voice was familiar, light but not high-pitched.

Richard took a gulp of his coffee and saw that his other line was flashing.

'Can I help you?' he repeated with more firmness.

His secretary dashed out of the door and the light stopped flashing.

'Richard. It's me, Mary. Risen from your past.' She laughed a ridiculous nervous screech. She was tempted to put down the telephone like a naughty child who's dialled 999.

'Mary? Mary Fellowes?'

The maiden name brought back the past more clearly. He sounded agitated. Disbelieving. Which was perfectly natural.

Richard picked up the biscuit placed beside the coffee cup and saw NICE was written across it in elegant letters. 'It's nice to hear from you,' he said. Was it? His heart was jumping peculiarly. He thought of the eighty-eight stairs up from the underground. They made his heart jump if he took them too fast.

'I'm glad.' Mary found tears in her eyes. Nice. What did he mean 'nice'? 'I'm just ringing on impulse.' She added untruthfully. 'For no reason.'

For no reason. Richard found he had crumbled the biscuit into tiny pieces which were now dropping through his fingers onto his suit. He brushed them off vigorously. 'How did you find me?'

'I rang the office. And asked for you.' She was quite right. He was easy to find. Whatever had changed in his life, it wasn't his work. Not yet. Thirty years in the same company.

He was right to question. Mary changed the telephone receiver to her left hand and shook out her clenched fingers. She had never telephoned him at his office. Even in her most desolate moments, she had waited for him to ring, sitting by the telephone hour after hour – sometimes all night. She had never known when he'd be free. 'Of course I never used to call you at the office.' She laughed, not quite such a screech this time.

Richard felt his face flush. The light from his other line was off now, he noticed. 'Are you well?' he asked, allowing his voice to relax a little, show a little warmth.

Mary heard the change of tone and relaxed a little too. 'Yes. Very well. Work. Home.'

'You're married, of course?'

'Oh yes.' She didn't want this over the telephone. Facts. Information swopped into machines. This was not what she wanted. She made herself take two or three long breaths. 'I thought perhaps we might meet? Have a drink.'

'Meet?' What did she want? He was tired. She sounded energetic, positively bubbling with energy. She was much younger than him. No younger than Cherry certainly, but then Cherry had far more energy than he did.

Mary heard his nervousness. She didn't mind that. It made her feel better. She was nervous too. 'I'm just in London for the day.' Why was she saying these things? She wasn't just in London for the day. She lived and worked in London, she had done for the last seventeen years. Yet it felt true. She was just in London for the day. 'And I suddenly felt like ringing you. I'm sorry if I've upset you.'

'No. No.' Just in London for the day. Richard admitted, because he felt less threatened now, that he had been nervous before. 'I'm not afraid of the past.' He laughed. A flush of excitement replaced the other. 'Let's meet, although I've changed so much we'll need carnations.'

'Not just you. I'm fat, greying and wrinkled.'

'Impossible!'

'I promise you.'

'I've gone the other way. I'm balding, bent and thin to scrawny.'

'How lovely!' Mary laughed. 'Well you always were the older man!'

They both became silent again.

'Where shall we meet?' said Richard eventually. Some of his nervousness returned but with it a feeling that he must see this Mary from the past.

'I don't mind.'

'Dingle's Wine Bar, then. Twelve forty-five.'
'Fine.' said Mary. 'I'm wearing a red cloak.'
'And I'm wearing a suit.'
Mary was not sure if he was making a joke.

David sat at his desk in the window. The cottage was absolutely silent, absolutely peaceful. He couldn't remember when he'd been on his own like this. It almost made him wish that Mary was going up to London for more than one day. Perhaps she would be delayed and miss the last train so that he could have the whole night to himself. The prospect made him feel light-headed.

David went to stand by the window. Patches of green showed through the whiteness. It hadn't snowed again since that day which might have killed him and had produced that girl. Mary's bastard. The word, not thought by him before, in her absence, popped into his head, giving him a malicious satisfaction. Mary was not perfect – as he was not perfect.

Strange though how he had gone off the idea of Veronica or anyone else. It was as if Mary's lack of perfection had made her more desirable. She had looked so beautiful as he'd dropped her at the station. Even the pallor and smudges of the early morning had flattered her face, softening the outline so that she looked like a tired girl rather than a competent middle-aged woman on her way to sort out a problem at the office. Not that she ever seemed quite convincing in that role.

David returned to his chair. It was unlike him not to settle immediately to his work. But then the events of the last few days were likely to unsettle anyone. When the girl had driven away yesterday, taking Jo and Lucy with her, he had thought that their youth gave them more in common with each other than they ever could with him. Even Lucy, his own daughter, wanted to be with them, felt it more natural than to stay with her parents.

Richard arrived at the wine bar early. He immediately regretted choosing it as a meeting place. It was so full and noisy, a kind of synthesis of young, ambitious London, not at all suitable for a sentimental tryst.

He decided to wait by the door and snatch Mary off to somewhere better.

But Mary had also arrived early. She had nothing else to do, nowhere else to go. She sat at a table further in the restaurant, giving herself courage with a glass of wine.

Twelve forty-five came and went. Mary had assumed he would appear in front of her, claiming her like a prize. She had kept her red cloak around her shoulders just in case but she hadn't really thought he would fail to recognise her. She didn't feel different at all, just a little more experienced, a little more used.

Richard looked at his watch for the third time. The idea of a practical joke struck him. He fingered his tie. It was one Cherry had given him for Christmas, blue and yellow, flashy, not really his taste. Mary had never given him anything, although he had brought her a present almost every time they met. He had felt so rich in those days, so pleased with his company car and his successful masculinity.

He supposed he was no less rich and successful now. Richard stood up and went to the bar with a determined expression.

Mary wound her cloak round herself and headed for the door. She would not ask for him.

'I'm looking for a Mrs Tempest.'

'Did she book?'

'No. I . . . '

The barman turned away, bored. 'Look round for her, if you like.'

Mary saw him, curved crossly over the bar. She went up and touched his shoulder.

'I'm here.'

She remembered how they'd smiled at each other when they'd met. It had always been so wonderful, after the hurdles of his marriage, her guilt. They had been smiles of relief, enormous, innocent, childlike. No-holds-barred smiles.

He was tall, thin, entirely grey. His face was creased but not very wrinkled, although the eyes were hooded by the lids. It gave him an animal air a little sinister, a little lecherous.

He turned to face her more fully. He was wearing a bright tie which seemed strange to her but the suit she recalled like his face. She had always been so impressed by his suit, by the contrast between its well-cut formality and the eager body underneath. Men, boys, her age had not worn suits. A man in a suit was something special, something remote, like an actor or a spaceman. She didn't remember telling him this but perhaps he knew anyway which would explain his, 'And I'll be wearing a suit.'

'Mary!' His exclamation was filled with happiness. He put his arm round her and kissed her on the cheek. 'I was beginning to think I'd invented your phone call.'

'No. I'm sorry.'

'Don't be sorry!' His arm stayed round her, taking her to the door.

He had always been like this, physically commanding, making her feel cared for.

'This is a terrible place. Far too youthful!'

Mary laughed. 'But you suggested it.'

'Brainstorm. We'll go somewhere much nicer where we can talk.'

She'd been a girl before, seventeen, eighteen, nineteen? He wasn't sure. Now she was a woman, heavier, more confident. What did she want from him?

Mary shivered violently as they went outside. He had taken his arm from her shoulder and put it through her arm.

'Cold?'

'No. I started early from the country . . . '

'Tired?'

'Yes. I suppose so.' She looked up at him. 'Nervous.'

'Oh yes.' He led her along briskly so that it was difficult for them to speak.

'I hope we can get a table.' They approached a striped awning above a narrow entrance.

They had eaten out together seldom, for fear of recognition. This seemed odd to her now, perhaps not the true reason, for she lived in Oxford at the time and knew barely anyone in London, while he could hardly be known in every city eating place. Perhaps he had wanted her to himself, in that little room he'd rented. She had been flattered by his need. Was their love all about flattery and need?

The restaurant was expensive. Richard felt more confident immediately. Expensive restaurants were one of the few places in which he still felt rich and successful.

Mary, sitting across the table from him, with a tentative eager expression, might have been a client, the wife of a client, the wife of a friend. He would charge the lunch to the company.

'Champagne?'

Mary flushed. He had always spoilt her, giving her a taste for things that were quite alien to her other self, the girl at home, the student. He bought her silk underclothes, leather-bound books. Donne, she remembered, was his favourite poet.

'Champagne would be perfect. But I'm not very hungry.'

'I shan't force you to eat.' It was the first time he had smiled properly. They both felt its effect.

Mary looked down at her plate.

'There is a reason I wanted to see you . . . '

Richard held up his hand. 'Not till after the champagne, please.' Now that he was less tense he felt perversely irritated by the idea of 'a reason'. A reason made their meeting seem almost official. He wanted to say 'We never needed a reason before' but was sensible enough to keep quiet.

'You look very well,' he said. 'More beautiful than you used to.'

'Thank you.' Mary suspected he felt obliged to pay her this sort of compliment but felt irrationally happy. She believed she was more beautiful now, even with her wrinkles and heavy hips. Last time he had seen her she had been six months pregnant, an anxious, thin girl with a bulge.

'A toast?' Richard lifted his champagne glass.

'To the past?' Mary smiled to show she was joking.

'No. No. No! That's far too depressing. Let's drink to the future!'

'The future!'

Playing a game, they leaned forward to touch glasses. They were close, smiling, but neither looked at the other's eyes.

David, finding to his surprise that he didn't want to drive to the pub, made himself cheese on toast.

Elizabeth sat in her hotel room. It was small and not very warm. Really it was only acceptable if you sat *in* bed. The telephone buzzed and just at the instant the noise reached Elizabeth's consciousness, or even a hair's breadth of time before, she had a new precise thought, 'Why don't I find out about my father?'

'You see.' Mary hesitated, rolled up her napkin as if it were a rug. Her fingers were competent, Richard noticed, blunt-ended, not delicate. He thought they had used to be fine and sensitive.

'You see.' Mary began again. She thought that if you were going to deliver a bombshell you might as well throw it with panache. 'Our daughter called to see me.'

'Hello.'

'Hi. It's me, Lucy. And Jo. Shall we come up?'

'Sure. If you can fit. This room's the size of a closet.'

But a father isn't as important as a mother. Is he?

'Our daughter?'

Richard's bewilderment was unexpected. Left with an unexploded bomb in her hands, Mary felt disinclined to explain.

Richard had not truly forgotten. But twenty-two years was a very long time and the memories that gave him pleasure were of loving afternoons in the little room he'd rented. Ten pounds a week it had cost him. The bed was so small that they had to lie entwined together.

Mary sipped at her champagne. She tried to think how much she minded he'd forgotten, or pretended to forget, but failed. He was there, in front of her and, as before, she couldn't judge him as she would others. After that first moment of recognition, she did not even see him clearly.

Richard allowed the real memories to return and flushed. Had she come to reproach him? It seemed a strange thing to do after all these years. He had had two more children since then. Blond boys, Daniel and Nicky, now nineteen and seventeen. He had been present at their births, held Cherry's hand, encouraged her with her breathing.

Mary put down her glass and leant forward. 'Please. I've not come to make you feel guilty. No! No! On the contrary.' She became agitated, her voice breaking, her eyes glistening.

Now Richard saw the girl again. How well he remembered that distressed look! She wore it whenever she wanted to say something and couldn't find the words. It was a painful moment for her but always made him feel particularly loving, particularly protective. 'Perhaps I didn't want to think about it,' he said gently. 'After all, the baby came between us.'

'Oh, I don't know.' Mary had resumed control of herself. She was a little cross at showing him so much vulnerability. Now she leant back and spoke calmly, even smiled. 'It would have had to end sometime.'

'Would it?' Richard drank some champagne. It seemed to affect him more quickly these days.

'Our affair,' said Mary boldly.

'Is that what it was?'

The sadness in Richard's voice suddenly made Mary very happy. She looked into his eyes. They were green, brown, grey. She had never known which. There was grey in the eyelashes.

'We always said it would never be that.' Richard was serious.

That look of concentration when he made love to her.

Richard watched her eyes and knew what she was feeling. Did they still have that effect on each other? It seemed impossible, absurd.

'Love. Of course, we talked of love.' Mary's voice was squeaky, hysterical. She couldn't be sitting here wanting to go to bed with this old lover, this old man. It was laughable. She laughed, unconvincingly. Or was that why she'd come? Looking for sexual passion.

'Eternal love.' Richard's mind whirled from Mary's face to an image of his secretary waiting in his office, his bedroom in the house he shared with Cherry, the room he had once rented for Mary. He felt his heart pumping, pumping.

'Leek soup?'

The waiter might have been standing there for some time. Mary looked up at him with amazement. Could he possibly have ordered leek soup?

'Thank you.'

The bowl was laid in front of Richard.

'Smoked trout?'

The fish was laid in front of Mary.

'Bon appétit.' The waiter withdrew.

'Where were we?' Richard tapped his glass with his knife. 'Order. Order.'

'Yes.' Mary picked up her fork. 'I think we were getting rather carried away.' She regretted the words as she said them. They had a dull, middle-aged sound, the sound of reason.

'This girl.' Richard spoke between gulps of soup and Mary thought how seldom they'd eaten together despite always meeting over lunchtime. He was not a hungry man. Or he had not used to be. Gulp. He swallowed the soup noisily. 'This girl. Does she have a name incidentally?'

'Elizabeth Crocker.' Mary's voice expressed reluctance which Richard registered without analysing. How could he understand that Mary was using Elizabeth as an excuse to meet him?

'And is she nice?'

'She's American.'

'The two things aren't incompatible.'

'She's nice without being especially pretty or clever or charming.'

'Oh dear.' Richard could not think they were discussing a child they had created so his voice was light, unconcerned.

Mary, wanting to talk about themselves and not about this stranger, this American, felt even less enthusiasm. But Richard had said 'Oh dear' and it was her duty to defend the girl. 'She was nervous, of course, jet-lagged. But Lucy liked her so she can't be all bad.'

'Lucy?'

'My daughter.' Mary had forgotten he knew nothing about her life. They stared at each other again but this time as strangers. Mary made an effort. 'I married David Tempest, a barrister. We have one daughter, Lucy.'

'And you're still married?'

'Yes.' Mary looked surprised at the question. 'Oh, yes.' She spoke more definitely. He had always been so very married. The unspoken basis to their relationship. His marriage. His children. His wife.

'Susan and I split up, you know.' Richard looked down as he said this but since Mary made no response he looked up again.

She wore a childish expression of bewilderment.

'Susan?'

'My wife. My ex-wife.'

They had both finished their first courses. There was nothing to eat, no diversion.

'When?' asked Mary.

'Years and years ago.' Richard's voice was casual. Why shouldn't it be? It was all so long in the past. 'My two younger children are nearly grown up. Boys.'

'So you married again?'

Richard laughed. 'I like women.'

Despair is a feeble word, thought Mary. Resentment would be more appropriate. So Susan, she had always thought it a hateful name, wasn't the wife of his life, the forever wife. If his sons are nearly grown up, he must have divorced and remarried soon after we broke up. He wasn't so very-very married. Resentment. She looked up at him still so handsome.

'Who did you marry?'

'Oh, Cherry's a real career woman. Cherry married me, really. She always gets what she wants.'

Bitterness? A bad marriage? Did she want to think of his problems? His problems which had nothing to do with her. But most of his life had nothing to do with her. Fantasy. This whole meeting was silly fantasy. 'And are you still married to her?' Mary's voice was businesslike. She might have been interviewing him for the BBC. Lines of the interview set down formally.

'Oh, yes. I'm very fond of Cherry.'

They both looked outward into the restaurant. Clear-sighted now, they watched the waiter approach with their main courses. Before he had cut into their passion, now he found them becalmed, each on their own stretch of water. Being Italian and sensitive, he felt unconsciously disappointed and tried to make up for the lack with his own fervour. 'Vitello parmigiano con fagiolini al burro. Che bel burro!'

Mary responded with a vague smile. What beautiful butter! seemed an odd statement even for an Italian.

'Trota affumicata alle vongole con insalata di pomodori e spinaci.'

Richard watched his food settle in front of him without enthusiasm. What more could they say to each other? Perhaps he should tell her about his retirement plans.

'Thank you,' he said bleakly. The waiter hovered round like a dragonfly. Swat! Swat! Richard imagined vicious physical action.

Jo and Lucy sat on Elizabeth's bed. She sat on the floor.

'But your Bob might not be so keen on us.' Lucy was planning a summer visit to America.

'You'll be my guests.'

'But he'll be your husband. His flat.'

Elizabeth laughed. 'Oh, no. It's not like that in America. We're equal partners.'

Jo lay on his back looking at the ceiling. He couldn't think why Lucy was so keen on this American girl. Since coming back to London, Elizabeth had lost her snow-maiden prettiness. She was prim and talkative without being lively. Besides, when the two girls talked, Jo felt curiously absent, as if he was a bit of old furniture.

'Fuck!' Both girls turned to look at him which was satisfactory. Having no particular communication in mind, he added at an even higher decibel. 'Shit!'

'What's the matter?' Elizabeth who swore out of feminist principle sounded less surprised than he hoped. 'Have you forgotten something?'

'You,' said Jo, ignoring the second question to answer the first.

'You could hardly forget us,' said Lucy, deliberately misunderstanding. A little flutter of excitement started in her breast. She had never been able to tease Jo. He was so strong and, besides, she was in love with him.

'Fuck you!' enlarged Jo and found the momentum of emotion had swung him upright and off the bed. The room being so small, there was nowhere much to go but out of the door. He turned the handle half-heartedly.

'Did we say something?' Elizabeth turned to Lucy. Who shrugged. Then smiled.

'Christ! Christ Jesus!'

Lucy half rose off the bed. She saw herself restraining his departure with a loving hand. Wasn't love everything?

'He wanted to go,' commented Elizabeth as the door slammed shut. 'Men are like that. Moody. Suddenly wanting to be on their own. Women are much more rational.'

'Oh, yes,' agreed Lucy, who'd previously thought exactly the opposite. 'They're so self-indulgent. Jo absolutely never admits to being wrong about anything.'

'Now Bob isn't like that.' Elizabeth joined Lucy on the bed. 'He's very good at recognising his weaknesses. Of course, I've helped him a lot, talking it through with him. I guess it's all about statements of independence. Have you tried talking to Jo?'

'No,' admitted Lucy, a little weakly. Burning the toast was the nearest she got to a statement of independence.

'Studying psychoanalysis got me started,' said Elizabeth consolingly. 'Personally, I think all prospective marriage partners should go into analysis before they settle down. It would save a lot of divorces.'

'Yes,' said Lucy, feeling pathetically young. A spark of life reasserted itself. 'As a matter of fact I'm not sure I believe in marriage.'

'That's a very reasonable position to take up.' Elizabeth crossed her legs under her but continued to sit very upright with a serious businesslike expression on her face. 'However it must, in the last analysis, depend on your definition of marriage.'

'Oh dear,' said Lucy who had just noticed something under the bed. 'Jo's left his bag. He will be upset.'

CHAPTER EIGHT

Mary and Richard left the restaurant arm in arm. The touching was strange, like the feel of a close relative after a long absence. They did not look at each other. After its becalmment in the middle, the lunch had picked up, moving into the more impersonal channel of work. Richard had been impressed to find Mary a successful executive. He would not have predicted it and yet she had always been strong-minded in her own way. No gradual unwinding, no reconsiderations, no contact of any sort.

'You said: "I won't see you again,"' he reminded her.

The champagne and wine no longer gave Mary a sense of exhilaration but had the effect of separating her from her thoughts. He held her arm as they walked along the pavement. If there was a reason, a motive, on either side, she couldn't bring herself to face it.

'Did I say that?' she at last replied.

Richard held her arm closer. They passed the entrance to a large and expensive hotel. Richard led her through the door. He let go of her arm and went up to the desk. Asking no questions, Mary stood waiting for him in front of the lifts.

Richard returned holding a key. 'I said we were between flights, needing a sleep,' he said, smiling.

Mary smiled back. If they were to make love, it should at least be done with good humour. They stood in the lift side by side, not talking.

'I'm afraid it's the best they could do. At such short notice.' Richard was still smiling as they stood at the threshold of the room.

Mary supposed, rather gloomily, that he might be feeling a macho sense of achievement at having brought her to this bedroom. The room was not big, the bed not wide but grandly

69

achieved with an abundance of beige and scarlet pelmets. 'It's very nice,' said Mary, laying her handbag on a chair.

Richard stopped smiling. Men of approaching sixty made love but not too often and not under such a weight of memory.

'Darling!' He caught Mary by the shoulders and pressed her close to him.

The meeting of their two bodies comforted Mary. She still felt no sexual arousal but there was a warmth and happiness. His cheek was rough on hers, harder than David's. His body was hard too and held her strongly, more strongly than David ever did.

Richard pulled himself away, flung back the bed covers and began to undress himself. Mary, left to herself, hovered indecisively.

'I want a pee.' Richard, stripped to his underpants, left for the bathroom.

Mary sat on the edge of the bed and took off her shoes and her coat. And her sweater and her tights. When he reappeared, she scurried past him into the bathroom. He flinched away a little, as if surprised by her haste.

Mary sat on the lavatory, glad of the momentary respite.

Richard lay in the bed with his arms behind his head. He reminded himself that making love was the one area where he'd never suffered from self-doubt.

'Hello! Helloah!' After calling a few times Helen discovered the cottage was not locked and walked in. After all it belonged to her husband and she was responsible for its upkeep. She poked about the kitchen and looked for signs of David.

In the bedroom, David continued to snore comfortably.

Mary and Richard lay side by side, naked under a single sheet. Both their hearts beat furiously but neither made a move.

'Darling Mary. Darling.' Richard began to kiss her. At once she was filled with joy and delight. Kissing, stroking, making love. How she and Richard had enjoyed themselves!

'Darling.' They held each other so close, mouth to mouth, breast to breast, thigh to thigh. They struggled to get closer, pressing each other on the back. It had always been like this. They had always wanted to merge into each other, lose the burden of separateness.

She had not come to David in the same way for, with him, she had wished to preserve her independence. She had come fully-formed, armed, aware of the need for self-preservation. She had not given herself to David as she had to Richard. He had not wanted it.

Richard remembered Mary's body now. The shape of her shoulders, the feel of her neck under her hair, the slope of her hip, the softness on the inside of her thighs. His hands, bony and shaking a little, began to explore. Impatiently he threw back the sheet.

Mary smiled and smiled, although her wide-open eyes glistened as if with tears. This was why she had come; to have someone worship her – worship her body, it didn't matter which. It didn't matter he was married, he had married again, she was married. She felt as though she were tumbling over and over with happiness, like a child on a lawn, although in fact she lay and smiled while he explored.

I am everything to him at this moment, thought Mary.

She is a gift, a gift, thought Richard less selfishly, and I'm alive to touch her and kiss her and love her. He felt puffed up with desire and very, very young. Her breasts are so round and her skin so smooth and if I turn her over like this I can feel the way her backbone runs down between her buttocks and all the way to her cunt.

'Richard. Richard.' Mary whispered and wound her legs and arms round him. She felt nineteen, eighteen, seventeen.

Lucy and Elizabeth walked through Hyde Park. It was beginning to get dark but the sun had set slowly leaving a burnished backcloth to the black trees.

'I love Jo, you see,' said Lucy.

'Love. Love.' Elizabeth sounded impatient.

'When I'm with him, he fills me up so I can't think of anything else,' explained Lucy earnestly. 'Isn't that love?' Her voice became a little wistful.

'That's sex,' replied Elizabeth briskly. She gave Lucy's arm a squeeze. 'Bob and I got over that feeling in our first year.'

'Got over?' Lucy felt a sudden sharp stab of dislike. 'I think you just don't believe in love!' She flung back her head, defiantly.

Those eyes above her. The wrinkles making them small but the expression as she remembered, serious. As serious as a child's. Such hard work, such concentration, all for her, all out of desire for her. Perhaps out of love.

'Richard. Richard, darling,' she murmured, pursing her lips, shutting her eyes, moving her hips, losing her thoughts.

'I love you. I love you. I love you,' grunted Richard as he always did when he made love to a woman. And he did. He did. He did. 'I love you.' He fell onto her.

She had not said it, although she was the one who had come to find him.

David stumbled out of the bedroom. Sleeping in the afternoon was so strange to him that he felt disorientated like someone in jet lag. But he thought he'd heard footsteps downstairs.

Helen looked upwards and saw David, half undressed with his hair standing on end. He was usually so tidy, so self-contained that the sight of him as a rumpled human being gave her a shock. He was attractive, she realised for the first time.

'I came to offer you tea and company,' she said smiling.

David frowned. 'Sorry. I was asleep.'

'I'm the one who should be sorry. The door was unlocked. Shall I go?'

'No. No. Tea would be nice.'

'Will you come over to us?'

David tied up his dressing-gown. 'Why don't I make it for you?'

Helen appeared to consider, which was deceptive since she had no intention of leaving. 'Ian's pasting up his photograph album. He takes it far more seriously than any report for the FO.'

'That's settled then. Tea and toast in front of the fire.' He descended a few stairs. 'Let the workers work and us be layabouts!' His voice was exhilarated as if the suggestion was daring. And for David the idea of being a layabout was as daring as a jump into a swimming pool would be for a non-swimmer. Over the last twenty years his work had filled every moment that he was not with Mary or Lucy. Every moment, every thought. But why shouldn't he have an afternoon off?

Mary was comfortable, her head resting on Richard's chest, her eyes shut, her thoughts pacified.

Richard was asleep, snoring, not firmly as David did but with a whistle like a bird. If Mary opened her eyes and swivelled them upwards, she could see the sharp edge of his chin and the grey stubble. She was glad he slept for it gave her a moment on her own to collect herself.

How would they part?

'Mary – is a wonderful woman,' said David staring into the fire. 'She combines absolute serenity with charm, beauty, intelligence and sensitivity.'

Helen was not sure that a paean in praise of his wife was exactly what she'd envisaged from this fireside scene – it was dark outside and they'd drawn the curtains so that the room was small, intimate. But she understood that for David it was extraordinary to talk so frankly, even if it was only about the virtues of his wife.

'You're very lucky,' she said and, thinking it sounded feeble, added quickly, 'it's so extraordinary the way the right people find each other.'

'Yes,' agreed David, prodding a piece of toast with a fork. 'I knew I wanted to marry Mary as soon as I met her. Although she wasn't as she is now.'

'Really?' Helen became more animated. 'I assumed she was one of those amazing women who are born perfect from their mother's womb.'

Not noticing Helen's tart tone, David continued with utter seriousness, 'She was beautiful but disorganised, charming but completely without confidence, intelligent but an emotional mess.'

'And you sorted her out?'

'I fell in love with her.' David suddenly turned from the fire and gave Helen a sharp look. 'You think I'm ridiculous.'

'Certainly not. But I'm interested you can see everything so clearly. I don't think women ever see anything as clearly as that.'

'It's my lawyer's mind.' David smiled and turned back to the fire. 'There'd been this man. We never talked about it properly but I knew anyway. He was much older than her. And married. I don't think she really loved him but she was very young and he seemed glamorous.'

'That's usual.'

'She had a protected childhood. She was very romantic so when she got pregnant . . . ' David broke off. But Helen finished the sentence for him.

'She had the baby.'

'Is that usual too?'

'No. But it makes sense from what you said. And Lucy's that baby.'

'*What?*' David turned.

Helen looked away and sighed and tried to think how she could deny her words. 'Nothing.' David had heard what she said and was looking at her with a most peculiar expression.

'Lucy's *my* daughter.'

'Yes. Of course.'

'That's not the problem.'

'No,' agreed Helen eagerly, though thinking, Ah so there is a problem.

'Mary didn't want her child. By this man. I guess she thought he would divorce and marry her when she had the baby. And when he didn't she turned against him.'

'Very understandable,' commented Helen who despite her insatiable desire for just this kind of conversation was beginning to feel a kind of embarrassment. This baring of the soul seemed unnatural in someone as restrained as David usually was.

'So she had the baby adopted at birth. She never saw her at all.'

'Oh.' Helen could think of nothing else to say. And why had he chosen her for his confidences?

'Have some toast.' Helen crouched forward to take the toast and looked at his face. It was bland, except for the prominent nose, smooth, over-fed, under-exercised, the mouth a bit rubbery, the face of a man in sedentary occupation. Whose brain was used all the time and his body seldom.

David looked at Helen's face as she took the toast. He was struck by the sharpness of her features compared to the quiet symmetry of Mary's. And yet she was attractive, with button-black eyes, a bright complexion and red shapely mouth.

Helen returned to her chair and ate her toast in silence.

David came and sat on the arm of the chair. His sense of being out of normal time had not altogether dissipated. He wanted to hold Helen's hand and tell her about the dreadful Elizabeth. He wanted a woman's view on the situation. But Helen's face had lost its usual eager enquiring expression and seemed withdrawn, unwelcoming. Nevertheless, compelled by an instinctive need for the touch of a woman, David laid his hand on her arm.

Helen looked up. His face was kindly, gentle, anxious. She sighed. She always thought she wanted confidences, longed for confidences, but when they came, really came, she sighed and

74

wondered whether anyone's emotional life was as interesting as her own. Perhaps she was a confidence-teaser, flirting for the overture, only to turn away disgusted.

David noticed the sigh and took his hand away.

'I've been married to Ian ten years. We have two children but I've never lived in a home of my own.'

'That's bad luck.'

'You see, we only had one home-posting.'

'Where did you live then?'

'In a rented house.'

'What about these houses?'

'I mean a *London* house. That's what I tell Ian. I wish you'd tell him. He respects you.'

David rubbed his eyes. If he couldn't talk to this woman properly or hold her or be held by her, then he wished she would go. He stood up and looked at his watch. 'I wonder if Mary's caught the 4.40 p.m. More tea?'

'No thank you. Ian will be wondering where I am.'

'Doesn't he know?'

'Oh, yes.' Now Helen took hold of David's arm. Her dark eyes peered at him sympathetically. 'Does she often think of the baby?'

'What?' David stared at her blankly.

'The adopted baby.'

Had he really told her that? What disloyalty to Mary. For a moment by the fireside, she had seemed someone special to whom he could tell his fears but now she was Ian's wife again, bright, inquisitive, a casual not particularly liked acquaintance. 'I'd be grateful if you didn't mention it to anyone else,' he said gruffly.

'Of course not.' Helen squeezed his arm, leant closer, 'Not even Ian!'

David saw she wanted to be kissed and bent forward. Their mouths met and, although both were thinking of other things – supper in her case, train timetables in his – their flesh made contact with a certain warmth and pleasure. They smiled as they drew apart.

David patted her shoulder. 'You must come round more often.'

Helen's smile widened flirtatiously, 'If I'd known what a dab hand you were with the toasting fork I'd have come round days ago.'

Mary and Richard were making love again. I'm too old for this, I'm too old for this, puffed Richard. But making love was such a pleasure.

After this we'll part, thought Mary. And is this passion I'm feeling? Is this what I came to him for?

'I love you. I love you.' Who was saying it to whom. Or was it in their heads.

They lay together, so closely, so tenderly, so exhaustedly together.

Outside it had become dark. Inside too. Vague silver moons danced in front of Mary's eyes. She felt Richard stir. She could feel him gathering himself.

'You always made me feel like this.'

'How?'

'Outside myself. Outside everything.'

They fell silent again. This time Mary rose.

'Were you planning to go back to the office?'

'Of course.' She could hear him smiling.

'I was planning to catch the 4.40 train.' He could hear her smiling.

They were both awake now, aware of each other's thoughts bustling around them.

'I suppose I should ask you,' Richard's voice was not altogether calm, 'why you gave me up?'

The darkness was helpful, comforting.

'I was very young.'

She felt Richard's hand at her waist. It stroked her hip. 'I'm sorry.'

'Yes.' Mary let him stroke her for a little and then rolled back again and kissed him gently on the cheek. 'I forgive you.'

'And I forgive you.'

They sat up then and Richard put on the bedside light. He looked absurdly old for their situation with his grey hair wildly awry, his wrinkles, his bony shoulders and legs. Yet he was still her Richard Beck. Besides, she must look pretty ragged herself.

'I love you.'

He smiled his lecherous crocodile smile and went to the bathroom.

Despite resolutions of immediate activity, Mary lay back to enjoy the moment. She had been right to come and find him.

From the bathroom, Richard whistled *Abide with me*.

Elizabeth and Lucy were making scrambled eggs for supper.

76

'Your mother's made a beautiful kitchen,' said Elizabeth carefully. Tomorrow she was going back to America. Tomorrow she wouldn't have to talk carefully about 'your mother' but freely to Bob about 'my mother'.

'She cares about things like that. Her surroundings.' Lucy flopped the over-cooked eggs onto two unwarmed plates. 'I sometimes think she must be a cold sort of person to care so much about what things look like.'

'Perhaps she's unhappy,' said Elizabeth less carefully.

'Unhappy?' Lucy dumped the two plates and came to sit at the table. 'Mummy?' Her voice expressed amazement.

'Mothers can be unhappy.'

'Oh, I'm not that naive.' Lucy took a large mouthful of eggs. 'Other people's mothers are dreadfully unhappy – apart from Jo's who's just stupid – but my mother is far too settled to be unhappy. She has her husband, her job, her house, her daughter in that order of importance and it would take a bomb to shake any unhappiness out of her. She's complete in herself, in her life. Complete people aren't unhappy. They just are.'

'Wow.' Elizabeth took her first bite of eggs with the look of someone who needed reviving. 'I guess you don't like your mother very much.'

'Of course I like my mother!' Lucy scraped at her plate energetically. 'Just because I can see her clearly enough to analyse her character, it doesn't mean I don't like her. Or even love her. Of course I love my mother. She drives me mad. What better proof is there?'

If Lucy hoped for a laugh, she didn't get one. 'I admire your mother,' Elizabeth said seriously. 'I think she's a sensitive person who finds life a sort of difficult proposition.'

'Oh, yeah. Yeah.'

'She was very kind to me, a stranger arriving on her doorstep.'

'I've been meaning to ask you that. How did you come to know her?'

Lucy had finished eating and was staring at Elizabeth curiously. Although generally too self-absorbed to investigate other people's lives, she was suddenly struck by the way this girl had popped out of nowhere into the centre of their lives.

Elizabeth finished and pushed back her chair. 'I guess they met in London. My parents.' This was true as far as she knew. Elizabeth's studies in psychotherapy had taught her an acute aversion to lying. Even in a good cause. She did it badly, emotionally and without conviction.

77

'Your father and your mother met my mother, you mean?' Lucy persevered with the nose of a dog on the scent. 'Were they very good friends?'

'I don't know. I guess so.'

'They must have been for you to track down my mother all these years later.'

Elizabeth stood up. 'Would you say you were emotionally secure, Lucy?'

Lucy smiled. 'Sounds as if you're interviewing me for a job.'

I am in a way, thought Elizabeth. The job of being my half-sister. 'You've had a very secure upbringing.' The words came out like an accusation.

'I'm sorry,' said Lucy, still smiling. She was used to that sort of jibe. Jo made it all the time. 'I'm doing my best to unsettle myself.'

'No. I didn't mean that.' Elizabeth tried to be more honest. If she was going to tell her it must be on a basis of total honesty. 'I'm jealous of you.'

'Do you think I'm, what did you say, emotionally secure?'

'I don't know. I think so. But I'm not altogether sure. That first night. You cried so hard.'

'Don't emotionally secure people cry?' Lucy couldn't keep up Elizabeth's level of intensity. She began to parody her. She talked such jargon, such nonsense.

Elizabeth sensed her lack of sympathy and felt suddenly consumed by rage. Spoilt bitch! 'You know I'm your mother's daughter,' she cried out, adding so there'd be no mistake, 'your fucking sister!'

Richard and Mary were quiet and very careful with each other. They didn't want to deny what had happened in the hotel bedroom but they didn't want to make too much of it. Make it impossible to continue things as they were.

Mary straightened the bed. Richard hung up towels in the bathroom. As they moved slowly about, they had time to become separate again, capable of independence.

Richard put on his jacket. Mary put on her cloak. She did it reluctantly, giving Richard time to come to her and smooth it over her shoulders. She leant back against him wondering as she did so why this man whom she'd loved for a short time twenty-two years ago should give her a greater sense of security than her own husband. Her husband who had loved her continuously over so many years. She couldn't understand such a contradiction but she equally couldn't deny that was how she felt it. She wondered if he felt it too.

'Thank you for ringing,' he said just before they left the room and they kissed gently.

'And now you'll rush to Cherry,' said Mary gaily over her shoulder as they went one behind the other along the corridor.

'That's right,' agreed Richard. 'And you'll go to David.'

'Exactly,' smiled Mary, absurdly glad that he'd remembered her husband's name.

Lucy's first thought was that this would show Jo that she didn't come from a boring bourgeois family. Her second was that she didn't want Elizabeth as a sister. And the third that she'd heard wrong.

'I shouldn't have thrown it at you. I'm sorry.' Elizabeth's tone of regret was contradicted by her air of satisfaction.

Lucy wanted to throw her out. Anything else was a compromise between dislike and good manners. She could not be her sister.

'I came to see my mother,' continued Elizabeth in the face of Lucy's silence. 'You couldn't understand that, having always . . .'

'I can understand very well!' snapped Lucy, cutting off reasonable explanations. 'If you must know, I think you're behaving extremely badly!' This was better. Colour and energy flooded her face. 'Who asked you to come blundering into my life like this? Who gave you the right? It seems to me you're the most monstrously selfish, unpleasant person I've ever come across and I wish you'd get out of this house and go back to where you came from!'

Lucy watched Elizabeth's reasonable manner crumple under her assault.

'But you can't talk to me like this!' Her voice was choked with outrage. 'I've only told you the truth.'

'The truth is of no interest to me whatsoever,' said Lucy, now becoming the calmer of the two. 'The truth does not exist as any halfway intelligent human being knows. Truth is relative and your idea of truth is extremely unlikely to coincide with mine.'

'But . . . .'

'But nothing. I have to say that you strike me as a supreme example of someone who has been educated beyond their intelligence, thus doing lasting damage to their brain.'

Elizabeth had never heard anyone talk like this. She felt on strange seas without a guiding light.

79

But Lucy was under full sail, blasting ahead.

'It seems to me there is something of the devil in you. First you try and kill my father . . . '

'No. No.'

'Then you attack my mother.'

'I'm not attacking your mother. I admire . . . '

'Don't speak of her. You have lost all right by the brutality of your . . . '

'*Brutality!*' Elizabeth felt like screaming and might have screamed had not a sound interrupted her.

It was the front door, a mere thin wall away in one direction, an angled window in another, being opened. But opened so ineptly, so noisily that Elizabeth, with her New York training, thought of burglars and Lucy thought of Jo.

It was strange, thought Mary, the effect on her of satisfactory sex. No, she must not be so vulgar, so superficial. Yet is was strange how satisfactory sex made her clumsy. It had always had that effect when one might have assumed the reverse would be true, that one's body, well-oiled, pleased with itself, would go into a new efficient gear in which physical co-ordination would be supreme, Porsche-like, bionic. At least she should be able to unlock her own front door.

But here she was, dropping keys to the ground, unable to turn keys in the lock. She was like an unco-ordinated youth, a colt, not a mature, satisfied . . .

'Oh, Mother!'

'Darling.'

'I thought it was Jo.'

'Oh yes. Hello, Elizabeth.'

The energy of the emotions broken into by this unexpected meeting gave the three women a certain momentum which carried them through greetings and explanations.

Nevertheless this was not entirely helpful for, although Mary and Lucy and possibly even Elizabeth, at this stage, longed to be alone to work out what had just happened to them, the same momentum of events took them into the sitting-room with a cup of tea.

'You're off tomorrow, aren't you?' said Mary to Elizabeth. She had hoped never to see her again.

'Yes,' agreed Elizabeth, subdued. What would Lucy say now?

She had decided, reasonably on the evidence, that her new sister was decidedly unstable, emotionally speaking. She glanced at her nervously.

'I didn't know you were coming to London?' Lucy accused her mother. Is that the worst she would have to accuse? Or would they have to 'have things out' like some horrid TV programme. 'I thought you and Daddy were having a month away from it all.'

'Oh, yes.' Mary gushed abstractedly. These lies were throwing her back to her youth.

Elizabeth stood up. 'I'd better be getting back to my hotel. Packing, you know.'

Coward, thought Lucy. Coward. Coward. Coward. 'You are a coward,' she said in a voice so calm it surprised her.

Mary, by the telephone, laughed a polite conversational laugh.

Lucy knew the laugh. It meant her mother's thoughts were as far removed from this room as if she were on top of Ben Nevis. 'Coward!' she repeated with more emphasis though no anger.

Mary concentrated on dialling the cottage. She could hardly remember it since all her visual images were filled with the events of the afternoon. She thought it was odd how she could see herself as well as Richard as if they were in a film or a play. Did this make it less real? What was he doing now? Speeding towards Cherry? Cherry. What a ridiculous name!

The two girls stared at each other.

'Why are you always standing up?' said Lucy crossly.

'Because I'm on my way out.'

'You're always on your way out or your way in. You're a terribly restless person.'

Elizabeth told herself Lucy had just sustained a severe phsychological trauma. She must be kind. 'I'm sorry.'

'Pooh!'

English people were so childish. 'If it would help you to talk this over . . .'

'Pooh!'

'With your mother.' Elizabeth glanced in Mary's direction but even she could tell she was as little on their wavelength as the man in the moon. 'Perhaps when you've had time to assimilate the news. When you've calmed down.'

'Calmed *down*!' Lucy leapt to her feet. Having got so far, some other action seemed called for and she advanced on the smaller girl, fists clenched.

Mary raised her blind eyes from the telephone. 'Whatever are you two squabbling about?' But then the telephone was answered.

'Darling!' David lay on his back on the sofa. He had still not dressed and his dressing-gown fell open across the floor. He had a feeling of undergraduate lounging, and memories of his rather too intimate conversation with Helen. Was that her name? 'Darling. I was wondering when you'd call.'

She was later than she planned. The 6.10 arriving at 9.20 p.m. She was apologetic, strained, in need of care. 'I'll meet you. Don't worry. And I'll put something from the freezer into the oven.'

There was no freezer, he'd forgotten that, but it was the offer that counted, a reflection of his feeling for her. They would start their holiday afresh when she arrived. 'It's been a lovely day but I missed you. See you soon, darling.'

On the 5.25 p.m. from Victoria to Beckenham Richard Beck slept with his newspaper on his knee. Before he dropped off, he hoped that his two children would not be home that evening. Cherry he didn't mind. Cherry never asked questions. She didn't have enough interest in him.

Lucy did not explain her unfriendly behaviour towards Elizabeth. She would have if her mother had shown even the faintest curiosity. But after she'd put down the telephone, she dashed about the house for a while and then dashed from it. A few words streamed behind her like a scarf. 'Come soon. Do. So long. Lovely. Happy. Jo. Night.'

Lucy picked up the telephone and dialled the number of a friend where Jo sometimes stayed. Why had her mother never told her?

Elizabeth, lying on her hotel bed, shut her eyes out of sheer bliss. Blissful relief.

'What's up, Liz? Are you still around?' Bob's voice acted on her like a sedative. She realised she'd been living a nightmare ever since she'd arrived in England.

'They're all crazy, Bob. Crazy as Silver's crazy.' She named a medic they all knew as the epitome of the screwed-up male.

'Good old Silver!' Bob laughed.

Oh, what joy to have a common language, an understanding, a warmth, a comradeship. She might even begin to believe in love again. What a mixed-up person that sister, no, not sister, half-sister, was.

'Well how about it? What was she like? Did she kill you for coming?'

'Her?' Mary's qualities, good or bad, now seemed less important than the behaviour of her daughter. 'She was fine. A little sad. Very very English. It was her daughter that was the pain.'

'That sounds heavy.'

'This is costing a fortune. Will you meet me, Bob?'

'At Kennedy? But we agreed.'

'I know. I know. But I feel so low. She kicked me out. Almost assaulted me.'

'OK. OK.'

'Bob. Do you love me?'

At that moment they were cut off. Elizabeth was to spend quite a few of the next twenty hours hoping that they had been cut off before that last pathetic, out of character, plea. What had that Lucy done to her?

David and Mary hugged each other enthusiastically. For both of them it seemed a longer parting than a day. The dark, cold and deserted station wore an air of expectation, as if it required more than a mere marital peck. Mary felt David's muffled body around hers with a sense of relief. It was all right. She loved him at least as much as she ever had, perhaps more.

David enjoyed the feeling of her cheeks, soft and warm from the over-heated train against his, cold and hard.

CHAPTER NINE

Mary slept against David's back. It felt like curling round a tree trunk, the thickness solid and comforting. She was asleep but vague images of sheep huddled together in a storm, of bare hillsides, of lonely desolation, passed through her visual imagination. She held David closer so that in the half-light of early dawn, he groaned and hit the side of the bed with his free hand.

Mary rolled away from his agitation and opened her eyes, still blurred from sleep. She smiled. Richard Beck. She loved him. He loved her. They loved each other. They had loved each other. Yesterday. It was ridiculous but true. They had nothing in common except a past (Mary did not think of Elizabeth) but nevertheless they loved each other. They had shared the feeling of oneness about which poets write. They understood each other without words. They had always loved each other and always would.

Mary lay awake, eyes shining, waiting for the time when she could start the lovely day in which both she and Richard Beck existed.

'Breakfast.' She kissed David gently on the cheek. 'The sun's coming out and the snow's all gone.'

Ian, Helen, David and Mary had lunch together in town. After the second bottle of German Riesling, Helen raised the subject of youth. Mary, who had never felt younger, took a calm almost patronising interest. Ian mistook the subject for childhood and prepared to give his lecture on the virtues of organisation. David sighed and thought with longing of his table and books. He had never known what it was to be young, except in the person of Lucy.

Lucy was young. Perhaps that's what he loved in her most. Mary had been young when he had fallen in love with her.

'Not our children,' Helen gave a spirited groan. 'It's ourselves I meant. What we were like. How we have changed.' Not far from her consciousness Helen knew that she was pursuing this line in the hopes of discomforting Mary with memories of her misspent youth as divulged by David the day before. Helen could not bear to see women wearing that particular look of radiant self-satisfaction presently plastered all over Mary's features. She hoped to see a return of the wild, questioning creature who had come in out of the snow for a glass of whisky.

'Is this the Truth Game or something?'

Helen gave her husband a look full of hatred. This did not reflect her feelings for him in general but accurately demonstrated her reaction to the prosaic side of his nature. Ian did not notice because he was thinking that Mary was one of the prettiest women he'd seen since he'd been Third Secretary in India – every woman was pretty then – and he wouldn't mind playing the Truth Game with her. Or Strip Poker, if it came to that. Ian's youth had been much filled with games and his first sight of a naked woman had been at the age of sixteen during a game of Strip Poker. It's good to know I'm still a randy old sod, he thought to himself, still eyeing Mary appreciatively. He almost gave a jump when her lips opened in his direction.

'I'd hate to be young again. I was so unhappy.'

'Oh, really?' On the trail, Helen's button eyes gleamed.

'I should imagine you were very good at being young,' Mary continued to address herself to Ian.

'Still am!' Ian could not resist a small leer. Too small. In the settled format of his regular features it passed unnoticed.

'Why were you unhappy?' Helen's face expressed friendly sympathy.

David felt uneasy. What was this talk of unhappiness, over lamb cutlets and peas, when they were on holiday? 'Mary has a most contented nature,' he said, as if it were dogma. 'That's why I married her.'

'I am lucky,' agreed Mary, smiling the smile of inner tranquillity which so irritated Helen, 'I do feel contented. But I was unhappy when I was young before I met David. In fact I assumed everyone felt the same before they decided what they wanted to do in life.' As she spoke she turned to David with a look of what Helen described to herself as mawkish gratitude.

The look perfectly disguised Mary's inner feelings. Am I such a liar? she was saying to herself.

'Don't take any notice of Ian.' Helen was still impatient. 'He went straight from Oxford to the Foreign Office. He stopped having feelings when he was a boy imagining the pain tadpoles felt when their tails dropped off.'

'Darling. So witty.' Ian tipped the remains of the bottle into his wife's glass. He seemed genuinely more admiring than upset.

David and Mary looked at each other with understanding. They would not talk to each other like this and did not enjoy it in others.

'Time to go.' David stood up.

But now Mary felt disinclined to follow him. Their cottage was small, stuffy. It was a place to work and sleep in. None of these possibilities appealed to her. She felt restless and unwilling to settle into such a routine. The look she had exchanged with David had again reflected a habit rather than the truth. The truth was she felt sympathy for Helen's probing and irritability. If it had been within her nature, she would have liked to try the same technique herself. Inner contentment, she thought, mis-quoting David and then reverting to schoolgirl language. What bilge he does talk!

'Mary.' David did not like being left standing without support. It was unlike Mary and suggested she was catching the disaffected atmosphere.

Mary stood up. But her face was reluctant even obstinate. 'There's an auction on today. How about looking in?'

'An auction!' David looked at her as if she were mad. 'Of what?'

'Oh, I don't know. Bits and pieces. In an old Presbyterian Church. I saw the sign.'

'I love auctions.' Helen stood up. 'Let's all go.'

'But we don't want any bits and pieces.' David suddenly sat down again so that the two men were facing each other across the table with the two women standing above them.

'We'll go!' cried Mary decisively.

'In my car.' Helen echoed her tone of voice.

And they were gone, without a farewell look behind them, as if making a break for freedom.

'We might as well have another bottle,' suggested Ian after a moment of silence.

'Certainly,' agreed David.

The 'bits and pieces' were unutterably depressing, some, disgust-ing. Stained mattresses, cracked mirrors, broken irons, scratched chairs, desks, tables. The star of the show was a formica-topped sink unit with both taps intact.

'Any advance on ten pounds?' the auctioneer's voice was understandably without hope. 'Five pounds?'

'Let's get out,' whispered Mary.

'But it's fascinating,' said Helen. 'Do you realise people have actually bought this junk. Look. They've stickers on. Sold. Sold?'

Mary shivered. 'Let's go?'

'OK.'

But Mary's movement had caught the auctioneer's eye.

A thrill of hope brought energy to his hammer-laden hand. 'Bang' the hammer was down. The unsaleable unit had been bought by the pretty lady in the red cape.

'You've bought it,' hissed Helen in a horrified voice. 'He thinks you like it.'

'I know.'

Already an assistant was making his way towards her, winding in a practised manner between lavatory bowls and electric fires. This is what happens, thought Mary, when you revive youthful love, when you make love in a hotel in the middle of the afternoon with a man you hardly know. This is exactly what happens. You buy a formica-topped sink unit for three pounds fifty. She began to laugh.

Mary expected David to be working when she returned. That was how she imagined him, at his desk, mind solving problems with well-oiled ease. She was prepared to tiptoe a little guiltily but only a little and make a delicious and slightly, but only slightly, apologetic cup of tea. In fact, he lay on the sofa and said, as she opened the door, 'Come and sit down a moment.' His tone was welcoming, loving. He made a place beside him on the sofa. Nearby the fire, half-burnt out, grizzled in the darkening room.

Mary had planned to make him laugh with the story of the sink unit. She would tell him it was waiting there for him to fetch – although actually she had paid a fiver to dissociate herself from its future. But the atmosphere was so peaceful, he was so moody and tender, that she couldn't bring herself to bandy words.

He put his hand round her hips, stretching so that his finger lay on the top of her thigh. Her body was so conscious now that she could feel each finger imprint, even the nail on the little finger which was turned sideways. She shut her mind to contradictory thoughts and sat quietly as he wanted.

Richard Beck was on the train again. Sometimes he thought there was a Richard Beck who never got off the train, so strong was his image of himself in his suit with his newspaper, sitting in corner seat 24H – except when some ignorant alien got in there before him, plonking down on his ghostly presence. Or was it his life which was the haunting, the wistful meander down meaningless corridors?

At home in the country – Cherry's home, not his, the childrens' home, not his – at home he put away his suit but held on to his newspaper, token that he would be back aboard the next day or Monday.

'Hi, darling!' Cherry had a breezy manner. It was what had attracted him to her in the first place. He felt as if he were taming a natural force and she had been so pretty. She was still pretty.

'Did you remember, it's my Oxfam night?' She kissed him. Sometimes he thought they lived on their absences from each other, coming together with some affection and parting with nearly as much.

'I met an old friend yesterday,' he said from an unusual impulse to interrupt her smooth exit.

'Oh, you didn't say anything yesterday.' She was only a little interrupted, her head turned to him, her body turned away to the door. She reminded him of an arrow winging over his left shoulder. She was straight and slim, her fluffy fair hair like feathers at the end.

'There's no need to shoot out the moment I come in.'

'But darling, I explained. You know I did.'

Her breeziness would rise to gale force if he persisted. 'Of course. You go.'

'Tell me about the old friend tomorrow. I'd love to hear.' In victory, she was always generous.

'Have a good evening.' It was not that he was weak but that he didn't care enough. Or perhaps that was a definition of a weak person.

Richard put down his newspaper and went to pour himself a beer. Once upon a time Cherry and he must have loved each other a great deal or why else would he have divorced Susan? Now they lived together. The change had been too gradual for him to know the reason why. Perhaps they were too compatible.

Richard took his beer to the kitchen where his plate was laid with two others, indicating the boys were around tonight. For a moment standing under the kitchen's bright spotlights, he thought sentimentally of Daniel and Nicky. It was easier to do this in anticipation of their large and unresponsive presence. Youth was enigmatic, Richard thought tolerantly. He sat down, not without a sense of contentment. It was hard to believe in the existence of Mary Fellowes. What was her married name? Travers? No. But something like that.

Lucy had judged Jo correctly. He was ecstatic at the idea of a family skeleton.

'Glorious bourgeois hyprocrisy,' he said with relish and repeatedly. 'It also explains why you were so keen on such a dreary alien. Blood will out. Blood will out.'

Lucy, who had been genuinely suffering, found his reaction a relief from her own feelings. Besides whenever Jo was excited, whether over the degeneration of England into a Fascist police state or the price of Mars Bars (for which he had a passion), his emotions soon turned into a desire for sex. Lucy, always compliant in a way she recognised guiltily as against the trend of the woman's movement, couldn't help seeing this as the ultimate compliment. Anyway she liked sex.

'It's the Watergate aspect of it that's so disgusting,' said Jo, resting his head comfortably between Lucy's thighs.

'Mummy should have told me.' Lucy's voice was inappropriately lazy and unconcerned. She could hear it herself. But she was so filled with Jo that she couldn't feel the pain. It was there somewhere, she supposed, waiting. 'Don't Jo, you're tickling!'

'Tickling. Tickling. Tickling.' He sat up on his haunches as if insulted. 'I was merely checking to see if you were properly defended against the seed of a bastard.'

'You know I'm on the pill.'

'Like mother, like daughter.' He fell flat, lying beside her with his mouth to her ear. 'And in her bed too. The bed of a fallen woman.'

'It's bigger.' Lucy giggled. 'We always make love in their bed.'

'But before we didn't know,' he lowered his voice to a dramatic whisper, 'what had gone on . . . '

'It was before she was married, Jo. She must have been awfully young. Elizabeth is older . . . ' But at the mention of her half-sister's name, Lucy suddenly felt a return of that terrible moment when she first understood what Elizabeth was telling her. She had not been her mother's first baby, not her only baby.

'Oh, Jo. Jo!' Shivering and tearful she pressed her soft naked body against his.

At first he lay unmoving, neither rejecting her nor offering comfort. But after a second she felt his arm come round and cradle her in a way he never had before. 'I'm sorry,' she whispered gratefully.

'That's OK.' His voice made his chest vibrate under her. How could they be closer than this? A gentle coupling that made the act of love seem so violent and selfish.

'That's OK,' he repeated. 'You've always been puerile where your parents are concerned. Luckily, you've got a pretty cunt.'

'Oh,' gasped Lucy. And then 'Oh!' again. Somehow the idea of a gentle coupling lost its appeal.

Richard Beck sat watching television with his two sons. It was unusual that they should both be in on a Friday evening. Even the youngest, Nicky, who was seventeen and still at school, had a regular girlfriend without whom he appeared unfinished, like half a sandwich. He was never talkative but when she was not there, he wore a suspicious, almost hostile look, as if expecting an attack on his open sandwich side.

'Where's Georgie?' Richard leant towards his son.

He appeared not to hear and then spoke without turning his head from the television. 'Working.'

'On a Friday?'

'Sshh, Dad.' His eldest son, Daniel, spoke firmly but without rancour.

Richard smiled to himself. He loved his sons but he also felt curiously detached from them which he did not consider altogether his fault. Even Daniel who was an aggressive character and had talked himself out of school and into a job with an ice-cream company at the age of seventeen, never tried to approach him directly. Perhaps it was his age, or perhaps it was this commuting, up and down to London, always just going or just coming, which put them off. Or it might be that they followed their mother's lead. She did not wish to be intimate with him any longer.

None of this depressed Richard unduly. Or so he told himself. He had never had very high expectations of life. In fact he had done better with his job than most of his contemporaries, his school-friends whom he read about in the yearly issue of the Old Boys Magazine. He had read it out loud for laughs, first to Susan and then to Cherry, but lately he had found himself taking it more seriously, even considering offering his own encapsulated life:

Richard Beck. Northumberland House, 1944. Just missed the war, went into business. Married 1948. First marriage, the most secure and happy time when he earned most in relation to his age, had most women, had Mary Fellowes. Was she different to the others? She must have been for he didn't rent a room for his other women. But then they were older, more able to look after themselves, often already with husbands. Like the Mary who had come to him the day before: complete.

Richard stood up suddenly, blocking his son's line to the television.

'I'm taking Marshall for a walk,' he said, although their concentration had not altered, merely the position of their heads as they craned round him. 'I won't be long.' He paused at the door.

'Bye Dad.' Startled he saw Nicky's face turned towards him smiling.

'See you later, Nick.' Did children know the power they had over their parents? Calling for the dog, Richard went cheerfully towards the back door.

'Your skin is so soft.' David stroked Mary's neck and shoulder. They lay close and comfortable in the rather small double bed.

Mary turned her head to try and see his expression but the darkness was too complete. Why was he so loving, so newly appreciative? Was it a reflection of her own new awareness of her body? How ironic! She felt too warm, too lazy to try and make sense of it. She loved her husband and he loved her.

Slowly they turned to each other, thigh to thigh, mouth to mouth.

Why did the bed shake? She must stop or David would wake. Mary stuffed her fist into her mouth but her body, however much she held it rigid, continued to vibrate painfully. Tears, so hot she felt they should steam in the midnight cold air, gushed and flowed. Really, she was behaving like a child. Utterly ridiculous. Oh Richard Beck!

Marshall, the banana-coloured labrador, shivered at his master's side. It was too dark for walking, too late; his basket, with its soft tartan rug and unrolled corner which he liked to chew, seemed infinitely desirable. A pair of headlights came towards them, their yellowness cross-hatched by layers of icy mist. It was a horrible night.

'Richard, whatever are you doing?' Cherry opened the door a little so that she was spotlit. Her fair hair stood in curls around her white face, her eyes were bright, her lips very red. She looked remote and beautiful like a china mask.

'I'm walking Marshall.'

'You *were* walking Marshall.'

The dog, seeing his chance of warmth and comfort, had already slipped into the car.

'It *is* cold. I'll come too.'

Cherry talked merrily as she drove back. She entertained her husband with views and gossip culled over the evening. She told stories well, with energy and panache. Richard was grateful she bothered for him.

'So, tell me about the old friend you bumped into.'

'What? Oh. It was nothing.'

'I thought . . . '

She wasn't really curious, he thought, merely polite. How about trying a bit of truth? 'It was a woman I hadn't seen for twenty plus years.'

'Someone you cared about?'

He thought of the words to tell her but suddenly the smooth and brilliant face looked like a mask of tragedy. The sight frightened him, suggesting that the breeziness could blow itself out and leave something more complicated revealed.

Richard, who was generous, put his hand on her arm.

'It was years and years ago. Before we even met.'

'Oh, yes. Yes, of course.' Her impatience was a relief, so was the garage, a safe hutch for a conversation that might have become dangerous. After all, he hadn't been unfaithful to her for several years now.

'Darling!' Richard leant over and kissed her on the cheek. He could smell the smoke, the hot room filled with people.

Marshall broke them apart bounding out between them, his large warm body reminding Richard of his sons. He must remember to ask if Nicky had broken with Georgie. But not now.

'Darling,' he said again, tucking her arm into his; it was nice to feel protective, nice to feel he could give her something more than the statutory role of husband.

'I am tired.'

'You work too hard.'

92

'We both do.'

Richard thought of the train, his suit, the stairs at the underground station. Work? Meetings, letters, decisions. Train, suit, underground. The casing as important as the contents. The business didn't need him anymore. When he left – he didn't think the word 'retired' – he wouldn't be missed.

CHAPTER TEN

The snow had melted away. Underneath the grass was flattened and unhealthy-looking. Like hair when a hat's been taken off, thought Mary as she walked away from the cottage along the stone-filled track. On either side small fields rose up to the sky. Although they had only just finished lunch, the sun had already dropped behind the left flank, gilding the blue sky so that it became a greenish-yellow. Mary walked faster. She would have to be quick if she wanted to get to and from the village shop before dark. Just as before, she had been enjoying the small sense of purpose which approaching night brought. A small sense of purpose, she thought, is about all I can manage at the moment. On the other hand, she was happy, looking upwards to the steady outlines of earth and hedge and sky.

'You'll ruin your eyes.' Richard's secretary brought in a cup of tea and switched on his desk lamp. Was this an aggressive action, a sign of caring, loving even – all his secretaries used to fall in love with him – or a merely neutral task such as a well-programmed robot would perform?

'Thank you.' He sat back in his chair. 'Have you ever come across this?' He looked at the paper on his desk. 'Snyderman? His report's much better than the usual. He's actually come up with some very reasonable suggestions for improvements.'

'Oh, Snyderman!' The secretary raised her eyes.

Richard scowled. 'What do you mean, Oh, Snyderman?' She was an attractive girl, her eyes big and blue, even if too protuberant.

'Everyone knows Snyderman. You know Snyderman actually.

He's always popping in here, although he's supposedly based at Harmondsworth.'

'How long's he been with us?'

'I don't know. Before me. Shall I find out?'

'No. Yes. All right.' He should know things like that. A bright young man whom he must have hired himself at some point. A bright young man who was filled with good ideas and the energy to carry them out. Seeing that his secretary was still waiting, he stood up and impulsively went over to her.

'Come with me and get a drink?'

Her surprise was not altogether flattering. 'But . . . '

'But what?' He smiled at her, put his hand on her shoulder. He was her boss, The Boss, managing director. At least she'd have something to tell the other girls.

'But it's only half past four.' She looked at her watch in confirmation. 'I just brought in your tea.'

'So you did.' Richard walked away from her to the window. It was not very big and looked out onto the large and rising wall of a post office but he could just see the sky above. 'It's so dark.'

'Yes.'

Since she still stood waiting, Richard realised that, after all, she did want to come with him for a drink – for whatever reason. But her initial questioning had made it seem like too much hard work. He continued to stare out of the window.

'We could go to the hotel bar. It's open. I use it quite a lot. It's nice.'

Suddenly she was so keen and the keener she became, the less keen Richard became. After all she was a good secretary, efficient, even-tempered, about thirty or so and married. Why run the risk of spoiling a good working relationship based, as it was, on a lack of personal information?

'Another day.' Richard sat down and picked up his tea cup. It was too late for hotel dalliance. Time on his mind, he turned over his cup as if it were a watch on his wrist. Warm tea gushed over his arm, his knee, the floor.

'Oh, Mr Beck!' The secretary ran forward, crouched at his feet, pulled coloured tissue out of the sleeve of her sweater like a magician.

Richard took out his own large white handkerchief and began scrubbing at his jacket and trousers.

'It's lucky it wasn't hot!' exclaimed the secretary whose pretty face wore a puzzled frown.

'I thought it was my watch.'

The secretary peered up at him, the pupils of her eyes swimming upwards in her large orbs.

Richard, avuncular, patted her on the head. He regretted arousing muddled emotions. She might have been his dog, friendly and willing.

'I'll get a proper cloth.'

'You do that.'

While she was out, the telephone rang. It was his son by his first marriage, inviting him to his grandson's birthday party but really wanting advice on a company in which he was interested. Richard declined the invitation and gave the advice, following it with an invitation to meet for a drink after work.

'Oh dear,' commented the secretary returning with a cloth and wiping off the desk, 'I'm afraid you've badly marked Mr Snyderman's report.'

'Never mind.' Richard's voice and manner became suddenly cheerful. 'There's plenty more where they came from.'

Taking the corner of the report which ran with brown rivulets, he dropped it neatly into the waste-paper basket.

Mary walked as fast as she could along the rutted track. It had become entirely dark on one side and the hedges and trees had turned to black cut-outs, like floats on either side of her in a grand theatrical production. But to the west there was still a pearly edge to the night which made it possible for her to find her way. She looked at the bright little digits of her watch and saw it was only five o'clock. In the cottage, David would still be working but his mind would be on a cup of tea. He would imagine her ghostly presence bringing it up to him, and miss her. In a quarter of an hour he could have her, tea and biscuits, body and soul, but just at the moment, she was out of reach, on her own, under the night sky.

Mary stopped and looked upwards. She put down her shopping bag which was heavy. Although the air was cold, sharpening itself on her nose and chin and ears, her body was warm after her long walk, almost hot.

'Booh!' A dark figure, legs splayed like a paper puppet, jumped out of the hedge.

Mary did not think of robbers or murderers but nevertheless took several quick steps backwards. The figure dressed in an anorak over the head and body, with boots below, waved his arms and continued to shout 'Booh!' and 'Yahoo!' and something that sounded like 'Tallyho!'

'Ian?'

'Is it so obvious?' The figure's arms and legs dropped down so it stood stiff and still as if the puppet's strings had been dropped all of a sudden.

Mary laughed. 'Whatever are you doing?'

'I might ask the same question?' Ian's voice was sulky. Why did no one play games anymore?

'I was shopping.'

'No car?'

They began walking side by side. 'No car.'

Ian pushed down his anorak hood.

'You look more human now.'

'It's extraordinary to think there are people who do this sort of thing for a living.'

'Walk alone in the dark?'

'Jump out on people, although of course they'd have guns. I was approached by MI6, you know. I was tempted, the training and the physical discipline – I've always been interested in fitness. I was running, you know, when I saw you. I admire fitness. But somehow I couldn't get over the feeling that all this undercover business wasn't quite fair.'

'Well, it isn't fair, is it?'

'No. Quite.' His face, pale in the dark, turned to her. 'Not at all. That's why I became a diplomat. Cards on the table.'

'Cards on the table?' repeated Mary. And she thought of her afternoon with Richard Beck. It was the first secret she'd ever had from David. 'I don't like secrets either.'

'Oh, I don't know about that. Secrets are essential. People can't exist without secrets. Countries couldn't function without secrets. It's a case of self-preservation. On both sides too. If someone's tempted to reveal a secret, I run a mile until the temptation passes. It usually does.'

'But surely that's the beginning of the road to what you were describing, MI6?'

'Possibly. They say everything leads somewhere. Would you mind awfully if I ran the last bit? Otherwise I'll be down on the day's exercise quota. Silly, I know, but that's how I am.'

Mary watched Ian pound off into the darkness. It seemed extraordinary to her that he didn't break an ankle on the loose stones and uneven ground.

The point about Richard Beck, she thought as silence returned, was that he was a re-creation of the past, an answer to the sudden appearance of Elizabeth. Their afternoon together was a secret from the past, not of the present. That was why it had made her purely happy and not separated her from David. She could have told David all about it and he would have understood.

To her right she saw the lights of the cottage.

David kicked the desk and then, finding that unworthy of such attention, kicked the bed. Still unsatisfied, he flung off the bedclothes onto the floor and tugged at the flimsy chintz curtains – which were not as flimsy as all that since they held firm to the rails. He then descended the stairs with the noise of Hannibal crossing the Alps and proceeded to the kitchen. There he found more scope with clanging saucepans, kettle top and taps. Even so, it was not enough and, eventually, he snatched his coat off the peg by the door, and headed belligerently for the car.

Mary saw the car swing out from the garage and come bumping angrily towards her. She was surprised and stepped out, waving her arms.

David stopped and leant out of the window. He mouthed something in the area of 'Grrh!'

'What's the matter?' Mary's tranquil picture of domesticity did a kaleidoscopic shake-up and re-formed in tragedy and confusion. Lucy hurt, the house on fire (but there were no flames), herself and Richard Beck discovered . . .

'Grrh! Ugh! Work!'

Work? Could difficulties with David's fraud case really make him so distraught? So hysterical, so furious? Yes. The answer was yes. While Mary walked and pondered life's imponderables, David was working, caught in a life and death struggle between one piece of information and another.

'Want to come for a drink?' It sounded like a threat.

His anger was not directed at her but it was anger nevertheless, churning the calm air.

'You go. I'll cook.'

'Right!' He drove off, too fast, pebbles throwing out from under the wheels.

Now Mary clattered and banged about the kitchen. She'd had her solitary communing, now she wanted a good-tempered husband, someone to talk to.

Banging and clattering, she didn't hear Helen come in the door.

'Oh, hello?' She knew her voice sounded unfriendly.

'I've been saying "Hi" for ages.'

'Sorry.'

'We wondered if we might do an à quatre tonight?'

'David's gone for a drink. I don't know when he'll be back. He's in a rage.'

'How exciting!'

'Not at all. It's with his work.'

'I can't imagine David being in a rage.' Helen sat down as if she planned to stay. 'Not even with his work.'

'Oh, he's just as bad-tempered as anyone else.' Mary sighed and got out a bottle of whisky.

'Ian has terrible rages. Sometimes he even hits me.'

'I'm sorry.'

Helen laughed. 'No. It's not like that. He doesn't hurt me. In fact I'm more likely to hurt him. I was captain of lacrosse, you know. That's why Ian fell in love with me. Our relationship is almost entirely physical.'

'Oh,' said Mary, unable to think of a more suitable rejoinder and with an instinctive sense that the details of Ian's and Helen's physical relationship must be avoided if at all possible.

'That's why I don't like him running.'

'What?' Mary sipped at her glass. She saw it would not be possible. Helen had come to talk and talk she would.

'He's hardly much use to me after he's run ten miles.'

'Oh, I see.' Mary thought of the hooded figure, flapping out of the dark. 'I thought athletes were always at it.'

'That's different. They're young.'

'But you're young. Younger than us anyway.'

'Yes.' Helen gave Mary a look in which complacency was reluctantly dispelled. 'How old are you?'

'Nearly forty.'

'You look younger.'

'Thank you. Shall we go and sit by the fire?'

David chose a new pub. It was filled with young men who held large glasses of beer and wore nothing but T-shirts despite the vile January weather. David ordered a double gin and tonic in retaliation and decided with some bitterness that the only point of youth was to make the middle-aged seem coarse and weary. When his work let him down or, to put it more positively, defeated him as it had this afternoon, the world took on a distinctly hostile hue. It was on such an occasion, he remembered, that he'd realised he was in love with Mary. He had actually loved her for some time but it took a Sunday afternoon, when the preparation for his first big case for the prosecution kept putting him on the side of the defence, to make him realise it. They had walked beside the canal near the Kensal Green cemetery – he had a flat off Harrow Road at the time – and afterwards he had asked her to marry him. That was when they were in her flat eating hot buttered toast. He had asked her about a photograph of herself with a man, asked her if it was her father and she had answered, no, it was my lover. And then, as if shocked by herself, she'd blushed scarlet and turned the photograph face downwards. Strange, that he'd asked her to marry him then, just as she told him about her lover. Perhaps it made her seem available. After that the photograph had never reappeared, although he'd elicited the facts from her. Witness for the defence. Or was it prosecution?

All that because he'd felt as he did now. Empty. David put down his glass on the table in front of him. Beyond it he saw the legs of a girl, dressed in high-heeled boots, jeans and, as he raised his eyes, a leather bomber jacket. (Veronica, his girlfriend in the office, was also a product of a non-productive work condition.) The girl moved her legs. She was so slim that there was a gap between her thighs where they met her crotch. David imagined putting his hand there. The coarseness of the jeans seemed inappropriate to such a tender part of a woman's anatomy. Mary never wore jeans and very seldom trousers. But he was not inclined to feel aroused at the thought of his wife who was linked with the desk in the bedroom and the books and the reports and the statements. The statements were the worst, filled with inaccuracies based at best on woolly thinking and at worst on sheer lies.

The girl moved. Turning from back to front, she heaved herself onto a round stool in front of the bar. Her jeans and leather-clad legs crossed just above David's eye level. An old man's occupation he thought, watching the thighs and crotch of a young girl. Who has a boyfriend too, he noted, as the next stool was filled by an identikit though broader, version of the first. Yes. This must be a sign of old age, this lascivious spying with no intention of doing anything about it.

'Double gin and tonic, please.'

'Visiting are you?' The barman was the same age as his clients. He wore one earring and his hair was shaved on one side, with the other decorated by wisps six inches long. Style apart, he had a pleasant country boy openness.

'Yes. Just visiting.'

'You should try the devil first?'

'Sorry?'

'The Devil First. It's a night-club. Just opened. This lot,' he indicated the youths, 'all go on there.'

'I see.' Had his encompassing look particularly emphasised the thin-thighed girl? 'It's not even seven o'clock.' David swivelled his watch with a sense of panic.

The barman shrugged, turned to another customer.

'My wife's cooking supper!' cried David, in a voice like a frightened child's. But the barman was finished with him.

David sat at his table but his view of the wide-spaced thighs was spoilt. He finished his drink hurriedly and pushed through the door. Only then he was struck by his four gins and what had happened last time he'd driven away from a West Country pub.

'Have you got anything to eat?'

'Crisps. Nuts.'

'No sandwiches?'

'No sandwiches or rolls or sausages. Crisps and nuts.'

David thought of telephoning Mary but couldn't remember the number.

Everybody said Richard's eldest son looked like his father. True he was tall and slim and dark but otherwise Richard had never been able to see the slightest resemblance. He always looked so settled.

'Did you ever wonder why your mother and I split up?'

'Not at all,' replied his son briskly. 'I was only surprised that you stayed together so long.'

This was not what Richard meant. He had wanted to lift out, as it were from tissue and pink ribbons, the image of Mary. Mary was why he'd left Susan, although he'd married Cherry.

'The other thing that always surprised me,' continued his eldest son in his honest man's voice, 'is why, having divorced mother, because she was so jolly and energetic and didn't pay you enough attention, you then went and married another woman a little jollier, a little less energetic, who paid you even less attention. That *did* seem perverse.'

'Oh, really!' said Richard, regretting that he'd started the conversation. 'Cherry was so sexy. We were at it two and three times a day.'

His son, usually steady under fire, jolted back a little. 'Well, that does explain it.'

Richard sank back in his chair. Mary had talked of a daughter. An American and yet she had not seemed much interested and then they had both become diverted.

'What are you smiling at?' Richard Beck's eldest son sounded distinctly disapproving.

'Nothing. Actually Cherry and I are exceptionally compatible and, in her own way, she pays me a great deal of attention.'

David was drinking coffee in a fish and chip shop. He'd baulked at the fish and chips, despite the owner's assurances that the fish came up daily from the coast. As he spoke he indicated a large plastic lobster on the display counter which did not further his argument.

'I only want coffee.'

'Oh, well, then.'

David was beginning to see the cottage in a more cheerful light. Even the desk with the papers scattered in anger did not seem entirely a symbol of defeat. The lobster was the sort of violent orange colour in which a child might paint the setting sun. Beside it lay a hunk of smoked haddock of an equally unlikely yellow and beyond that four or five red-eyed scallops. Something began to clutch inside David's stomach as if smaller replicas of the orange monster had escaped and taken refuge.

'Excuse me!' He pushed past the fish and chip man looking for a lavatory.

'Where do you think you're going?'

'I'm going to be . . . ' Putting himself into quick reverse he dashed for the outer door and just made it to the gutter. 'Sick!'

Bent and shaking, David found a handkerchief and wiped his forehead which was wet with perspiration and then his mouth. So that was it. He was ill. That was why he had felt so dreadful, so defeated, why his mind had refused to work. On the whole, although his legs felt like smoked haddock and his eyes like scallops, he was relieved. Besides now he could drive home perfectly safely. He even smiled while making a fairly quick getaway from possible officers of street hygiene in the direction of his car.

Mary would put him to bed and bring him a hot water bottle and perhaps tomorrow he would feel up to a nourishing soup. David was seldom ill but, when he was, he reverted without intermediate steps to the feebleness of a small boy.

David slept upstairs. Obviously he had a temperature. His skin was hot and sticky. He smelled sick. Ugh. Mary prowled about from kitchen to sitting-room. Nurse to a sick man. Ugh. Ugh. Dangerous words came into Mary's head. I want to be with David when he's loving and well. Richard Beck, I love you. I want to be with you now. What I most don't want is to be with David when he's sick and ugly and smelling. Smelling. Smelling. Smelling. Mary banged her temples and poured herself a large vodka and tonic.

CHAPTER ELEVEN

Mary picked snowdrops for David's breakfast tray. His flu was lifting a little and she felt better disposed to him.

'I'm going to do some shopping in town.'

'Am I quite spoiling your holiday?'

'Of course not.'

Richard looked at his desk calendar. He couldn't call her. She had appeared and disappeared. Even her married name had disappeared from his memory.

'Yes, I will have tea. And a biscuit.'

'She doesn't seem real.'

'Uhm. Ah.'

'Of course I was there such a short time. And it was all so crazy. I suppose I shouldn't have gone.'

'Can't you sleep?'

'It's morning.'

'It's Saturday.'

'I think of her daughter, Lucy, more than I do of her. But then I suppose I saw more of her.'

Bob sat up, his hair fanned about his face. Without his glasses he looked so much younger. Elizabeth patted his hand placatingly, 'I went looking for a mother and came back with a sister.'

'Come on!' Even Bob's tolerance of all things self-analytical (hadn't he accompanied her almost willingly to group therapy sessions?) had its limits.

'You don't think I should write to her then?'

'Elizabeth! You told me she hated you, she screamed at you, she threw you out of the house.'

'In a way. But that was shock. That wasn't her real self.'

'You don't know her real self.'

'We're sisters.'

'OK. Write.' Bob flopped back into the bed pillows.

Poor Bob! He worked so hard. It was unfair to torture him with her problems on his morning off. 'I have written. Last night.' Elizabeth eased herself out of bed. 'Would you like a cup of tea?' Bob's silence could be serious disapproval or merely assent. On the whole it seemed more positive to assume it was assent. Sometime he would have to learn that she didn't always behave as rationally as either of them would like.

'We've got to get ourselves together.' Jo, lying naked in Mary's and David's double bed, put his hands comfortably behind his head. 'What time is it?'

Lucy unwound the clock from a tangle of sheets and clothes – they had gone to bed late and in disarray. 'It's stopped.' She shook it. 'Now it's started again.' She looked out of the window. They had not drawn the curtains and the ghostly light of winter shone from on high. 'Midday, I should think.'

'We should organise ourselves. It's this house. It's organised for comfort not for positive action.'

Repressing the urge to apologise, Lucy sat up, giving some care to the position of her head. They had taken positive action in the direction of her father's wine stores the night before. 'Your friends suffered from the same problem last night.'

'How long did you say your parents are away?'

'We don't have to stay here.' She thought of adding, You don't have to stay here, but he was her lover and she wanted him with her. 'It'll teach you to understand the problems of being born middle class,' she said instead with as much acerbity as she could manage. Even when he was rude or difficult or silly or all three, she wanted to follow his lead. Besides, she agreed with him, the political system was unfair. If it hadn't been for the especially good education bought for her by her parents, she'd never have got into university. Things should be different. Someone should change them. 'Wasn't there that Anti-Apartheid Rally this afternoon?' she suggested hopefully. Protests always put Jo in a good mood.

'I'm beginning to think South Africa is a red herring devised by the right to divert attention from the problems at home.' He spoke in his severest manner so that Lucy didn't dare suggest he was joking. Instead she pulled on a sweater and went to find some food. Jo was so much cleverer than she that he must be right. Staring at the pile of unwashed dishes in the sink, she found herself thinking of Elizabeth. No doubts in her life. A direct path through life with a career to guide her. Jo had hated her. As far as he allowed himself to believe any human being important enough to hate. This was the point where Lucy became muddled about Jo's beliefs. They were all to do with the rights of the individual, fighting racism, sexism and all the other thoroughly awful injustices. And yet he said the individual had no importance and it was the 'cause' which must be served. At least that seemed to be his position.

Abandoning the washing up, Lucy found a packet of biscuits and returned to bed. 'This is all I can find.'

Jo lay where she'd left him, hands behind head, eyes staring at ceiling. She was sure he was cogitating on some matter of importance to the human race but she couldn't help admiring his extreme good looks – the pure wholeness of his skin, the muscled well-shaped arms, the strong manly jaw, the straight nose, heavy eyebrows, large dark eyes, red chiselled lips. She sighed and kissed away a crumb. There just wasn't the opportunity anymore to be a silk-shirt-and-jodhpur-heroine.

'Do you know, you're voracious.' No one had taught Jo not to speak with his mouth full. 'And I'll tell you something else.' He pulled himself upright. 'You're corrupting me. And I'll tell you something else,' he continued firmly over Lucy's open-mouthed expostulation, 'I like it.'

'You like it?' Lucy felt her mouth one huge gape.

'I like it,' repeated Jo without shame.

Mary carried the food from the supermarket and then saw the telephone kiosk. It was too tempting. The sun was out and she felt rested and pretty and just about able to manage anything. Back at the cottage, David was neatly tucked into bed, lovingly cared for, on the road to recovery, almost smug in his sense of well-being. Smiling at the image, Mary entered the kiosk.

She had written the number in her diary.

'Could I speak to Mr Beck, please?'

'Will you hold?'

'Beck!'

Mary put down the receiver.

Who was this 'Beck!' shouting at her with so much antagonism? Capable and confident, just about able to manage anything, she found she was shaking, her palms sweating.

'You weren't gone long.' David put down *Phineas Finn*.

Was he disappointed? Probably. He'd been enjoying a rare time of peace and relaxation.

'Tomorrow I'll have to start work again.'

'You enjoy working.' Mary didn't sit down.

David looked up at his wife. He knew she found it difficult to look after him when he was sick – not that it happened often – but she'd been so gentle with him the last few days. Kind and caring as she'd been when they first met, in the early years of their marriage before she'd begun to work. Now she stood with her legs a little apart, her back very straight, the stance of a schoolmistress, a soldier nurse, not gentle any longer.

David caught Mary's hand which dangled at about his eye level. It was crisp with cold and seemed to tingle in his grasp, not just because of the cold but as if it wanted to escape. Obviously, it was time he got up.

'I'm afraid I'm not going to be much fun. These days off have put me behind. I'll have to work like the devil.'

'Don't worry. There's always Helen.' She might have said, I'm used to it, but that sort of sharp honesty was not part of their marriage. Besides she liked David's obsession with his work. She respected him for it and would have hated a husband who drifted through life without occupational purpose. 'If it comes to that, I should do some work myself.' This was true. She had promised to go through a drafted report on reverse discrimination within the organisation.

Mary wrote:

Dear Richard,

I have to be in London again in the next few days. Perhaps we might meet? If you're not too busy. You can write to my office but mark it personal so my secretary doesn't open it.

With love Mary.

Mary was pleased with this letter. She felt it placed them on equal footing. It was the sort of letter a man might have written to a girl. It was a mature, confident letter, unemotional, undemanding, rational, precise. In short, it dared to ask.

Richard's mail never arrived on his desk much before eleven. It was one of the problems he had sworn to solve when he became managing director. Ten years later his secretary, smiling, still came in with it at eleven and he was still irritated. Lack of staff was the cause, he'd been told, but he could hardly recommend an extra wage packet just to ensure his letters arrived at a reasonable hour. No one else seemed to care. Not even Mr Ambitious Snyderman. Unless he'd found a way round the system. That was always possible, of course, but not for the managing director.

'Thank you.'

'There's one marked "personal", I'm afraid I began to open it before I realised.'

'Don't worry.'

Of course she hadn't worried. The only 'personal' notes Richard received were from his family. There had been a time when things had been different.

On Monday morning, when Richard read Mary's letter, Mary sat in the living-room and opened page one of *Under the Greenwood Tree* by Thomas Hardy. 'To dwellers in a wood almost every species of tree has its voice as well as its feature. At the passing of the breeze the fir-trees sob and moan no less distinctly than they rock; the holly whistles as it battles with itself; the ash hisses amid its quiverings; the beech rustles while its flat boughs rise and fall. And winter, which modifies the note of such trees as shed their leaves, does not destroy its individuality.' She sighed deeply, smiled, took a sip of coffee. She'd been barely twenty when she'd last read those lines.

Richard sat on the train re-reading Mary's letter. He felt puzzled by it.

'Darling!' exclaimed Cherry when he came through their front door. 'You do look under the weather.'

Cherry's smiling face, her healthy youth and confidence, combined with the atmosphere of the house which seemed filled with the kind of brisk air blown through tree-tops and over grass, acted on Richard as a sharp stimulant. He kissed his wife's firm pink cheek and pulled out Mary's letter from his pocket.

'I'll get myself a drink and you read this.' He waved the letter towards her.

Cherry took it eagerly; she liked the positive, practical side of their relationship. She liked advising him about work, clothes, people, she liked reading his letters.

'It's very short.' She sounded disappointed.

'Short and sweet.' Richard poured himself a beer without feelings of disloyalty. He sat down on the sofa. The yellow room reflected Cherry's personality.

'She wants to meet you. Who is she?'

'Someone I once knew.'

Cherry laughed. 'Darling!'

'Before I knew you.'

'Ah. The one you started to tell me about the other night. Do you want to meet her?'

Suddenly this pretence at honesty seemed less appealing. If Cherry had really cared it might have had some point. As it was it merely emphasised the depressing lack in their marriage.

'Give it to me.' Wanting to make some faintly violent statement, Richard snatched back the letter, tore it across several times and threw the pieces into the fire.

'Howzat!'

Cherry walked to the door. 'I presume you're in to supper?'

'You're the one who has evening meetings!'

'Not as often as you pretend,' said Cherry good-humouredly before closing the door.

Like a child, thought Richard Beck, she treats me like a child. Taking off both his well-polished city shoes, he flung them across the room. To his great delight one joined the letter in the fire, while the other, hurtling upwards with glorious abandon, swept three or four ornaments off the mantelpiece. 'Howzat!' he shouted and, since Cherry did not return despite the noise which was considerable, he was able to contemplate the wreckage of a china cupid, a glass bell and an ornamental egg with solitary satisfaction. He did, however, retrieve his shoe from the fire.

That was fun, he thought to himself, I should do it more often and incidentally, I will write to Mary. It was then he again realised he still didn't remember her married surname.

'What a peculiar letter!'

David was an early riser. He liked getting out of bed while Mary still slept. Downstairs he took a long time making tea, warming the pot and often the cups too, and even then he was often ahead of the postman.

'What a peculiar letter!'

'What darling?' Mary didn't open her eyes.

'It's been forwarded from your office. "Mary" that's all it says.' David laughed. 'Typed and marked "personal". Do open it.'

'Not now.' Mumbling and grunting, Mary rolled over onto her side. 'I've got a headache.' As if irritated, she pushed her mail onto the floor.

'I'm sorry.' David put down the teacup he'd brought for her. 'I hope you haven't caught my bug.'

'Uhm. I'll be all right. Just give me a moment.'

Just give me a moment. Give me a moment! Go downstairs. Leave me alone. Please. Please, darling!

David went downstairs.

Mary ran to the lavatory, clutching her letter. How ridiculous! How humiliating! Trembling, she opened the envelope.

'Why are we meeting in this terrible wine bar again?'

Mary laughed but, as she looked at Richard Beck, a feeling of gloom doused her silly sparkle. Last time she had been too nervous to see him properly, too blinded by her own image of the past, too aghast and terrified and romantic. Now she saw a once-good-looking man, gaunt and wrinkled and grey, his expression, under the tension of the moment, without life or originality. She was too good for him, she thought, and dropped her eyes to study her finger nails.

'You wrote to me. You wanted to see me.'

Richard saw the flush of excitement die from under the rouge on Mary's cheek. She looked at her nails so he looked at her as if at an enemy and said accusingly, 'Why did you want to see me?'

Mary couldn't answer, didn't know the answer.

'Just for a fuck, was it? Your husband a bit lacking in that area, is he?'

Mary put a shaking hand up to her face. She supposed he spoke like that to make her leave but she felt as incapable of movement as speech. Why had he known she was despising him, regretting their meeting? Did he hate her? How could he speak to her like that?

Ironically, now that he spoke to her so violently, his face looked alive again, reminding her of the man she'd loved. Was all her love in the past?

Richard wanted to break some more china. He hadn't guessed she would have turned into such a silly, self-indulgent woman. Writing to him out of some idiot whim and then horrified when faced by the reality. He pushed back his chair.

'Oh, no!' Mary managed to gasp.

'What do you want?' He sat down again with an exasperated sigh. She was pretty, certainly, soft-looking. Last time they had met, they had been like lovers. But that had seemed to be an unrepeatable experience, out of the blue, no hold's barred. Remembering, his expression changed.

Looking up at last, Mary saw it and attempted a smile. 'I don't know why I wrote to you. I wanted to see you again. I'm sorry. It was a stupid idea. You can't go back.'

'We did.' Richard spoke matter of factly. The words echoed.

'Yes.' Now they understood each other again. They both looked down, said no more.

In a way, Richard thought, more as self-protection than because he believed it, she has come for the fuck. Well, why not? I love Cherry, our children, my previous children, even my previous wife, but there're not too many of them who are loaded down with her kind of love. She loves me. Or at least she wants to. Perhaps we can make each other happy. He stood up again. 'Let's get out of here.' He put his arm round her shoulders and lifted her to her feet. He kissed her cheek and stroked it.

In the crowded and noisy room Mary shut her eyes and felt the peace of physical affection. 'I love you,' she said softly enough so he would not be able to hear it.

David enjoyed feeling well again. He was pleased to be able to cut out the world with his plastic containers of files. However, as he boiled the kettle to make an afternoon cup of tea, he did wonder why Mary had gone to London for a second time. It was not like her to worry about problems in her absence. One of her gifts was a sense that she was the centre of the world. It made her relaxed about anything outside her immediate sphere – Lucy, the London house, her job. Perhaps there was something especially wrong she hadn't told him about. He would ask her when he picked her up from the station. Guiltily, he admitted to himself that he had never been the slightest bit interested in anything to do with her job.

'Is that nice?'

'Yes.' Mary gasped. The whole thing was ridiculous. Except she felt she loved him. She always had. 'Darling.' He had always made love to her so beautifully, so carefully, so tenderly, so attentively. 'Ah!' The first man to touch her naked body. The first man to love her, when she was just a girl. 'Darling Richard.' She smiled, stroked his cheeks above her, touched him.

Richard thought of Cherry, her slim whiteness against the sheets, her pale hair. It was weeks since they'd made love. When they did, he felt the need to apologise, although she kissed him sweetly when it was all over.

'Ah!'

What must Mary's husband be like? A cold fish, presumably, one of those Englishmen who are feebly ashamed of their animal passions. Or perhaps he was proud of them and uncaring about Mary. How lovely she was! How soft! How pretty! How receptive! If only a moment like this could go on forever.

'Oh, oh!'

'Darling!' They fell together in a heap. Like a pack of cards, built too high, tumbling down. Richard, breathing heavily, sprawled across Mary. Mary, pinioned in sacrificial pose, hardly breathed at all. Eyes shut, smiling, they groped for each other's hands.

Richard fell asleep. Outside it was already dark. Only a dusky orange glow from a street light seeped around the edges of the heavy hotel curtains. Traffic noises, vanquished by love-making, rose up again into the room. Mary, comforted, exhilarated, despairing, lay quietly with her eyes open. Was this happiness? She remembered lying with very much the same emotions in their little rented room. The curtains had been flimsier with a few tiny holes through which light had pierced like stars. The traffic noise had been closer for the room was on the ground floor but less intense because it was on a little side-street, not like this smart hotel in the middle of town. But the sensation of lying with the world returning around her but at one remove because of Richard's presence, because of their love-making, was just the same.

Richard shifted sleepily and cuddled her to him so that she lay in the crook of his arm.

Surely she must have felt like this with David, at least at the beginning? Why else would she have married him?

Fraud is peculiar, thought David sitting at his desk, I deal in an amoral world. He picked up a heavy weight of papers and put them down again. I wonder if it has corrupted my own sense of morality.

Unhappiness. Desolation and unhappiness. That was why she had married him. She had had a baby by Richard. The same Richard who was lying beside her, snoring now without shame. It had wrecked her university career, wrecked her relationship with her parents, wrecked her life. She had wrecked her life for love of him. A particularly loud snore woke Richard but only long enough to throw an arm more securely around her.

Then David had come along. David, so strong, so determined, so hard-working, so clever, so kind, so remote, so unthreatening, so much in love with her. It was no wonder she'd married him.

Richard sat up suddenly. 'Whatever time is it?' Without waiting for an answer, he swung out of bed and strode off to the bathroom.

Mary recalled this physical decisiveness. David was not the same. Putting thoughts of David away, she wrapped her arms about herself, replacing Richard, replacing any man. In a moment she too must spring up, break out of this cocoon, join the traffic, the lights, the world out there.

'Are we going to meet again?' Richard sat on the edge of the bed. He pulled on his socks, his underpants. His voice was unemotional, as if asking for a point of information. He kept his eyes down, on the job. He was going to make her decide, as she had all along.

'Do you want to?' Mary sat straight, sheet grasped across her breasts.

'Yes.' Richard wanted to say more, saw that more was called for, but baulked at insincere protestations of love. He had loved her when he was young and she was younger.

Mary leant forward and stroked his back. The same thought

struck her with an unwelcome question and a welcome answer. If she had wanted a lover why had she not chosen someone young and beautiful, someone like Lucy's Jo, for example? Answer: because she loved Richard Beck with his sinewy calves now clad in rather too long navy socks and his skin, darkened and freckled with years of summer sun.

'I love you!' She let her body flow forward, curving across his back, as if he was going to lift her, carry her, like St Christopher, across a stream.

Richard paused. He had to pause because the next stage was putting on his shirt. Having paused, he was struck immobile by the thought of how little he knew this woman draped across his back. Their first association, although lasting two years, had been hampered by his marital status, by her nervous youth, her love, his love, the briefness of their encounters, the urgency of their love-making. If they had exchanged information about themselves, he hardly remembered it. Besides, at that stage of his life he did not associate an exchange of information with love affairs. Friendship had not seemed a very vital part of intimacy. But he had not then been married for seventeen years to a woman who was more friend than lover.

Mary had said, 'I love you' so Richard mumbled something that could have been 'And I you' or 'And I do too' or, just possibly, 'Do you?'

David, driving to pick up Mary at the station, noted that a cold akin to snow had returned and silver sprayed his car windows, back and front.

'A fine night!' A railway-blue figure met David at the entrance hall. He seemed entranced by the night, staring up to the sky with abandon. 'Look, there's Epsilon Indi and Capella and Antares.' He used the names with a familiarity that David found irritating. 'Makes you think, doesn't it!'

Indeed the sky glistened with light, as if strong beams were shining through a dark curtain.

'Is the train on time?'

'Too cold for snow,' said the porter.

The train was over-heated even though it was almost completely empty. Mary pressed her hands to her hot cheeks and tried to concentrate on the evening paper. But the light was dim and her eyes had a non-ocular spongey quality. Instead she laid her face against her cool image in the window and let her eyelids drop, lid to lid.

Twenty minutes late already. Despite his aversion to the porter, David came out of the gloomy waiting-room in search of further information. Immediately a bell rang and the blue-coated figure strode briskly down the platform. His head was turned slightly up and David could imagine his eyes swivelled still further, searching celestially for the meaning of life.

The train crept in with infuriating lack of energy. Carriage after carriage, glowing and empty, passed where he stood looking for the opening door, the smiling wife. At one point he gave a start: there, sleeping face pressed against the glass, was a woman extraordinarily like Mary. A woman, blurred and youthful and not Mary, of course, but like her fifteen years ago.

The train stopped. No door opened. The porter came marching back again. 'Missed it, has she?' His certainty galvanised David.

'Certainly not!' He strode alongside the train. And there she was, fast asleep by the window. The train gave a lurch. 'Stop the train!' shouted David.

Mary woke up. The porter signalled to the driver. David wrenched open the door.

'I'm so sorry. I am so sorry.' Mary shivered and shook on the platform. The train moved off behind her. 'I am sorry. I must have fallen asleep.'

'Fell asleep, did she?' The porter stamped his feet and clapped his hands while his eyes remained fixed on the departing train. 'That's it, then, till six. Night all. Night all. And what a night!'

David propelled Mary from the station.

'Why are you pushing me? What's the matter?'

'Blast it! I'll have to scrape it all over again. Do you know your train was half an hour late?'

'What's the matter?'

David made angry attempts to clear the windscreen of its layers of frosty coating. His behaviour increased her sleepy sense of unreality.

'Fuck!' exclaimed David, catching his nail against the scraper.

Mary sat in the car and watched his antics through the glass. It did not cross her mind to wonder if he had discovered how she had spent the afternoon. She felt curiously guiltless as if the two men met different women, neither taking anything from the other. Besides her need to see Richard was so great that it couldn't be wrong.

They drove back in silence, David too angry to talk, Mary too tired.

'I'm sorry,' she said again as they entered the house. 'Have you eaten?'

'What were you doing in London?'

'What?'

David flung off his coat as Mary stared at him, open-mouthed.

'What were you doing in London? Why did you have to go to London?'

Mary turned away. 'You know why I went to London. Have you eaten?'

'What should I eat!'

'I'll make something then.' Mary opened the fridge and stared at its contents with a feeling she would like to cry. Why was he bullying her when she'd come back to him, so worn out, so ready to be a good wife?

David went into the sitting-room and poured himself a strong whisky. He sat down on the sofa in front of the burnt-out fire. Already he felt calmer, his outburst a little unconvincing. By the time Mary came in with a tray, he was ready to pat the seat beside him and hold out an arm.

Mary sat down, not too close. 'I've made a salad.'

'Good, good. Darling. I'm sorry.'

'Yes.' Her face was sober.

'I missed you.'

I don't love you, thought Mary, looking at his face dispassionately but all the same found herself moving closer into the circle of his arm. Without conscious will, she found herself laying her head on his shoulder. 'Darling,' this unconscious person said and turned so she could run her lips down the side of his cheek. 'I'm sorry I left you alone.' David stroked her face, the warm skin under her hair. The familiarity of their two skins set up contacts down their bodies. Mary, alive already from Richard's touch, felt herself too soft and malleable for much resistance. 'What about the salad?'

'I had sandwiches.'

'But you said . . . '

'I was cross.'

'Why were you cross?' Words without meaning. They walked

upstairs close together. Mary, eyes almost closed, stumbled at the top step. David supported her.

Was this how he had led her into marriage? Had he looked after her and comforted her and made her feel secure and brave? But then she had been a miserable young girl while now she was a woman, almost middle-aged, running her own life with as much conviction as anyone else.

'You go to the bathroom first.'

She turned obediently.

CHAPTER TWELVE

'And aside from all that, you can't throw off the past. You have to confront it, learn what it means and then make it part of your present.'

'Darling Lucy!' Mary shook the telephone receiver in protest. 'You don't believe all that jargon, do you?'

'I'm just reading her letter to you, Mum. This is what she wrote. I'm reading it to you because it upset me and Jo won't listen.'

'It upsets me too.'

'I'm sorry.' Lucy sighed. Usually her mother's lack of caring, as she saw it, made her a comfortable and consoling confidante. She would listen, accept and suggest that the problem was not worth very much attention and certainly no emotion. But today it was she who was being emotional. 'Of course, Elizabeth is your daughter.'

'Oh, no!' Now Mary stood up in irritation. 'She's not my daughter. Not in any way that matters. I don't think of her as my daughter at all.'

'Well, she thinks of you as her mother.' Lucy sounded dull and sulky, or perhaps it was just that she had let the receiver fall further from her mouth.

'This is an impossible conversation to hold over the telephone!' cried Mary.

'You should have told me,' said Lucy, sounding even further away.

'But she doesn't exist! She's of no importance. I was so young. I never thought about a baby.'

'Oh, Mother.'

Mary stopped ranting and considered what she was saying. Never thought about a baby. Could that really have been true? She was eighteen, not so young, only a year younger than Lucy. It was impossible to think of Lucy or any of her friends making so ridiculous a statement. No wonder she had groaned, 'Oh, Mother.' Lucy had been on the pill since she was sixteen.

'Why don't you come down here again?'

'I thought you and Dad wanted a holiday on your own.'

'We always want you. And we could talk.'

'What shall I write back to Elizabeth?'

'Don't.'

'But Mother!'

Mary found tears in her eyes. Surely, that afternoon of Ian's bonfire, she had defused Elizabeth, turned her into a dim relation, well-intentioned but peripheral. 'I'm sorry, darling. I'm truly sorry.'

'But I'm not going to London. It's nothing at all to do with work. I'm going to Oxford.'

'In our last week here, on our own together, you're going to Oxford! Why are you going to Oxford?' David, previously warm, comfortable, well-fed, lying beside the fire at eleven o'clock at night, felt doubly aggrieved at this disloyal stirring. 'Why are you so restless?'

'I'm going to see my house. My parents' house.' Mary stood, determined.

'You're going to see your parents' house? Are you crazy? Why should you want to see your parents' house all of a sudden? It's a nasty house and you were unhappy there.'

'It's my holiday, too. You're working all the time. Why shouldn't I go back and see my old home if I want to? I'll get a taxi to the station if that's what's worrying you.' Mary's face was bright and red. She looked raw and ugly, silencing David who had never seen her like this.

She left the room, shutting the door behind her, treading up the stairs immediately without her usual check at the stove, check at the door, wipe-over round the sink.

What is this all about? thought David, too lazily. Is she cross because I'm working all day? But there's nothing new in that. He picked up the daily paper and then put it down again for Mary's contentment was necessary to his contentment. He switched off the lights and followed her up the stairs.

Sun mixed with the pale frosty air and shaded everything with a diaphanous glow. Mary had been unhappy in Oxford but she could admire the buildings, the spires and towers, the libraries, court-yards, and gardens, everything that made up the university town. This had not been her Oxford. Her Oxford, which she had come to visit, was composed of rows of brick houses, set behind dark hedges, inside driveways, filled with clever, spying families who knew about each other and placed newcomers before they placed themselves.

Mary's parents had bought their house when they married and lived there for the rest of their lives. It was too big for them but they had always thought they would have more than one daughter. Both of them were schoolteachers and they wanted Mary to go to the university, which neither of them had attended. She felt their presence constantly, encouraging, planning, marking her success or failure.

At first the house seemed unchanged. Only the ugly privet hedge replaced by a low brick wall, it's welcoming properties – as seat or child high-wire act – defaced by a pattern of large nails zig-zagging across the top. Mary realised that her home had become institutionalised, the front door ajar on an easy access mechanical spring, neon lighting making silver stripes across the rooms, curtains flimsy or non-existent. It was probably some sort of tutorial establishment for girls, not as well off for brains as they were for money. The educating spirit of her parents hovered still but diluted into this public place, this empty piece of Edwardian brickwork.

Mary turned away and started to walk at a desultory pace in the direction of the station. She could have gone into the house easily enough, walked upstairs to her old bedroom but what was the point? She could imagine it all easily enough, both as it was and as it would be now. What she wanted to imagine was herself as she'd been, lying awake in that high-ceilinged room, looking at the red diagonals in the curtain, pulling the pink eiderdown over her head.

Richard and she had met first on a street in London. He had been introduced to her by a friend of her father. Theirs had been a London love affair and she'd been away from her home and her friends.

The lights were already shining in the centre of Oxford, shop windows slashed across with SALE signs, lights from shapely windows in old buildings, street lamps in graceful iron rods, traffic lights, and traffic directions at too frequent intervals. When Mary grew up the city was darker, the spires more visible against the night sky. Why had she loved Richard so suddenly and so completely? And why, becoming pregnant, had she not either kept the child or aborted it? And why after all that had she refused to see Richard ever again?

The train was not due in for half an hour. Mary could hardly believe it was only five o'clock. She felt as if it were midnight, except that then the platform would have been peaceful, empty, while now it was crowded with determined travellers. Feeling very undetermined, she went to find herself a cup of coffee and something to eat.

Richard had kissed her when she told him about the baby, had laid his head upon her naked stomach. He had kissed her breasts and said that now he could see they were swollen and more beautiful than ever. But what had he said that made any practical sense? When she lay in the bedroom? Nothing. He had taken no interest or responsibility beyond love and sympathy. That seemed to make him a monster.

A noise, like chain mail unrolling, made Mary turn round. A particularly ugly man with peony-coloured cheeks and bulbous nose grinned at her from behind the bar. At once she recalled the scene played out in front of that same bar – Richard had come to see her just before she went into hospital – his one visit to Oxford. He had instigated the arrangement, telephoning her at home which he had never done before.

Realising that the man was looking at her oddly and that she must be staring at him, she went over and ordered a cider. The room began to fill. And she remembered that also, how Richard and she had been alone one minute, whispering in secretive undertones, and then suddenly surrounded by laughing, talking, end of day travellers, so that they had to raise their voices. But what had they been saying to each other?

They had hardly met those last few months. She had been due to take her Oxford university entrance exam in November but, of course, she had not, her stomach seeming reason too obvious and indisputable for even her parents. She had been three months pregnant in June when she'd taken her A levels. Was that the reason she'd not considered an abortion? It might have interrupted her studies, caused her to explain at that awkward time to her parents who were so keen on her doing well. She had told them after her results came when they were excited with her A's and S's, talking confidently about university. She had said, 'Actually, I'm going to have a baby round about Christmas so I won't be trying for university.'

'Excuse me, do you mind if we share?' Two boys joined Mary at her table. They were undergraduates, she thought, looking at their loutish manner and clothes which failed to disguise their ambition, intelligence and sensitivity. It was to avoid just such a terrifying combination that she had fallen in love with Richard. He was a man of the world, unintellectual, physical, all the things her parents are not. Mary smiled into her glass. It seemed that she'd loved her parents so much that she had been scared stiff of failing them. So she had failed them.

The boys across the table were talking about a girl.

'It was rolling up his mattress each morning that browned her off.'

'Imagine old Lenin rolling up his own mattress.'

They both laughed.

Mary understood that the girl, presumably an undergraduate, had her boyfriend sleeping on her bedroom floor. That would have been impossible twenty years ago but what struck her more was the relaxed attitude of the two boys. They were recalling the scene not because of its sexual content but because the social implications of the boyfriend's refusal to roll up his own bedding appealed to their sense of humour. They were Lucy's contemporaries.

What was it Lucy had said when she'd tried to explain that Elizabeth was not her daughter? 'Oh, Mother!' 'But Mother!' Nothing much, yet expressing a sense of impatience as if she were the silly child, Lucy the knowing adult.

It was time to catch the train. Mary walked slowly down the stairs and through the underpass. As she came out again onto the appropriate platform, she remembered what Richard had said to her in front of the bar. He had said: 'I want to marry you and be with you and bring up our baby together.'

David was making love to Helen. Even as he held her, stroked her back and kissed her cheek, he wondered why he was doing it. The foolhardiness, the danger, the guilt were with them on the sitting-room floor but also some kind of weighty inertia which made their act of love and betrayal inevitable. It's the third time you've left me, Mary, during this, our special holiday all alone together in the country.

Richard Beck had a late meeting outside the office. He decided to walk, hoping for the coolness of a light drizzle to wash away the aridity of the office. He considered the idea of retirement as an opportunity for long walks in the countryside. The evening before Nicky had come with him to walk the dog, Marshall. It had been a surprise to have this tall youth at his side. They had not talked intimately for Richard had learnt with his first family that questions from an adult are considered an unacceptable form of bullying. Instead he told him a little about his job, not so much because it interested either of them but as a kind of anonymous bridge. Nicky was his last child; in retirement he would like to know him better.

Cherry had told him that Nicky's separation from the girlfriend was truly due to work and only temporary but even so he didn't presume to raise the subject. Who better than he knew the secret tenderness of love?

'Thank you for coming,' he'd said at the end of their walk.

'That's all right, Dad,' Nicky had looked at him with his mother's bright eyes. 'Without Georgie I find myself a bit spare.'

So he could be open and unabashed. Suddenly deeply touched, Richard turned his face away to hide his expression.

Now as he walked through the dank London, he remembered that moment of emotion and raised his face a little more hopefully to the rain. With this hopeful lifting of the spirit came an image of Mary's naked shoulders and breasts.

Lucy and Jo were working. Term started soon. They had chosen separate rooms in order not to be distracted by each other's company but while Jo bent over his books in a position of dedicated, not to say, exaggerated, concentration, Lucy swung back on her chair, sighed and began to count the hairs on her head.

'Two hundred and three, two hundred and four . . . '

'Shut up!'

The rooms were not far away.

'How can I be expected to unravel the workings of the fifteenth-century mind when I can't understand my own mother – my . . . '

'SHUT UP!'

Lucy who had been allotted the kitchen, stood up and found herself a chocolate digestive biscuit. It was one of those late January afternoons when daylight had never been strong enough to turn off the street lamps. It was now drizzling slightly, merging the falling night with waves of damp, not glistening but soft like inky strands of wool. She could imagine that if she went out the air would be like a muffler pressing against her face.

'Let's do something!' She shouted at Jo from the sitting-room door.

He didn't look up. 'No.'

'But your work's so dull. Everyone says Political Theory is the dullest subject on earth.'

'Just because you can't work, don't try and stop me. You're behaving like a child.'

'I am a child. Why shouldn't I behave like a child?'

'Shut up!'

'That's a childish thing to say.' Lucy came into the room and wound her arms round Jo's shoulders. She could see herself doing it, imitating a crass heroine of an American serial. Unfortunately she did not have long to enjoy her imaginings.

'Get OFF!' Jo flung himself backwards, one arm making painful contact with her cheek. 'What are you trying to DO!'

Exaggerating her hurt, even this was better than staring at her books, Lucy huddled on the floor. 'You don't love me. You couldn't behave like this if you loved me.'

'What are you fucking talking about?'

'Love! I'm talking about love!'

Jo, suddenly calm again, turned back to his desk. 'Love.'

'Yes. Yes. Yes.' Shaking her head from side to side, Lucy worked herself up into a passion. 'Don't you have any sympathy? Any understanding . . . There's my mother . . . There's that girl, Elizabeth. She's my sister, my mother's bastard . . . '

'I don't see what that's got to do with love.'

'Everything's got to do with love. You're inhuman, that's what you are!' Now Lucy no longer needed to act. Tears poured down her cheeks and her hands clawed in the air. It was such a relief to lose control. She didn't care what Jo thought. Let him despise her! This was her real self, the one that was filled with feeling and longing and sadness and, yes, love! This was the self that could not be reasonably expected to sit down at a desk and interpret the four-hundred-year-old self-doubts of a green knight.

Jo turned round again. Didn't she yet realise that he had to work? It was no game for him, as it was for her. Without a good degree he'd have to return whence he came. 'I believe you're mad. Clinically mad.'

'Mad! Because I talk about love. Yes, I do believe you think it's mad to talk about love. And you know why? Because you don't know what love is, because you've never loved anyone. You don't love me! You couldn't love me! You're, you're programmed. A machine!'

Indeed Jo's continued calm in the face of Lucy's ever-increasing passion surprised even himself. She seemed to be blowing up like a huge red balloon, becoming featureless and monstrous. 'Love.' Why did she think that word so important, more important than anything else in the whole world? It reminded him of a conversation he'd once had with a Catholic girl. They were not talking on a religious subject but he'd become aware that there was a barrier between them. Afterwards he realised it was because the girl saw everything in the context of a spiritual belief, life everlasting for ever and ever. Amen.

Now he was faced with a red balloon screaming about love so he said, in a voice of a lecturer on political theory, 'Love is a concept introduced by the bourgeois to divert themselves and their less fortunate comrades from the realities of human existence.'

Jo watched, almost surprised, as the balloon gasped and subsided. Lucy was so sweetly naive and took his every word as gospel. One day he must take her to meet his mother.

The train was full. Mary sat in the midst of a family consisting of three small children and their astonishingly youthful parents. The father had orange red hair which he had passed on to all his children, even the few wisps on the baby's head gleamed as bright as well-polished copper. At first Mary was cheered by their exuberant energy. The children never sat down for a moment, nor stopped talking, while the father was continually back and forth to the buffet. But gradually as their conversation, all form and no content, impressed itself upon her – 'No, Michael! Stop it! Jenny!' – she began to see their energy as a reflection of a brain vacuum. The mother didn't even have the kind of animal calm you might expect from someone with such a young baby. They were like the slightly deranged, eyes too bright, movements sudden, voices too loud. In front of Mary's weary eyes they began to assume the appearance of monsters, of family clones which might soon fill the whole world.

In a series of non-sequiturs, head clogged with exhaustion, Mary remembered how she had reacted to Richard's invitation to marriage. For the first time the baby inside her had seemed real. She imagined the little girl or boy swinging between their two hands as they, a married couple, walked along between an avenue of trees, in a park, a university garden. They were married, Richard and she, coupled in marriage, becoming with the child a family unit. The image, which should have been pleasant, made her begin to shake, not with pleasant anticipation, but cold-blooded fear. She did not want it. She did not want Richard's child. She did not want to be part of his family.

What had she said to him, sitting in that dim waiting-room she had just left behind? She could remember how he looked, the tired lines on his face, the slightly greying hair, curling below his ears as was the fashion at that time. She could remember wanting to kiss him, put her hand inside his well-cut suiting even as she was rejecting him for a family future. But what did she say? What had he said?

The onus had been on her. An offer of marriage was like a contract, both parties had to sign, without passion, in cold blood. But she didn't love him in cold blood. So what had she said?

'I'm so sorry. She's just worn out, that's the trouble.' The baby was kicking Mary's legs and squealing. 'We've been travelling all day one way and another.'

'She's very good really,' said Mary, the bigger the lie, the more convincing. The baby's face was fierce and contorted as she tried to stretch her legs to reach Mary's knees.

'I'll take her off for a little stroll. Now Cath!' And she was off, up again, trailed by the other children. The father had already gone up the train to divert himself with a can of beer.

In the quiet of their absence, Mary remembered another quiet. She had not answered Richard Beck's question. It had been so unlikely that she had been able to look at him, as if he hadn't meant it. It was possible for her to give no answer and for him to think that she didn't believe in his offer. She gave no answer. She merely looked at him and he had not asked her a second time or pressed her.

What had he seen in her face? Had he seen the fear produced by that image of the family walking hand in hand between the tall trees? Or had he been taken in, as she herself had been by her lack of belief?

'I've got to catch my train now,' he'd said, standing up in either anger or love. He seemed detached already.

They'd walked together to the platform, not talking until the train came in and he'd opened the carriage door. 'I hope it all goes well.' He was referring to the baby, of course, but Mary was suffering from the physical pain that separation from him always gave her and could not concentrate on his words. She'd have swopped the baby for him any day. That thought passed swiftly. Not something she could say.

'Goodbye, darling.' He had kissed her, their flesh together for one last time. She had known it was the last time and said 'Goodbye' without a 'darling' in order to harden her heart. She had not understood what he was thinking and did not understand it now.

Had he felt the same pain which caused her to stand absolutely still on the platform even after the train had left? A movement, arm or leg pushed out from the centre, felt as if it must cause the disintegration of her whole body. Yet, remarkably, after a few minutes, she had moved without conscious effort, an instinctive setting of one foot in front of the other. In that state she had gone home and gone to bed.

Richard and two other directors were listening to Ronnie Snyderman talking about the future of the company. His tone was brisk, confident and forceful. He was small and plump with girlish eyes and dark curling eyelashes. His voice, which was heavy and low, contradicted his appearance in a way Richard found unappealing. But then Snyderman was to be his supplanter, heir to his company, the repeat story of his life. For how many years had he sat in just such sterile offices talking about the future of the company? Always the future, never the past or the present. Thirty years ago he had been the one to lecture. Now he listened, nodding at the good ideas, making notes, reacting to Snyderman's eyelashes. He wasn't envious of him, because he no longer wanted to use the energy necessary for playing that role. He didn't want to be Snyderman.

At the same time he felt the sadness of nostalgia, of déjà vu. Perhaps it was time he got out.

'How much more have you got there, Ronnie?' Richard looked at his watch. He could do that sort of thing now, an older man who was not expected to miss his train for however important a meeting.

'Nearly finished, Richard. Sorry about the length. Just thought it needed saying.'

'Of course. Of course. I'm in no hurry.' And where would he be hurrying to? In the old days his energy in the office had been parallelled by his energy outside it. How he'd loved women! Truly loved them, not just loved fucking them. He could never harm a woman. On the contrary he'd wanted to give them everything. He'd seen them as different, special. He'd loved their nervousness, their boldness, their smell, their taste, their gentleness, their brittleness. And Mary, who'd reappeared, how had he loved her?

'That's backed up by the figures, is it?' One of the other directors asked Snyderman the sort of question he was so capable of answering.

'Oh yes. It's all in this folder. I had some extra copies prepared in case you were interested.'

Oh, yes, indeed! He'd married Cherry, met and married Cherry so soon after Mary disappeared. Or it seemed soon, looking back after so many years. Had he loved Mary more than all the others? Is that why she had come back to him? Is that why he booked hotel bedrooms at not inconsiderable cost and inconvenience?

'So that's about it. For now anyway.'

He knew he'd done a good job. Richard smiled at Snyderman in congratulations. In his time he had received smiles containing just the same careful lack of rancour. In his time. Was Mary merely a pathetic old man's last fling?

David thought Helen much prettier after he'd made love to her. She abandoned the stridency which was so wearing and which was probably the reason for his escaping into sex. He couldn't have faced another intimate conversation.

'Oh dear!' she muttered, sitting cross-legged on the floor.

David saw it was 'Oh dear' too but hung on as long as possible to contented irresponsibility. 'What a pretty petticoat!'

'It's new. I got it for Christmas.'

'It's very pretty.'

'My beloved husband bought it for me. At least I bought it but it was his present.'

'That's nice.'

'Oh dear,' repeated Helen, after a short pause.

'I know. But I wouldn't worry too much.' David patted her sympathetically on the shoulder. She was a very pretty girl.

'I'm always telling myself this sort of thing shouldn't happen.'

'Of course it shouldn't.' David shrugged, still feeling warm towards her. 'We've behaved badly, I'm afraid. Who seduced whom, if it comes to that?' He smiled.

But she began to dress, not exactly in haste but with a sense of imminent removal. When she was all done up, lipstick reapplied and hair brushed, she turned to him with a look of severity, although not, as it turned out for him. 'Ian isn't very interested, you see.'

Mis-hearing, David demurred, 'On his own subject, he can be pretty convincing.'

'Not interesting, interested. I meant he's not very interested in sex.' She stood, looking down at him with, it seemed, much of her old menace returned.

'Ha!' David blinked in what he hoped denoted emphatic sympathy rather than his real embarrassment.

'He prefers running.' Helen was now at the door.

'I'll show you out.' David leapt up, his long shirt drooped round his naked thighs. He put his arm round Helen and took her to the door. She was a nice girl, who, like everyone, had her problems.

The night was cool but not cold, the air moist but not wet. Mary and Ian told each other what luck it was that they'd both arrived from London on the same train. Ian thought how pale and exhausted Mary looked. He wanted to advise her about eating habits and exercise but suspected it would not be the best moment.

Mary thought that Ian could drive her to the house, thus avoiding David's bad temper when he came to fetch her from the station.

She sat in his car with her hands folded in her lap, so still and silent, that eventually Ian couldn't restrain himself.

'You look dreadful!'

'Oh. I'm sorry.'

'I didn't mean that.' Ian laughed. 'I just wondered if I could help.'

Mary put her hand to her head and, without any intention of doing such a ridiculous thing, burst into tears.

Too late, Ian wanted to explain that he had been making an exclusive reference to her physical health.

'I went home, you see. My home when I was a child.' She spoke between sobs but the words were still unavoidably clear. 'I had a baby . . . I was in love . . . Long ago . . . No. Now. Elizabeth came, you see . . . '

Ian drove the car out of the town and into the absolute blackness of the countryside. The agonised voice, the sobbing, the heaving and choking, reminded him of Helen. Sometimes he would be woken by her in the middle of the night but she had never been able to explain. Personally, although he had never discussed it with anyone else, he thought women were different. They needed a level of emotion which was entirely irrational. They linked it to love and the man who was their husband or lover, but he thought it was a temperamental imbalance. Not that he liked to hear a woman crying. One evening when he'd run through dusk and into nightfall he'd been shocked by a scream coming from behind the hedge. He'd wanted to stop and find out what was wrong but his stop-watch was ticking on his wrist so he hadn't been able to. He still thought about it, now and again, even though in the light of the next morning he'd made a special trip to identify the spot but had only seen a field full of sheep and known it must have been one bleating in feminine imitation. He should have stopped.

'Look, I'll pull over for a moment and find you a hankie.'

The road was narrow and overhung with trees as big and black as wings on a set. The car seemed very small, cosy and secure. Mary, worn out with crying, took hold of Ian's hand that held the hankie. 'I'll just tell you about it,' she said in a calm voice, 'and then in the morning we can pretend it didn't happen. After all it's nothing to do with you.'

'No,' agreed Ian, successfully hiding his trepidation.

Part Three

CHAPTER THIRTEEN

Ian was very keen to follow Mary's commands and forget all about the terrible intimacies of her life. When he arrived back at his cottage, he shouted in a bluff no-nonsense voice – not at all the voice of someone who was party, if an unwilling party, to passion and intrigue: 'Hi ho, Helen! The poor old traveller's back!'

He was unsurprised to receive no answer. When he returned late, Helen often took the opportunity to retire early to bed with a book. After all, he enjoyed making do for himself in the kitchen, mixing the ingredients for a perfect welsh rarebit, experimenting with smoked oysters and scrambled eggs. He whistled as he cooked, imagining himself, not too vividly, in the mess of some explorers' camp, perhaps part of a naval team returning into Antarctica.

By the time he went upstairs, he really had forgotten the intricacies of Mary's love life although she had sunk irretrievably in his regard.

'Darling!' Helen was huddled in the bed, asleep he assumed. His returning husband's peck, on what part of the cheek he could discern, was received without movement, but then that too was not unusual. Ian went to the bathroom, remembering, virtuously, not to whistle.

Helen's bed began to shake. By the time Ian returned, it was springing noisily on the polished floor. For the first time Ian regretted the cottage's single beds. In a double bed he could hold her without enquiries or speech or too much discomfort to himself. But now it seemed he must crouch beside her, like a suppliant on his knees. He must speak.

'What is it Helen? What's wrong?'

Fleetingly he recalled Mary's tears. But this was his wife.

'Why are you crying like that?'

At last he put out his hand to her in more than dutiful compassion.

'Oh, Ian! Ian!' She flung herself at him, the strength of her lunge almost knocking him backwards onto the hard floor.

'Gently, now.' He crouched on the boards, she half in bed, half out, torso slung across him, legs still inside. It was an ungainly position, difficult to sustain. 'Come out now. Stand up.' With some idea of creating order, making her stand up like a man, reforming the wet and hairy mass that pinioned him, he tried to haul her out of bed.

'Come on. Open your eyes. Then we can talk and I can try and help.'

'So dreadful . . . I feel so ashamed . . . ' She was mumbling now, even more incoherent than Mary had been.

'Helen!' He spoke sharply. Perhaps she was hysterical, needed a slap on the face.

'I don't know why it happened . . . yes, I do . . . If I thought you . . . but you . . . '

'I can't hear what you're saying.' At last his clipped tones seemed to penetrate her miasma. She sat up in bed, drawing her legs under her and releasing Ian to get up and after a momentary hesitation, to sit on the end of her bed. He would have preferred still to get her standing up, in action out of thought as it were, but it remained only as a remote ambition.

'I know one should never tell. A woman should never tell. A woman's strength is her ability to keep secrets. A woman protects her man from what he doesn't want to hear.'

Although Ian tried to listen patiently he was tired and it was his second submission to a misguided woman's will in one evening. Besides all this talk of 'A woman's this and a woman's that . . . ' must be particularly calculated to irritate him. 'What are you trying to say, Helen? I can't help, if you don't make yourself clear.' Because Ian was threatened by emotions, he did not try to guess at Helen's meaning, rather waiting until she should choose to explain.

'It would never have happened if you and Mary hadn't been away at the same time.'

At the mention of Mary's name, Ian suffered a distinctly unpleasant sensation in his stomach. 'Mary and I. Yes, as a matter of fact, we met at the station so I gave her a lift back.' But Helen didn't seem to be listening.

'We'd always been attracted, I suppose . . . It's so difficult . . .

How can you ever understand? Someone like you . . . But I must tell you. I've got to tell you . . . '

'What?'

Helen looked at him, her eyes bright and shining in the dim light almost as if with happiness. 'We made love, David and I, on his carpet in front of the fire, in their cottage.' She stopped, perhaps her story unfinished but her attention diverted by Ian's expression.

'Love!' he repeated with a mixture of bewilderment, disbelief and anguish.

'No, not love.' She twisted her own face in unconscious imitation of his. 'Sex, sexual intercourse. I was wrong. We did not make love . . . although there was warmth, intimacy . . . '

This time she did not break off her own thoughts but was interrupted by Ian bounding forward and grabbing her shoulders with steely fingers. 'I'll kill you! I'll kill him!' The anguish had become anger. Ian had had enough. Anger, for him, meant action; he wanted to do something to stop the words and, worse still, the thoughts they suggested. Being non-violent by nature and belief, he'd have best liked to climb a mountain but, no mountain being immediately available, he shook Helen instead.

'No. No. Please. I had to tell you . . . but it didn't mean anything . . . it's just that you don't like that sort of thing anymore . . . not much . . . not often . . . and I do . . . ' Determined to finish her message, Helen rattled out the words between and above shakes. She knew Ian too well to be frightened by murderous threats, although she was surprised by the intensity of his reaction. Even if she had never admitted openly to her sexual infidelity before, she had always assumed he knew and condoned. 'Ow! You're hurting!' What she didn't know was that she was the second woman that evening to destroy his sense of a benign world.

'And now I'll go and kill him!' Releasing Helen suddenly, Ian raged towards the door.

Knowing he would do no such thing, Helen did nevertheless put her hands on her heart and cry out tensely, 'Come back, Ian, please! It's nothing to do with David. It's to do with us. Come back and we'll discuss it properly.'

But Ian, in need of air and movement, continued his downward rush until he reached the front door and stepped out into the cold night air. Then he stopped. Watching his dragon's breath wafting away, he became calmer. He could of course break into that other cottage. He could steam with righteous indignation. But did he want to? When it came down to the nitty gritties of the situation, did he want to involve himself further in the murky goings-on of someone else's bad behaviour? What would it effect? And how would he suffer?

Helen, leaning anxiously from the bedroom window, heard Ian return and then saw him set out, torch in hand, at a brisk pace along the track that led from the cottages. Sighing in a mixture of relief and disappointment, she returned to bed.

Mary and David lay as near the opposite sides as possible of the not very large double bed. Both had plenty to think about. Mary was now regretting her confession to Ian. It showed the kind of weakness she despised. It seemed odd, too, that she should have survived the whole traumatic experience of a love affair and birth of a child when still a young girl without feeling the need to confide in anyone. While now, as a mature and confident woman, she felt the need of unburdening her emotions onto a man supremely unfitted for the role of comforter. Marriage, she suspected, was the reason for this softening of the heart strings. She was used to sharing problems with David. She would like to tell David. She loved David. Mary's eyes filled with tears. Why was it she wanted to see Richard Beck?

David, back turned to his wife, was trying to overcome feelings of remorse. The incident with Helen had been regrettable, somehow more regrettable than his love-making at the office with Veronica who he'd made very sure had never met nor would meet Mary, but all the same, he told himself, it was not important enough for heavy beatings of the breast. Besides, Mary continued to behave in an unnaturally cool manner so he felt some measure of justification. It could be categorised as an act of foolishness rather than of wickedness.

David closed his eyes and soon slept, his mind already returning even in its unconscious to thoughts of his morning's work.

Mary also closed her eyes but did not sleep. She felt that she was presented with a puzzle, which, if only she concentrated hard enough and stayed awake long enough, she would be able to solve. Yet in the end she fell asleep without being able to solve anything or even being able properly to line up the pieces. I'll be glad to get back to work, was her last conscious thought.

Ian shook Helen's shoulder. Why should she sleep so comfortably when he'd been driven out to take a long icy walk through the night? 'Wake up!'

Opening her eyes unwillingly, Helen saw Ian like a giant towering and threatening. 'Aah! Help!'

'What's the matter?'

Why could Helen never react without emotion.

'You're so . . . enormous. It is you?'

'Of course it's me. I'm wearing my quilted anorak, that's all. I want to talk to you.'

'Why . . .'

'What?'

'Why are you wearing your anorak in the middle of the night?'

Ian saw that Helen was still half asleep and he must give her time to wake up. 'I'll be back in a moment and then I've some news for you.'

This, delivered in tones very unlike Ian's usual diplomatic calm, forced Helen into nervous wakefulness. Dragging her duvet round her, she followed Ian downstairs. What could he have to tell her? She found him pouring a brandy in the kitchen.

'Just to warm me up.'

He must not lose the whip hand.

'I'll have one too.'

In the interests of warmth Ian and Helen cuddled up together under the duvet on the sitting-room sofa.

'We could light the fire,' suggested Helen. 'Will it take long?'

Unused to instigating such matters, Ian didn't answer except to say in a desultory manner, 'How long is a chinaman?'

Helen waited, as patient as Ian had been impatient earlier.

'You women,' he said eventually without much excitement but with extreme bitterness, 'you're all the same. All determined on creating mayhem. The trouble is you don't work hard enough.'

'How can I work when I never know which country I'll land up in next?'

'What about Mary then?'

'What about Mary, then?'

'She could work.'

'She does work.' Helen couldn't help feeling a little mystified, although she could see by the flush beginning to darken Ian's face that he was approaching the nub of the matter. 'What about Mary?'

'She told me, tears pouring down her face, when she's always been so calm, so dignified, she told me about this man, this lover. Years ago when he was married and she was single, a young girl, they had an affair.' To Ian's relief he found the beat of indignation against that terrible creature called woman, carrying him forward. He flung off the duvet and began to pace up and down. He waved his arms and shouted. 'They didn't have just an affair, they had a baby. And that baby was Elizabeth!' He produced the name like a conjuror produces a rabbit from a hat and Helen reacted with appropriate shock.

'What!' She sat up, hugging her knees. 'Elizabeth, that American girl, is Mary's daughter. Well!'

'But that's not the most important thing!' continued Ian with no sense of betrayal of trust – not after what his wife had done with her husband. 'She met him again recently and they've started all over again.'

'Started all over again,' repeated Helen, tempted to smile at his terminology. 'Do you mean they're still in love?'

'Of course not!' Ian turned with a military sweep. 'How could they be after all these years? Love! You don't know the meaning of the word. None of you women do. It's just seeking after emotional gratification. It's avoiding facing facts. It's a puerile search for happiness. "Happiness"! "Love"! If I had my way I'd delete them from the language!'

'Yes, I know you would.' Helen felt depressed. So she and Mary and all the other erring women in the world were cast into an outer darkness of self-gratification. 'You would replace them with "responsibility" and "common-sense".'

'And why not?' Ian stood in front of her, legs apart, head thrown back. He looked brave and handsome, like a small boy who feels sure he's in the right.

What could she say? He was in the right. Except for his belief that all men were like him, fine, strong, upstanding, and all women like herself and the new almost unbelievable Mary he had revealed. But there was no point in denying him, any more than there was in arguing with a cocksure little boy.

Poor Ian! She had hurt him and he had no defence but a flag waving attack. If she apologised he would probably weep on her breast.

'I'm sorry . . . ' said Helen, opening her arms.

'Our last Saturday.' David appeared at the bedroom door carrying a breakfast tray. 'We must go for a walk.'

Mary pulled herself up in bed. She looked pale and appealing.

David felt more remorse this morning. He determined to make the end of their holiday together as happy as they'd planned to make it all. He just hoped that that Helen woman wouldn't make trouble.

'I'll miss this place. The cottage, the countryside, the absolute silence, the absence of people.'

Mary thought, when I get back to London, I shall have to make some decision about Richard Beck. He'll be there, a few streets away. We could speak daily, meet whenever we have time.

'I'd like to promise not to work so hard, but it's hardly possible.'

Mary tried to pull herself together as her thoughts of her lover mixed with the half-heard words of her husband.

It was a clear, sunny morning when they opened the door of the cottage. David wore the look of a determined walker but Mary dawdled. 'Look at the crocuses!' she cried just before they reached Ian's and Helen's cottage. She wanted to crouch down and study the tongues of orange but David strode impatiently on. 'Then I'll look at them myself,' she murmured but only stayed a moment before running to catch up.

Helen saw them passing energetically by. She felt frail and unloved. The brandy had been a mistake. She couldn't even bear to think of the things that had been said. This time next week she would be back in Jeddah. Trailing her dressing-gown sash like a tail hanging dejectedly, she went to run herself a bath. Ian had left much earlier, all set for a very long run.

Mary and David walked arm in arm. The sun was bright in their faces, making them half shut their eyes and not look too high or too far ahead. They heard Ian before they saw him pounding down the track towards them. He apparently wasn't aware of them either until he was near and they could see his rigid face down which sweat trickled and occasionally flew out into the light, and he could see their closeness to each other and sunlit smiles.

Then he came on even faster, holding the centre of the track as if it was his right.

'Careful there,' muttered David pulling Mary aside.

But she was slow, leaving her arm swinging outward as Ian passed. She had been watching him, half mesmerised by his feverish yet determined expression. Like a man making love, she was thinking, like Richard Beck. And then she reproved herself, half smiling. She was ridiculous.

Ian caught her look and slightly broke his even stride. His right arm caught Mary's left, throwing him more off-balance. He stumbled, recovered himself and then took what, to David and Mary's horrified gaze, looked like a straight dive into the rocky ground.

Helen lay in her bath. She had twice refilled it with hot water and twice watched bubbles collect under the taps, disperse and dissolve. Sometimes, in foreign lands, she spent all morning in the bath, rising only for lunch or to answer the telephone from which she often returned to the waters. The telephone had rung about half an hour ago but she had ignored it. Downstairs was cold and besides, it was probably only Ian's office.

Mary sat with Ian in casualty.

'Once it's in a plaster you'll be more comfortable.' Her voice was placating, like a mother with a child.

'Blasted nuisance,' replied Ian petulantly. 'Damned nuisance.'

'At least it's the left arm,' said Mary in the same agreeable tones. She did feel guilty at having been in some part responsible for his fall. But why had he come on like that, on and on, as if he wanted to wipe out herself and David? 'Although I doubt if you'll be able to run for a bit.'

Helen stood at the top of the landing wrapped in a bath towel.

'We tried to telephone and Mary even looked in but no one seemed to be at home.' David peered up from the bottom of the stairs. His mission was to tell her her husband had broken his arm.

'I was in the bath.' Helen's face was pink and round as if the water had swollen her skin, making it soft and childlike. 'I ran the taps now and again to keep the water hot. They're very noisy.'

'Well, the thing is . . . ' Was he supposed to shout the news up to her? 'Look, you get some clothes on and I'll wait for you down here.'

'Right.' Helen turned obediently. She felt dazed by her bath. He didn't want another go with her, did he? Not in her house surely? And if he did, why had he sent her to get dressed?

David sat downstairs wishing he was at his desk.

Helen, pulling her sweater over her pretty pink breasts, decided David had come back for more. There was no other explanation for such an exceptional visit. Perhaps he had fallen in love with her. She put on lipstick and patted scent against her neck.

'Darling David!'

David gave a kind of shudder as Helen swept into the room and pressed herself against him. Surely she could not think that was why he'd come? 'Sit down,' he said nervously as if it was his house instead of hers. And then added quickly, as best defence against Helen's apparent desire to sit on his lap, 'Ian's had an accident.'

'A bad accident?'

'He fell over running.'

'He's always falling over. Poor Ian. It hurts his pride more than anything.'

'No. He's quite badly hurt. Mary's with him at the hospital.'

Now at last Helen moved away, her face expressed real concern. 'What do you mean? What's he done?'

'Broken his arm, I should say.'

'His arm, I see.' Again Helen seemed to relax, though she said tenderly enough, 'He'll hate that. He hates any part of him being out of action, out of his control. It's for the same reason . . . ' She broke off and looked sidelong at David, lowering her lids in a way that made him stand up anxiously, though, he hoped, not impolitely. 'It's for the same reason,' she crossed her legs, staring up at him now, 'that he's not much good in bed. Or, shall we say, only intermittently interested.'

'I see.' David put his hands together with a lawyer's deliberation. Who could be more cold-blooded than a lawyer? But the effect was more like a priest, hands joined in prayerful supplication. Leave me alone, please! I love my wife, not you. What happened yesterday evening must be classified and forever put away, under the heading 'aberration', sub-heading 'trivial'.

But Helen, either not recognising or not wishing to recognise the plea rose to her feet and put her arm round David's neck, pulling his face to hers.

Faced with the alternatives of a kiss or a struggle, David, with the image of the orderly challenge of his desk at the back of his mind, felt frustrated, irritated and compelled to act decisively. Removing Helen's arm from around his neck with one hand, he pushed her firmly from him with the other.

Helen staggered backward. Her eyes opened wide. At first it looked as if they might fill with tears but then they changed expression and brightened spitefully. 'I see. That's how it is!'

'No. It's just . . . ' What did she want him to say? Did she want him to be cruel?

'If that's how it is,' repeated Helen in a high squeaky voice, 'then I've a thing or two to tell you.'

'It's better not. Really . . . ' David edged backwards towards the door. Veronica at the office never behaved like this. He even had a moment, while Helen gathered together her message, to pity Ian. Mary was never like this either, he thought further, not examining the idea that Mary had never felt herself scorned by him.

'You might as well sit down,' Helen advised, face flushed with determination.

'Actually I'm leaving,' said David, equally determined.

'I expect you love your wife?'

'Yes,' agreed David by the door.

'So you wouldn't like to know she's in love with someone else?'

'Oh, shut up,' said David going through the door. 'Shut up, you silly bitch!'

'She is! She is!' Helen ran after him. The high squeaky voice developed into a screech. 'She told Ian last night. It's Elizabeth's father. They met again. They're having an affair! They meet in London. They make love. She loves him. He loves her! He loves her! She loves him!'

David stood completely still while Helen, like a mad woman, tore at him. Her voice, as much as her hands, seemed to be clawing at his brain. He felt it tearing away at him, shredding his cells, pulling apart everything, everything.

Shaking her off, he walked, almost ran, through the kitchen and out of the house. When he got outside, he waited for his brain to re-form and deny the terrible things it had heard. But instead, the words repeated themselves. 'They meet in London. They make love. She loves him.' He must get back to his desk, sit down, lay his hands on his books, calm himself. The woman was crazy. The important thing was not to believe anything she said. 'They meet in London. They make love. She loves him.'

Mary rang from the hospital. 'Is that you, David?'

'Yes. Yes.'

'You sound strange.' Since there was no answer to this, Mary continued, a little brisk, a little fed up at their last day being spoiled in this way. 'Did you get through to Helen? Is she going to pick us up?'

'I . . .'

'David? What's the matter? The pips will go.'

'I'll pick you up.'

'Do. Come soon and we'll have a wander through the town while we wait for Ian. 'Bye darling.'

Mary rang Richard Beck. She hadn't spoken to him for four days and it seemed too good an opportunity to waste.

'Darling,' he said, 'darling Mary, I've missed you.'

'I've missed you too.'

'I love you.'

'I love you too.'

They didn't speak of meeting but they could do so when she got back to London.

Mary sat down in the hospital waiting-room and waited contentedly for her husband.

The day was no longer bright. Heavy clouds, overlaid on top of each other like layers of blankets, pressed down on the spires, the roofs, the grey roads and dim shop windows of the little town. David and Mary walked side by side.

'I'm hungry,' said Mary. 'Or at least I've got a headache, which usually means I'm hungry.'

'I'm sorry.' David walked slowly, head down.

'How about popping into this pub?'

'Why not.'

It was the same pub that David had sat in and watched the gap between a girl's thighs, while drinking a gin and tonic. At lunchtime it had a gloomy respectable air.

'They don't serve food here,' said David.

'Yes. They do. Look, salad and snacks.' She was so certain of herself and the world around her. It seemed impossible that she could be leading a double life. She was so calm, so untroubled.

Mary and David sat behind a small pub table. At last Mary was struck by David's silence.

'Is there anything wrong?' she asked with warm concern.

David fetched himself another drink without offering her one. 'Have you heard from Elizabeth?'

'Elizabeth?' For a moment Mary was genuinely perplexed.

'Elizabeth your daughter. That Elizabeth.'

His tone of sarcasm made Mary put out her hand to him, repeating with more concern, 'Is anything wrong?'

'I asked you a question.'

'No. No. She wrote a letter to Lucy. I told you. But I haven't heard from her.'

David was staring into his glass which he had nearly drained for the second time. Now he held it up to his eyes and looked at Mary through its double convex. Her face billowed out into porpoise cheeks. 'And what about her father?'

'What?' Mary felt as if someone had pulled a plug on her body. Her head seemed to sit, hollow like an old nut, on top of an empty shell. She flushed red for a second and then became completely without colour.

David watched this through the glass. He felt tears beginning to collect behind his eyes. It was true then what that bitch had told him. 'Her father,' he repeated with extreme difficulty. 'Your ex-lover. Your present lover.'

They had been too honest with each other for too long. Mary had no defence. This was not like sucking cream behind the fridge.

'He must be a wizened old man,' shouted David suddenly. 'What could you want with him?'

Mary's dry nut on top of her empty shoulders produced the word love, but not with enough strength to propel the sound outside herself. She remembered telling Richard she loved him less than an hour ago. What she said was, muttering painfully, 'I love you, David.'

'Love!' Now he put down the glass, not noticing as it smashed into his plate of food. 'A geriatric! Is that what you want? A doddering idiot who'll talk about love before he gets his rubber sheets.'

'I'm sorry.'

'Sorry, now, is it? Sorry! A bit late to be sorry I would have thought! Sorry! As if that was relevant. I bet you're sorry about all sorts of things not least that I've found out your dirty little secret!'

'Please.' Mary wanted to stand up but she had no strength in her legs or arms. She couldn't even push the table away. 'Please. Can we go home?'

'Home!' David used the word like an expletive. Mary crouched backwards. It seemed he must hit her next. Her reaction was automatic for it didn't seem to matter very much if she was hurt. Perhaps he would knock her unconscious.

'All right. We'll go to what you call home!' Again he shouted but this time the word ended in a wail as he took Mary's arm and hauled her to her feet.

The pub was almost empty but suddenly a voice bellowed across the space between the table and bar, 'Hold on! None of that rough stuff here!'

David let go of Mary's arm and took brisk strides to the bar where stood the same double-earringed youth who had suggested a visit to the The Devil First Club that evening a few weeks ago, and was now ordering him out of the pub.

'Fuck you! Fuck all of your silly youth and stupidity!'

Mary looked at David's back despairingly. He might be taller than the boy behind the bar but he was also older, flaccid, soft-hipped and physically non-aggressive. Not that this was obvious at the moment.

'David, please.'

'That's right!' said the youth, calmly. 'Listen to your wife and if you must give her a bollocking, take her home first.'

The blow, stretched as it must be across the bar, hit the boy's face with limited intensity. Not, however, as limited as might have been expected.

'David!' screeched Mary, hardly knowing whether she feared for him or the boy. That doubt was resolved as two more youths appeared, as if the original had cloned himself in adversity. All three surmounted the barrier of the bar.

'Come on!' screamed Mary, as David seemed inclined to hang around in oddly uncombative stance. 'Let's run!'

Just in time he turned and like two young gangsters, two rebels against the establishment of the country pub, they fled out into the street. Dazed for a moment by bright daylight after red-lamped gloom, they hesitated and were nearly caught again.

'This way!' Now David took command, grabbing Mary's arm and pulling her along the pavement. The weakness she had felt, sitting at the table, was only slowly being replaced by the adrenalin of fear.

'Lawyer lashes out in country pub!'

'We're winning!' David seemed elated. He let go of her arm but she could still feel where his fingers had clutched at the flesh. 'They've stopped.'

'Please. Can we stop?'

'When we reach the car.'

Richard Beck rang his wife, Cherry. 'I'm sorry, darling. I'll be late back.'

'But what about the school?' She was exasperated. 'We're supposed to be discussing Nicky's university entrance.'

'Christ. I forgot.'

Cherry said nothing which was particularly damning. She would go, of course, and ask all the right questions.

'I'm sorry.'

'So am I. So will Nicky be.'

'But you know it's not my fault. You know it's not lack of caring . . . ' Who could blame her for putting the telephone down?

Richard, feeling guilty and bitter, tugged out a bit of paper from his desk and wrote in capitals, 'HOW SILLY'.

His secretary, entering silently in her regular tea-bringing capacity, smiled politely as she read the message over his shoulder. 'I do agree,' and indeed her voice was loud and bright with agreement. Which gave Richard, who'd been too absorbed to notice her entrance, a nasty shock.

'Philosophy,' he said, recovering enough to hurl the paper into the basket. 'I may take a course in philosophy.'

'Ha, ha,' responded the girl as politely as ever.

Mary leant against the side of the car, sweating and trembling. She would have liked to faint, crumpling slowly down to the ground, dissolving into a puddle and disappearing under the car wheels.

David stood outside too but he was upright, head high, eyes glittering. 'I should run more often.' He paused, then slapped his hand on the side of the car. 'I should swing a punch more often.'

Mary now wanted to get into the car, sink her trembling limbs into the seat, but David had the key and seemed disinclined to open the door. Presumably he was enjoying a feeling of ascendancy. He wasn't too keen to restart their terrible conversation. Again Mary suffered the sense of draining in her body and the trembling induced by physical exertion was replaced by the ague caused by mental panic.

'I've got to sit.' She leant her whole body over the bonnet of the car. Perhaps her weakness would make him take pity.

'Oh, have you!' His voice was mocking and supercilious. 'You've got to sit. Of course you've lost any claims to my caring for you. You can't have a jolly time with another chap and expect me to be waiting around to do the caring and looking after.'

'What?' Fainting, which had been a good idea, seemed, now that it was almost on her, a miserable prospect. She had to show some grit.

'What do I mean?' said David in the same ugly tones. 'I mean that I don't have to provide a place for you to sit. A nice cosy seat in which you can forget your troubles.'

'Please, let's drive home.'

'Home again, home again, jiggety jog.' He came round and stood in front of her, staring with dispassionate criticism. 'You don't look beautiful to me anymore. You don't look remotely attractive or even interesting. You look like another middle-aged, middle-class woman who's had a drink in the middle of the day after a not very good night. You look ordinary, drab, dull, with grey in your hair, wrinkles round your eyes and red veins in your cheeks. Your stomach is too big and so are your ankles which used to be slim and so were your hips. You are an unappealing sight and I don't really see why I should let you into my car and drive you back to my cottage. I'm not at all sure I want to be in close proximity with you now I know what you're really like. Je m'en fou, as the French say.'

Finishing this speech which he delivered with a lawyer's emphasis, David bent down and unlocked the car. Once inside, he opened Mary's door and waited.

Mary got in, despite everything enjoying the relief of physical support. Of course he hated her now. She hated herself. She was everything he described.

David drove carefully, not speaking. After a few minutes they passed by the hospital where Ian was being treated. David stared straight ahead and Mary, although having a mental image of Ian in the waiting-room, arm stiff and white, did not remind him. It seemed proper behaviour towards friends was the first casualty of marital collapse.

Richard drove fast from the station. His car swept round in front of the school and stopped noisily. In a moment he was out, tall and elegant in his tight city overcoat.

Nicky, working late in the library, looked up at the noise but it was too bright inside and too dark outside for him to see anything.

Richard, racing to the door, caught sight of his son's pale raised face but in his haste did not quite believe his eyes, otherwise he would have waved triumphantly or given him an exuberant thumbs up. It felt good to be doing something for the family. Screw Snyderman!

CHAPTER FOURTEEN

Helen saw David's car coming back, with Mary sitting in the front seat but not Ian. Because she never for a moment thought David would confront Mary with her piece of information, she assumed there must be some complication with Ian's arm. Even she, however, did not have the gall to telephone the cottage for news. Both David and she had lost their tempers, of course, both behaved badly, but she suspected David's nature was not as forgiving as hers. Men were like that. She settled into an armchair and, after a few minutes of low-key wifely concern, realised there was no reason why she shouldn't contact the hospital.

David, staring from the sitting-room window, saw Helen's car going past. 'Bitch!' he shouted in what he felt must be his last flash of self-righteous anger. Already he could feel the weight of age, good sense, hopelessness crushing his gin and tonic spree of energy and power.

'What?' said Mary, coming from the kitchen with two cups of tea. Both question and tea took courage, the one because she dreaded any explanation, the other because it might be thrown in her face, wiping wet swathes across her guilt.

But David accepted the tea and sat down without a word. Mary still stood, 'Shall I stay?'

David looked up and saw her humility was not assumed. She really was accepting all the guilt and blame. If he told her 'Go', she would leave, probably only the room at this moment, since she held a mug of tea in her hands, but perhaps, eventually, the house. 'Do you want to stay?'

Honestly, Mary would have liked to take the tea up to her bed, drink it as quickly as possible and then pull the bedclothes over her head for ever and ever. 'Yes.' She sat down.

The tea was very good. David thought about tea plantations in Sri Lanka which he'd once visited. He considered the brilliant blue sky, the crisp mountainside air, the brightly coloured women putting the leaves into neatly woven baskets. That's why people went abroad, he thought, to contemplate other peoples' lives without the complication of understanding. He felt exhausted.

I feel exhausted, thought Mary. And what can I say to him? I've already said the only thing that matters, that I love him. I do love him. I want to stay married to him. I can say that to him. But should I deny Richard Beck? Do I want to deny him? Suddenly Mary sat up straighter and her cheeks filled with colour.

She caught David's attention and he looked at her for the first time since they'd come into the cottage. He remembered how he'd detailed her ugliness and he thought bitterly that he'd been wrong for she was a beautiful woman and always would be.

I hate Richard Beck! Mary could hardly contain her anger. He wrecked my life once and now he's going to do it again. Her hatred did not recall that it was she who had brought him back into her life. And he's not worth it! she thought. He's an ageing – no, old – untalented businessman who has no ambitions or interest beyond his first drink in the evening. I'm just a fuck to him which is almost cost free. Indeed if he puts down the hotel on expenses, which he probably does, then it is entirely cost free! I hate him! I hate him!

Extraordinarily, considering the violence of her feelings, Mary's face remained still and calm, only the flush and bright eyes suggesting something else.

David finished his tea. 'Well. Are you planning to leave me? Go off with your old man? Perhaps, fetch your daughter back from America and make a nice cosy family party. Don't let me stand in your way.' Although David's irony was horrible, it was no longer fired by fury. He would not hit her, shout at her, swear at her, not even insult her more than was reasonable under the circumstances.

Mary lay back in her chair. Her anger against Richard, produced in some sense as a balance to David's against her, disappeared, leaving her once more in the grip of extreme lassitude. 'I don't know. I don't know anything.'

'You don't know! That's funny. You're the one who knows,

remember? I'm the one who doesn't know. I'm the silly twit who's had the proverbial wool pulled over his eyes.' His irony had weakened further, even rising in tone as if it might eventually reach a childish whine.

'I mean I can't explain. I don't understand myself so how can I explain it to you?'

'In a moment you'll tell me it's your age. You'll talk of mid-life crisis and your perception of yourself as a woman.'

'No. No. I won't. Oh, David.'

David saw, with further sinking of spirits, that she wanted him to comfort her. She wanted him to hug her and tell her she mustn't worry so much and everything would turn out all right in the end. He could even imagine himself doing it, burying his real anger and unhappiness under a sham of civilised behaviour. To save himself from such a humiliating fate, he put down his mug and enquired in a severe tone, 'How often have you seen him?' Such was his lack of conviction, for he realised before the end of the sentence that he certainly had no wish for the answer, that the question mark was muted almost to extinction.

But Mary, with a kind of carelessness, as if it was of no importance, responded immediately, 'Oh, two or three times. Not much. He is married, you know.'

This was better than it might have been and David found himself asking a second question, 'Is he planning to leave his wife?' The question mark was stronger this time as if it took a charted route.

Lawyers are good at asking questions, thought Mary dully. But questions destroy. A good thing if they destroy whatever I feel or felt for Richard Beck but not so helpful if they destroy my love for David. 'No one's planning anything.'

David stood up with an amount of energy which stunned Mary. She felt small and weak huddled below him in her chair, although that feeling too was a form of defence. How could he turn against someone so obviously lily-livered? If it was evening, she thought, they could go to bed. If it had been summer, they could have sat in the garden, been healed by the sky and the trees. But it was four or five on a winter afternoon, a terrible time. She did not even feel like a drink. 'Asking all these questions, won't improve things,' she said with an effort.

David walked back to the window again. It had grown dark and only the blackest and heaviest shapes were still visible. 'I knew that girl was a disaster.'

'What girl?'

'First she tries to kill me.'

'You mean Elizabeth?'

'My instinct was right. She caused everything.'

Spurred on to think a little, Mary was struck by a question she wanted to ask, 'How did you find out?' She did not ask it vehemently for she expected no more than an admission of anxiety, an instinctive sense of misrule.

'That bitch Helen told me.' David, unusually for him, reacted without forethought.

'Helen!' Mary's surprised exclamation might have been followed by a further question. How could Helen know? Except that, as she opened her mouth, she saw herself weeping out her sad story to Ian. The rat must have told Helen. What a verminous rat indeed! So she must take the blame, as for everything. If she hadn't enjoyed the luxury of tearful revelation, David might never have known.

David, back turned to Mary, was suffering rather late in the day, from his own portion of guilt. He waited, indeed, for the question, Why should Helen tell you? The answer, she was his scorned lover, showed him in a distinctly unflattering light. His guilt was not the same as Mary's, he told himself, being rather a peccadillo beside a flaming wrong, but he realised she might not see it quite like that. It now also struck him with a dismal sense of responsibility that if he hadn't screwed Helen, he would never have known about what might, after all, have turned out to be merely a passing lunacy. Moreover it now seemed more or less incomprehensible to him why he'd ever laid hands on the loathsome girl, although he retained a dim sense that he'd been trying to avoid the thrust of her personality. Afraid! That was a joke.

Both Mary and David gave a startled quiver as he produced a loud syllable somewhere between a croak, a groan and a laugh.

The truth was neither of them wished to continue the conversation along its present lines. Silence, estranged and precipitous as it was, seemed a less dangerous alternative.

Nicky chose to return home in his father's car. Cherry drove behind them, her headlights striking at the backs of their heads. As usual Nicky was silent, although they could have talked about Edinburgh or East Anglia or York.

'Your teachers seem pretty satisfied with you.'

'Yup,' agreed Nicky. His pale hair was turned into a halo by the light. The sight, glimpsed out of the corner of Richard's eye, made him uneasy, with a disturbing sense of déjà vu. He put out a hand to touch Nicky's arm.

Helen, still excited by events and with only the merest hint of guilt for she had been vilely mistreated, drove Ian from the hospital to the cottage. Her sympathy for his woebegone face and rigid plaster cast arm, was lessened by the knowledge that she must bear his depression, in doubtless increasing doses, for two or three months, most of it, moreover, in Jeddah.

'What bad luck!' she said emphatically as they neared the turning to the cottage. 'And it was such a beautiful morning too.'

'I don't see what that has to do with it.' Nor, he might have added, did his accident have anything to do with luck. He had been angry because Helen had been unfaithful to him yet again and when he had seen David on the path, arm in arm with his charming wife who he, Ian, just happened to know was being unfaithful to her husband, his anger had risen up turning him into a roaring mass of hatred against humanity (in particular against Helen, David and Mary) and this rage, turning him into a small child who throws himself down in front of his mother, this rage had hurled him down on the stoney ground with the inevitable result that he, the only one on the path of righteousness, should end up with a badly broken arm.

It was not fair. The last few days of his holiday were ruined, although it was also true to say that he longed to be back at his desk, tackling other people's problems with efficiency and impartiality.

'You're such a slag.'

'What?' Helen was so amazed that she allowed the car to stop, settling down as if forever in a large pot-hole.

'I haven't bothered to say it before. But that's what you are, a slag.'

'You're . . . ' Words could not describe. 'Fuck you!'

'Slag.'

'Just because you've broken your fucking arm.'

'Slag!' Ian shouted, his face screwed up and red. The stretching of his vocal cords reached his arm, giving him a nasty twinge of pain. 'This would never have happened if you hadn't fucked that pompous fat-arsed prick, David, QC leg-over wicket.'

'And that would never have happened if you weren't such a

no-ball boy scout with a Holy Grail quest to run longer and faster than a cowardly ostrich.'

'Slag!'

'Get out! There's nothing wrong with your legs.'

'My pleasure.'

'And I hope you fall down a hole in your fucking no-good driveway and break your other arm!'

'Slag! Slag! Slag!'

Rattling and bumping, firing stones from its wheels and smoke from its exhaust, the car set off down the long dark drive, apparently in as bad a temper as its mistress.

Feeling very ill, cold and sorry for himself, Ian walked a few steps and then sat down on a boulder. Unused to self-analysis, his mind obstinately refused to face the fact that he was in the middle of a personal crisis and that Helen might leave him or the cottage or both. Instead he worked out the distance yet to walk and the risks of doing what Helen wanted, that is, falling and breaking his other arm. This deliberation fitted in with his picture of himself as a sensible man of action and slightly raised his spirits. Even more sustaining was the stoicism needed to rise above the ever-increasing pain in his arm and head. Stoicism had always been his strong point. The real challenge was not to pass out. On the whole he thought it better to sit tight, at least, for the time being.

Locked in their mutual silence, Mary and David both heard Helen return with the car. When running footsteps approached in their direction, they cowered with an identical and comic look of apprehension.

I'm miserable, fed up, unhappy, unloved, unloving, that's what I am. Helen's head filled with a jumbled jargon of marital breakdown as she ran from the car. If it wasn't for the children, I'd have left him long ago. He takes me to horrible places. I can't work, I can't have fun, I can't have friends. And what for? For him. For his career. Not for me. What do I have? Nothing. Or rather worse than nothing. Him. He doesn't love me. He doesn't see when I'm unhappy. Or if he does, he looks the other way. I don't love him. I hate him. I hate everyone. I hate myself.

'Helen,' said Mary as she burst through the kitchen door and from there on to the sitting-room. Now that she had broached the silence it came as a relief.

'Helen,' agreed David, his attitude of rigid apprehension unchanged. The woman had taken on the form of a witch.

Helen stood wild-eyed in the middle of the room. Her head flipped from side to side. Since Mary and David could not hear the gramophone record inside her head which had reached the 'I hate myself' line, they waited for her to speak, explain and, in David's dread, destroy still further.

Instead she gave a yelp, sank to the floor and burst into tears.

Mary and David looked at each other over her head. Mary thought, she's a pretty terrible human being but that doesn't mean I don't have a duty to find out what's wrong and comfort her. David thought, the important thing is to keep them apart. I must offer to take her back to her cottage. Simultaneously Mary and David took a step forward.

Helen looked up, grateful through her tears. 'It's the end, you see. And, although it's my fault, it isn't really.'

'Of course,' said David with such warm sympathy that both women looked at him, in surprise. 'But it'll feel better when you're at home in bed.' He took her arm firmly.

Mary saw he was simply trying to get rid of her and felt reassured. That warmth had been quite creepy. 'It's the shock, of course. But a broken arm's not too bad.'

'Fuck Ian!'

'What?'

'Fuck Ian. And his arm. I left him out there on the driveway. I never want to see him again.'

'But you can't leave him out there!' Mary was shocked. She ran to the window, as if she might be able to see him. 'It's dangerous. He's not in a fit state.'

David gave up trying to pull on Helen's arm, although not without a final exasperated tug. Let her have the floor then! What did he care? 'I'm going upstairs to do some work.'

'But David, we can't leave Ian out there.' Now Mary was tugging at his arm. The physical contact might have been reassuring after so much alienation but he was too exasperated by the sight of the witch, now rocking herself despairingly on the floor.

'That's her responsibility.'

'But look at her!'

'Then you go and fetch him. Personally I think a human being has to prove he's worth saving before being saved.'

'What do you mean? I . . . '

David stamped upstairs. Let her tell Mary everything. He was disgusted by the whole tawdry business.

Mary set out in the car to bring back Ian. There was no moon but the sky was clear and filled with stars. Again she felt a sense of relief after the nightmare of her conversation with David. Here she was, leaving him and the cottage on an errand of mercy but planning to return. Perhaps nothing irremediable had happened. Fleetingly she considered Richard Beck but this was not the moment, not the place.

Ian watched the car lights approach. So she had decided to come back to him, beg him for forgiveness, perhaps, and make things calm and happy between them. He got up from his boulder, although the effort made his legs shake and his head spin.

Mary said nothing as she stopped the car. She was there in the capacity of an ambulance man, just as originally she had been the transportation to hospital. But Ian's face of disappointment as she opened the car door struck through her anxiety and exhaustion.

'Helen's not feeling too good.'

'Not too good,' repeated Ian, getting into the car with some difficulty. 'That makes two of us.'

'I'm so sorry.' Mary drove slowly and carefully down the bumpy track. She wondered if there was any hope of Helen having removed herself from their carpet into her own cottage.

'It's all a bit disastrous,' said Ian, which was, for him, a statement of the end of all hope.

Mary, past recognising the niceties of another's personality, particularly one she didn't care for, merely nodded. She regretted making him her confidant. He had told Helen. Helen had told David. He had seemed appropriately impervious, the next best thing to talking to a wall but now his face had a deadly sensitivity about it. If Helen had not returned, she would have to help him into the cottage, make him a cup of tea.

Helen had fallen asleep. Or at least that was the impression she gave. David, unable to work, peered at her from the sitting-room door and then retreated hastily. Outside he heard Mary driving slowly past to the other cottage. He went to the kitchen, sat down at the table and clasped his head.

'Mind the door.' Thinking of other things, Mary still showed Ian tender care. She was unsurprised to find Helen's house empty.

Ian stood in the middle of the kitchen, glaring.

'Where is she?'

'In our cottage, I'm afraid.'

'In your cottage.' Ian's face was greenish white and his eyes bulged ferociously.

'Don't you think you should sit down? Or better still, lie down.'

'She's there with him!'

'What do you mean?' Mary sighed.

'She's there alone with your husband!'

'Not exactly. I mean she's in the sitting-room and he's gone upstairs to do some work.'

'Huh!' Spittle flew from Ian's pale lips, cresting towards Mary in a graceful arc. Try as she might to avoid his meaning with disinterested lack of sympathy, she could no longer do so.

'I see.' Mary sat down. But immediately had to spring up again for Ian's knees, bending with unnatural languor, had deposited him sideways on the floor.

The telephone rang near Helen's head. She twitched a little but otherwise made no sign of hearing it. After several rings, David came into the room, picked his way across Helen's prone body and lifted the receiver.

'Hello,' he found he was whispering, as if in the presence of the sick or dying. 'Hello,' he bellowed defiantly.

Helen groaned slightly and rolled away.

'What?'

Mary's voice was even dimmer than this had been.

'He's fainted. Passed out. Unconscious on the floor. I can't move him. You'll have to help.'

Without answering, David turned to Helen. 'Your husband's fainted on your floor. What is it with you two and floors?'

'Fuck my husband.'

When David turned back to the receiver, Mary had hung up.

David crouched down beside Helen. 'You may have problems, you and Ian. I can see you have problems. But I'd be very grateful if you did not let them ruin my life and happiness as well as your own. I am now going to go across to your cottage and carry your husband up to bed. And you are going to come with me.'

'No.'

'Yes. Then I am going to ring a doctor and after that I shall leave with my wife and return to this cottage where we will remain for twenty-four hours, before we return to London, entirely on our own. If you follow my instructions and make no more trouble I just might bring myself to believe you are a sad foolish woman rather than a mad, wicked woman, almost certainly possessed by the devil!'

The lights from one cottage stretched into the dark countryside for a while and then paled and lost their strength. The lights from the other cottage reached out but could not penetrate to where Mary and David stood. Why had they stopped? Neither of them knew, neither of them had anything to say. Perhaps it was the sense of being in a no-man's-land before entering the world of forced decisions again.

Mary made a salad and cooked pasta with meat sauce. They ate almost in silence, without even the heart to open a bottle of wine. Afterwards David watched the news and Mary went to bed. When he came up, she pretended to be asleep. She had not closed the bedroom curtains and David stood for a moment looking out at the moonless, although starlit night. It was odd, he thought, for once showing a lack of common-sense, that the moon gives so much light and the stars so little. Reminded of the star-gazing porter, he remembered how he had so foolishly met her from her adulterous jaunts to London.

Richard went up to his bedroom. He liked feeling energetic on his early morning starts and these days he seemed to need more sleep. Lying in bed on his own, he allowed himself the luxury of imagining Mary as a young boy might his lover. When Cherry joined him he flung his arm across her and, finding the slippery cool of her nightdress, quickly became more than half awake.

Downstairs, Nicky sat up in front of the television with his books open and his eyes half shut.

Lucy curled around Jo's warm sleepiness.

'They'll be back tomorrow.'

'You'd better change the sheets then.'

'Where will you go?'

'I haven't thought.'

'It's been wonderful living so close to you.'

'It's been OK.'

Lucy kissed his shoulder gratefully but couldn't resist trying for more. 'I didn't think you'd stay in one place so long.'

'It's a comfortable house.'

'I could ask them if you could stay on.'

'No, thanks.'

'But why not? They wouldn't bother us. They're both out working all day.'

'Just no thanks.'

Lucy took a strong-minded breath. 'OK.'

'OK it is.' Jo, suddenly rolling back, faced Lucy. She thought he might be smiling, although it was too dark to see. 'Sometimes I'm more sensible than you. And less greedy. We've had a good time, don't let's spoil it.'

'No.' Lucy agreed fervently, smiling and smiling till her legs buzzed. She felt so happy she didn't even need to say she loved him.

'She still hasn't answered my letter.'

'Why do you bother?'

'She's my half-sister. There's a tie. I have to work through it.'

'Balls.'

'Bob!'

'I apologise. But it drives me crazy. You know, Elizabeth, you're becoming obsessional.'

'Obsessional. I make one trip to find out what sort of mother God provided me with, I discover the existence of a half-sister, about my age, to whom I write one letter and you call that obsessional. It's clear you haven't ever studied the human psyche.'

'That's what you should be doing, studying instead of worrying yourself about these people who have nothing to do with your real life.'

'Real life? Real life! What do you mean real life? Mary's my mother, Lucy's my half-sister.'

'But they don't care about you. They have no interest in you. I'm your real life. Here in New York. I love you!'

In the middle of the night a wind began to streak clouds across the sky. A door banged in Richard Beck's house in the country. It banged again, waking the dog who began to bark.

'Do make your dog shut up.' Cherry nudged her husband, not rancorous but insistent.

There was never any point in ignoring Cherry's righteous demands. Richard buttoned up his pyjamas and felt for his dressing-gown. Ten years ago he had always slept naked even in the coldest weather.

It was the kitchen door banging. Marshall slept in the scullery beyond. Stumbling sleepily, he pushed open the door and switched on the lights. Nicky lay stretched out on the floor. One spotlight encircled his head as if he were on a stage. There was blood on his pale hair and a little coming from his mouth. Breath came from his mouth too, but irregularly, raising his naked chest for a fleeting second as if on the crest of a hopeful wave and then lowering it into an endless trough.

Richard crouched beside him. The door banged, the dog increased his barking and behind him an open window rocked against its hinges. 'Oh, no. Oh, no. Oh, no. Please not.' Richard blundered his way to the telephone.

CHAPTER FIFTEEN

The house in London was so big. Mary had forgotten how big it was. There was space enough for her and David to avoid each other, particularly as they were both back on their working time-scale, he leaving the house at nine and returning at seven or eight, she leaving at eight-thirty and returning at six. Their lives together were staggered, only joining for sleep or now and again for supper. But there they were chaperoned by Lucy who still had two more weeks before she returned to college. Quite possibly, they need never talk seriously again. Was that what she wanted? A cessation of hostilities, followed by a gradual but inevitable cessation of love?

Richard and Cherry sat beside Nicky's bed. It was hardly necessary for them both to keep vigil – the hospital clearly thought they should take turns – but they neither wanted to be separated from him nor from each other. They sat for thirty-six hours without resting and were still there when, without recovering consciousness, Nicky stopped breathing. Almost at once the police asked for an interview. Again they sat side by side but this time without hope.

'We picked up the suspect that same evening,' the policeman said. 'A boy. Drunk, blood-stained, hardly in control.'

'Nothing had been taken,' said Richard, making an effort. 'Nicky must have surprised him as soon as he came through the window. My dog was barking.'

The policeman wrote without comment as Richard described what he had found. Every time he pronounced their son's name, Cherry's body twitched so that Richard felt the movement in his own. Eventually she said, 'This boy, how old was he?'

'Nineteen,' said the policeman, looking at his notes.

'He must have been very drunk,' Cherry murmured and, in order not to cry, thought of Daniel who was alive and also nineteen.

'He must be mad!' cried Richard as the policeman closed his notebook.

Lucy was enjoying the relief caused by Jo's absence. She loved him, of course, but he was such an unrelaxing sort of person. He had gone up to his parents to pay a ritual visit so she didn't even have to worry about girls with a musky scent and snake hips – although why there should be no feminine temptation in his parents' home ground she didn't try to explain. Jo was away and Lucy slept, really slept, stretched out across her bed; worked, really worked, with the concentration of her whole mind; and, when her parents were around, became their loving daughter.

It was about three or four days after their return that she noticed they were hardly speaking to each other. With the emotion usually spent on wondering about Jo, she wondered about them instead and for the first time considered what effect the appearance of the horrible Elizabeth might have had. Although she felt warmer towards her father who was never critical and always ready to help her with advice or cash, she did not think of approaching him but decided to sound out her mother.

Mary sat on her bed, reading the evening paper and drinking a glass of wine. She also had a large folder filled with papers relating to a report on the future of local radio which she was correlating. This working at home was a new form of defence in which she imitated David's behaviour. It had also struck her that there was one more salary band in the BBC which she could hope to reach and that such an achievement would give her something to be proud of, something for her future.

'Hi, Mum!' Lucy flopped onto the bed with a fish-like lack of sinew.

Mary sat up straighter. 'Hi, darling. How was your day?'

'Fine. I decided I liked Middle English.'

'That's good.'

'I didn't even have to do it.'

'That's why I said it was good.'

Lucy flopped over onto her back and looked at the ceiling. She hadn't envisaged this as a difficult conversation. The only difficult conversations were with Jo because he was so important. She herself no longer thought intensely about Elizabeth. Once she had decided not to answer her letter, it had been easy to forget her. Jo had said one must always be ready to dispense with the counter-productive elements of a family.

Mary put down the newspaper. 'I expect you're looking forward to term starting?'

'In a way. Mother?'

'Yes.'

'Were you, you and Father very upset when that girl, Elizabeth, turned up?'

Mary looked at her daughter. Lucy's eyes, large, innocent, blue, gazed at the ceiling with such intensity that she was almost tempted to look herself, find some cobweb, crack or blot.

'Are you curious or sympathetic?'

Lucy blushed, making pink stalactites down her neck. Mary relented. Why shouldn't she be curious? It was her right to be curious.

'I'm sorry, darling. Yes. I was miserable. I didn't want to see her but she came anyway.'

'She would.'

Mary smiled. So Lucy was on her side. Lucy, seeing the smile, curled herself round in an almost human posture. When she was small, her mother had read to her every night, snuggling into her bed with her arm providing a rest for her head.

'A long, long time ago . . . ' began Mary. It was a bedtime story, thought Lucy.

'Go on, Mum.'

'A long, long time ago when I was about your age, no, younger and much, much younger in experience – I fell in love with a man. He was older than me and married. I was so shocked by my own behaviour that I kept it hidden from everybody, my parents, of course, but all my friends too. I told nobody. Then I became pregnant. I never even thought of an abortion. Not that I wanted the baby. I didn't at all. It was as if I lived all that time in a state of shock, unable to think clearly or act reasonably. I was about to take the entrance for Oxford but I gave it up, using my pregnancy as an excuse. I told my parents and they were almost as dazed as me. They looked at me as if I'd gone out of my mind. And perhaps I had. Eventually they suggested an abortion but it was too late. So I landed up in the Radcliffe Infirmary having a baby I didn't want.'

'Elizabeth.' Lucy looked at her mother. 'Did you call her Elizabeth?'

'No. I only saw her once when a nurse made a mistake and brought her along to be fed. She cried as they carried her away. I never saw Richard again either.'

'Richard?'

'The man I loved. The father. I just felt I'd had enough. I didn't stop loving him, I just didn't want to see him again.'

'But didn't he want to see you again?'

'I suppose so. But he didn't ring me.'

'He could have written to you.'

'Yes. Perhaps he didn't love me enough. Or perhaps he felt ashamed at what he'd done to me. Perhaps he loved me very much.'

'But how could you never look him up? Just stop, cold like that.'

'I don't know. It seems strange to me now. But I was young.'

'I'm young but I could never give up Jo like that.'

'Richard was never in all my life. He was in a secret compartment labelled "love" or "guilty love". I shut up that compartment and went on with the rest of my life. The following year I went to Brighton University which was brand new and exciting and forgot about him. Then I met your father.'

'And lived happily ever after.'

Mary picked up her glass and looked at the drop of ruby liquid collected at the bottom. 'That's right, darling.'

Lucy sat cross-legged and stared at her mother. 'But there's still Elizabeth.'

'That's right, too.' Mary sighed. And there was still Richard Beck. It seemed extraordinary to her that Lucy showed so little interest in the man she loved. Perhaps it was difficult or even distasteful to imagine your middle-aged mother passionately in love. Or ridiculous. She probably thought Richard was dead. Certainly it would be impossible for a girl her age to imagine that her mother spent hours trying not to telephone her old lover's office just as she had when they were both young.

Lucy stroked her mother's hand. She looked so sad and worn. 'Thank you for telling me the whole story. Now I see why you and Dad seem so cold to each other at the moment. Raking up the past must be awfully painful.'

'Darling.' Mary put her free hand on top of her daughter's. 'A hand sandwich,' she said lightly. 'And that reminds me, I'd better make some supper.'

Richard and Cherry lay in bed together. They had both taken sleeping pills and hoped the other slept, although guessing by the stillness that they shared a dreadful alertness. Four days after Nicky's death when his cold body lay at the mercy of the police pathologists, their own warmth and life seemed against nature. At two o'clock in the morning Richard spoke into the darkness, 'Why didn't I hear Marshall's barking sooner? Why didn't I go to the kitchen? Why didn't I get my brains knocked out?'

'Don't.' Cherry's denial was hardly audible.

'Because I'm old and deaf and lazy, that's why!' He was shouting now. 'Because I didn't care. Because I'd left him down there on his own. Why was he down there on his own so late? Because I'm selfish and . . .'

'Sshh. Daniel will hear.' Cherry spoke with more energy now. 'Sshh. Come here and I'll hold you. I'll hold you. There's no use in saying this. Lie quiet. Please.'

They were both so very tired.

David looked at Veronica's half-clothed body. She had a pretty body, less voluptuous than Mary's but neat and sweet-smelling. If her legs were rather short and her back rather bent as if with too much typing, what right had he to complain?

They were in her flat since her husband was abroad. 'I missed you,' she said, removing her remaining clothes.

'I missed you too.'

'Was the country very peaceful?'

'Beautiful,' replied David following her into bed. Peaceful it was not.

David had come to Veronica in search of healing affection. He wound his legs round her warm body in the hopes that the contact would unwind some of the crossed strings pulling inside his head.

David went up to bed, leaving Mary and Lucy watching television. They sat on the sofa, arms and legs touching comfortably.

When Mary came to bed, David looked up from his book, 'You and Lucy seem to be getting on well.'

Mary considered her husband's pale face, carefully blanked of emotion. 'She asked me about Elizabeth. How it happened. So I told her.'

'What? Told her what?'

'About Richard.'

'I see.' David shut his book and rolled over to switch off his bedside light.'

'I didn't tell her about now.'

'Oh, good.' The light snapped off.

Mary paused for a moment and then turned to go to the bathroom. Could she really love this cold, unforgiving man? Did she want to love him?

Mary telephoned Richard Beck's office. The secretary said, 'I'm afraid Mr Beck is away all this week. But we expect he'll be back on Monday.'

'He's not ill, I hope?'

'Oh, no.'

'On holiday then. Lucky him!'

The secretary made an assenting kind of noise followed by a not quite rude replacement of the receiver. Mary sat looking at it for a while. She felt rebuffed and frustrated. She had telephoned in a spirit of doubt, half hoping that he would not be there but now that he was unavailable for a week she felt a desperate longing. Childish. It was a ridiculously childish emotion. I want that sweet! She tried to smile at herself and return to work.

There was no need for the secretary to have been quite so unfriendly.

It was St Valentine's Day. Mary studied, as she did every year, the columns of loving messages printed in *The Times*. She disapproved of the increasing tendency towards ribald humour. Particularly irritated by 'Piggy Pinky longs to crackle with Roasting Porker', she turned back to the main part of the paper and found herself reading a small item in Home News.

John Douglas Dunn, 19, unemployed and of no fixed address, has been charged with the murder of Nicholas Beck. Beck, who was 17, surprised him in the act of burgling his parents' house at Beckingham, Kent, on February 6th and received a blow to his head. He never recovered consciousness and died two days later.

Richard opened another letter of condolence. Sometimes they helped, sometimes they made things worse.

Dear Richard,
    I'm so dreadfully sorry about the death of your son. I would have written before but only saw the report in the newspapers today. This must be a terrible time for you and your wife. Please accept all my sympathy.
    With love from Mary (Tempest/Fellowes)

Cherry took the letter from his outstretched fingers. 'Who is she?'
'An old friend.'
'But she didn't know Nicky?'
'No.'
Cherry took the letter to all the others. The growing pile seemed to give her some kind of comfort, almost as if they were a part of her son still remaining.

David said to Mary, 'Is that your Richard Beck, whose son was murdered?'
'Yes.' Mary looked down at her food. They faced each other across the table for Lucy had gone back to Bristol that morning.
'What a dreadful thing.'
'Yes. There can be nothing worse.'
'To lose a child. It makes one shudder. Have you spoken to him?'
'No.' Mary paused, picked up her fork. What did David's calm, sympathetic interest mean? 'I wrote him a letter. Just a few lines of formal condolence. But I haven't heard anything.'
'You were right to send him a letter.'
Mary nodded, eyes still cast down. Was it possible that the name of Richard Beck could be spoken between them without guilt and agony? Even though the circumstances were tragic, she couldn't repress a little lifting of the soul. As neither of them spoke but David didn't resume eating, she realised that he still had something to say.
'It struck me that your daughter Elizabeth is half-sister to this boy. This murdered boy.'
Mary looked up. She didn't understand. Why should he suddenly call Elizabeth her daughter? He had never admitted it before. Was he making some judicial comparison between her loss of Elizabeth and Richard's loss of Nicky? But she hadn't lost Elizabeth, she had given her away.

The sky was not quite dark when Mary arrived home from work. She thought that soon she could look forward to spring and that something more would have happened by then so that the odd sensation she had at the moment of living without reality would alter. She and David never touched each other; perhaps it was that that gave her a feeling of being bodiless. Sometimes she clasped her own shoulder, just to be in contact with the comforting warmth of human flesh. She was surprised how resilient its surface was, how fine and springy, so unlike the ragged confusion she felt within her. Richard still had not answered her letter.

David, who was waiting to go into court with his case, saw Veronica once a week, or sometimes more. She was a gentle woman, intelligent and sympathetic. She asked no questions, although it must have been obvious to her that David was in a state of confusion that hadn't been there before. David hoped she didn't love him because he would not have been able to respond. When he left her flat he felt tired and a little more peaceful.

An arrow of sunlight pierced Mary's office window. It was a notable achievement since the walls of two neighbouring office blocks appeared to cross in front of her. Somewhere there must be a gap, Mary thought, tippling her fingers on her sun-bright desk.

The telephone rang, the vibrations apparently raising a dust-storm into the air or was it her arm, moving forward slowly to lift the receiver? Why was she so slow?

'Mary Tempest.'

'This is Richard Beck speaking.'

'Hello. Hello. How are you?'

'Thank you for your letter I . . . ' He stopped. His voice was thin, frail, suffering.

'Such a terrible thing. The worst thing.'

'Yes. Look, the reason I'm ringing . . . ' His voice gained strength and then faded away again.

'Is there anything I can do to help? Anything?'

'Yes. You see . . . I wanted to ask . . . '

Why was it so hard for him to speak? In agony for his agony – conscious that she had not lost a child – Mary nevertheless could not quite suppress a miserably self-centred sense of rejection.

Rejected by husband and lover, where would she turn now? 'If I can help you at all?' She tried to put impersonal warmth into her voice.

On the other end of the telephone, Richard pulled himself up in his chair. He had not imagined it would be so hard to ask her but then he had been unable to think of anything but his son – until this idea had come to him.

'Could you get out now? Just for a moment.'

'Of course.'

The sun was bright in the street. Hard and sharp and cold. Mary walked briskly towards their rendezvous. A street or two away, she began to imagine Richard's state of mind and was ashamed of her energy. It was inappropriate to look forward to seeing him.

Dingle's was completely empty, a disconcerting contrast to its usual ebullient overflowing. Mary took off her coat and hung it on a peg by the door. Richard sat in the far corner drinking a coffee. He had not taken off his coat but Mary saw at once they were not going anywhere. She kissed him, held his hands and felt tears in her eyes. Despite everything, she could share his suffering in an unselfish way.

He began talking before she sat down.

'Cherry and I are going to America for a couple of weeks.'

'Yes.'

'It seemed a good idea, to get away. Neither of us feel able to do very much – work, I mean – so it seems sensible to have a break. Avoid the committal proceedings. Later there will be the trial.'

'How terrible for you.'

'I was ringing to ask you for our daughter's address.'

Mary began to shake, as if someone had turned a switch on her body. Sweat started on her palms and forehead and at the base of her spine.

'I thought I might go and see her since I'm over there. I have a feeling you told me she lived in New York?'

'Yes,' whispered Mary.

'What?'

'Yes. I'll look for her address.' Mary stood up and went to her coat. She felt in its pockets as if to look for her address book. So Richard, in his pain, didn't want to see her but he wanted to see Elizabeth. Elizabeth, that ignorant trouble-maker. If only she had never risen from the past. Should she tell Richard what a hateful child she was?

Mary came back to Richard. 'So your wife knows of her existence?'

'Yes. She was before her time, of course. We were before her time.'

And after, Mary added to herself. Had he forgotten? Why did she have nothing but unworthy thoughts? If only he would let her console him. She could console him, love him.

'Nicky's death made me look at things in a different way,' said Richard. 'Perhaps you can understand?'

'Yes,' said Mary. She had stopped shaking and the sweat had turned cold. She must continue to behave calmly and well. She must tell him nothing of her own problems. His son had died. Died. It was not the time now and probably never would be. 'I'll telephone your secretary with the number.'

'Thank you for everything. Do you want me to give her, Elizabeth, a message?'

'No. I don't think so.'

He stood up. 'Goodbye, Mary.'

No endearment. Nothing. 'Goodbye, Richard. Good Luck.'

'Yes.'

After he'd gone, Mary sat on by herself until the youthful crowds engulfed her and made her feel unbearably alone. Then she wandered back to her desk – where the dust was still dancing.

Richard was not impressed by the block on which he found Elizabeth's apartment. It seemed to him urban in a threatening, inhuman way. The buildings were immense, grey, almost identical. They lay back from the street which was almost as wide as a highway and along which cars went at a terrific pace. He said to Cherry as they stood on the pavement, watching the yellow cab that had delivered them rejoin the stream of cars, 'I couldn't imagine living here.'

'No,' agreed Cherry who had a map in one hand. 'But there's a famous park somewhere very near.' She opened the map for she was a good hard-working tourist.

'She'll tell us. Elizabeth.' Richard took her arm and led her towards the entrance of the building.

'Perhaps we could walk there. It's a beautiful day, even if it is cold.'

'Perhaps we could.'

Once inside the hallway, Richard looked around and saw a doorman and carpeting and elegant light fittings and he revised his opinion of his daughter. She was doing well to afford to live in a

170

place like this, even if it was in Brooklyn. Knowing nothing about New York, Richard floundered for clues to his daughter's character. On the pavement, he had felt sorry for her. Now he saw she might be an independent adult, wary of him, perhaps, or even hostile. On the telephone she had sounded not as surprised as he would have expected and brisk as if she were in a hurry. She was in a hurry, of course, on her way to medical school, she'd said. But this was Saturday, day off and time for shopping. Bob would be there but she'd send him out so they could talk.

Richard and Cherry took the elevator to the eighth floor. When the doors opened, Elizabeth faced them, a young woman in sweater and trousers, face pale and tired-looking, eyes blue. No smiles.

'I'm so glad to meet you!' Cherry took a step forward. It was generous of her to fill the gap. Even now, people were her strength, she liked people, whoever they were, she was always interested to find out what was the most important thing about them. When Richard had just met her, it was she who had made the running, telling him what was wrong about the world and her plans to make it better. She was strong, stronger than he, but now she cried in his arms.

'And I'm glad to welcome you, Mrs Beck.' She looked at Richard, her expression both curious and surprised. He was old, so much older than Mary and yet his wife, too, was young.

They walked into the apartment which had a kind of ordered cleanliness unrevealed by the hard sunlight. As promised, Bob was not around but Elizabeth gave them cups of good strong filter coffee, saying, 'Bob made it; he's better at that sort of thing than me.'

Then they were all sitting down silently. Even Cherry seemed unwilling to speak, thinking perhaps that now that father and daughter were together, they should be allowed to make contact.

Elizabeth, looking down, saw that her nails were chipped and ugly and that her hands were shaking. This meeting with her father and his wife was the sort of confrontation that she believed was necessary to mature development. She had sought for it in her journey to England and Mary. Now she was on the other end, not the seeker, but the sought. She felt frightened, her burrow menaced by strangers. Lucy had thrown her out of her mother's house. Forcing herself to leave her finger's alone, she looked up.

Both Richard and Cherry were staring at her but, instead of lively interest which was what she expected and half dreaded, she saw a similar kind of blankness, as if they only partly saw her.

Richard put down his coffee and leant forward. 'I should explain. Cherry and I . . . ' He paused and looked at his wife. 'Our youngest son died recently. He was only seventeen. We . . . ' Again he paused, this time without restarting.

At the words 'our youngest son died recently', Elizabeth, who was already tense, knew she would not be able to control her emotions. In a way she didn't even want to. Shuddering and heaving, she began to cry, tears instantly falling in streams down her face. There was nothing shaming in this feeling of sympathy at such a dreadful, dreadful thing.

Cherry put her arm round Elizabeth. 'Don't. Please.'

'I'm sorry. It's the shock.'

Richard put his head in his hands and tried not to lose control. Once he started crying, why should he ever stop? When he comforted Cherry she managed to stop herself but she was young, not old as he was, who had no future now. What a waste! What a waste! A waste for him too. He had loved his son but hardly known him. The images that played over in his mind, other than that last terrible scene, were of Nicky as a small boy.

Elizabeth, in Cherry's arms, raised her head now. 'I'll wash my face.'

'Yes, you do that.'

Cherry walked over to Richard and put her arm round him. How much they all touched each other now, seeking consolation and reassurance of their physical existence. Survivors. Making up for all the times he had not hugged Nicky.

'I'm glad we came.'

'Yes. I won't tell her more. About . . . what happened.'

'No.'

Elizabeth returned. Her face was very pale with red rings round the eyes but she had put on lipstick and was trying to smile. 'I'm so glad you came to see me. I'm so grateful.'

'That's very generous of you.' Richard managed a kind of smile. 'It's good to see you doing so well.'

'Yes. I've always wanted to be a doctor. It's very hard work but I like that. I like to be busy and to be clear about things.'

'I would like to help. That's why I came. To say that.'

'I see. But . . . '

'I know you have parents. But if you need money. Money or anything else.'

'Bob and I will be getting married soon.'

'Is Bob doing well then?'

'Very well.' Elizabeth's face began to lose the distortions of strain. 'He's financing me at the moment but I shall pay him back of course.'

'Does he live here?'

'Oh, yes. He'll be back here in a moment.' She paused, suddenly distraught again. 'I won't tell him . . . not now.'

'No,' said Cherry quickly. 'We won't.' She stood up and went to the window where the sun still pounded in light. 'There's a park nearby, isn't there?'

Richard, Cherry, Elizabeth and Bob walked through Brooklyn Park. There were still leaves from the previous winter, lying as crisp as ice on the ground. It was a large park, ragged and unfathomable.

Elizabeth talked to Cherry about the Botanical Gardens the other side of the road where, on warm evenings, she sat between lines of hedges and studied her notes. She did not mention Lucy or Mary. Cherry told her about Kew Gardens in London and said she must visit England again. Perhaps she would stay with them in the country. Elizabeth, eyes bright again, said she sometimes wished she didn't work so hard but Cherry said work was the second most important thing in the world.

Bob told Richard about his ambitions. He was deferential, frequently calling him 'Sir' and waiting until his sentences were properly finished before beginning his own. Richard told him how glad he was that Elizabeth had found such a good husband and that he hoped they would let him know the date of the wedding. Bob seemed surprised at this for Richard's tone was emotional, filled with unexplained appeal. It was embarrassing, making him turn away to point out a distant boat-house across a smooth lake. Richard looked, noting the classic symmetry of the white building which was fronted with pillars and a long row of steps, but it was a superficial impression, as was everything since his son's murder. He took Bob's arm. 'I'll come over for the wedding,' he said trying to see the expression in Bob's eyes, which was difficult for he was nearly a head shorter. 'If you would let me, that is.'

Mary received a letter in her office. Recognising Richard's writing, she did not open it immediately. She was working with her assistant that morning, a prying kind of girl, whose efficient energy extended to accurately assessing her colleagues' state of mind.

173

Eventually, unable to wait longer, Mary took the letter to the sterility of the Broadcasting House Ladies. She felt resilient enough to smile at the idea of a forty-year-old woman sitting on the lavatory reading a letter from her lover.

Dear Mary,

I saw Elizabeth in New York. And Bob. We went to their flat which was very pleasant and well organised. They were both friendly but as I told her about Nicky's death right at the beginning, she was unlikely to be anything else, I suppose. In fact she was so upset that I felt guilty afterwards, although not at the time as I very much wanted her to know. I wanted her to understand the reason I suddenly needed to see her and I think she did. If I'm not being very clear, please forgive me. I still find it difficult to organise my thoughts clearly. All the time, they return to Nicky and how he was when I found him. I'm sure you of all people will understand.

I am writing to you now for several reasons. I want you to know that Elizabeth is well and that I have seen her and that I shall continue to see her. I've never looked back much in my life. There never seemed any real point, no way of changing the past. But it struck me the other day, and please don't take this as a reproach, that you never gave me a chance with our daughter. Why was that? I remembered coming to see you in the waiting-room on Oxford Station. You would never let me come to your home. You would never let me into your real life. And I asked you to marry me. You were already pregnant, I think. I remember leaving on the train again but I can't remember your answer. You must have said 'no', of course, but I can't actually remember you saying it. And then it was the end. You went into hospital. I rang your home but your parents said you didn't want to talk to me. I rang the hospital, I sent flowers, I even came to visit you and the baby but they said again you didn't want to see me. I thought I couldn't force myself on you at such a time and, after all, I was a married man, 'the wicked seducer' who'd caused all your trouble. But I thought we still loved each other. Then I had that letter from your father. It was a terrible letter, filled with hatred. He said the baby was being adopted and that you never wished to see me again and that he trusted I would have the decency to leave you alone so that you could start a new life. I wouldn't have believed it except that you never got in touch. So I had no choice but to do what he said.

Why am I telling you all this now? Because of Nicky. Because of Elizabeth. Because we mustn't see each other again. Because I'm old. Because I used to love you and because of Cherry, my wife.

When I started writing, I didn't plan to be so honest but now it's there on the paper, I won't retract anything.

Before I met Elizabeth, I had expected her to remind me of you when you were young and so lovely. But she didn't. Or at least only physically a very little. Cherry said the same. She saw hardly anything of me in her. She was herself. And yet I am her father and for that I shall try and help her in her life and love her.

With all good wishes, Richard.

CHAPTER SIXTEEN

Helen rang Mary at the office. Hearing her high-pitched voice, Mary thought, not that silly irrelevant woman, before she remembered she had committed adultery with her husband which presumably meant she wasn't entirely irrelevant. 'Yes, I'll have lunch with you,' she agreed with a reluctant sigh. What was there to say, after all?

Veronica's character had never been very important to David but he did trust her. Except that he didn't wish to be disloyal to Mary, he would have used her as a confidante. In some ways he did, just by making love to her, by holding her body and stroking her flesh and putting himself into her. It was an unwelcome shock, therefore, when she turned her naked back on him one day and said in a muffled unhappy voice, 'I don't think I'll go on seeing you. Not like this anyway. Not so much.'

How could he argue? What could he say? If he tried to persuade her he might learn all sorts of terrifying things, he might discover that she no longer loved her husband and was looking for an excuse to leave him. She might cry miserably or rage against him. Yet he had never been able to offer her anything; theirs was a sterile relationship. Now he could only kiss her shoulder kindly and tell her she must do what she wanted.

'You're free,' he said, 'I have no rights over you. But I'll miss you very much.'

Helen wore so much make-up and was dressed in such a welter of colour and jewelry that Mary hardly recognised her. Her hair too was streaked with a kind of pale aubergine where before it had been all copper. 'I've left him!' she cried, the moment they were seated at a table.

As Mary gasped for appropriate reaction, she laughed and continued, 'Well, actually, he's left me, of course, for Jeddah. But I'm not going with him. Never again. I can't think how I stuck it so long, him so long!'

'Do you want a drink?' suggested Mary, in need of one herself. It seemed Helen had come to show off her new independent radiance. Her eyes whirled in their black-surrounded sockets as she surveyed the restaurant. She would have liked to announce her availability to every man in the place.

'You are brave,' said Mary, weakly, managing not to add, 'and what about the children?'

'Yes. All that in Somerset was the last straw. Do you know why I wanted to have lunch with you?'

'Perhaps you could catch the waiter's eye?'

'I wanted to apologise.'

'Apologise?' What a nightmare this would be if she could raise herself to the appropriate level of emotional response. But ever since Richard's letter, she had felt exhausted. All that in Somerset seemed very far away.

'Yes. I behaved despicably. But I thought you should know that I was on the edge of a breakdown. I mean you can only be married to a boy scout for so long. I'd packed everything – you can imagine what it was like with Ian's broken arm, he stood over me barking commands, – we were all set to go before I had this sudden revelation, I didn't have to go. Nobody could force me to go. Even from the children's point of view, I'm better here. I'll be able to see them more. I was just being a good wife. Except I wasn't being a good wife. I was going mad. It wasn't just that I'd stopped loving him but that I was beginning to hate him.'

'A bottle of your house white,' said Mary to the waiter, causing Helen to pause a moment. For the first time she looked at Mary.

'You don't look very well.'

'I'm fine.'

'How is everything? David? That's what I wanted to apologise for particularly. Of course I know it was totally unimportant.'

'Yes,' said Mary.

'I was hysterical, that's all.'

'Yes,' said Mary.

Again Helen looked at Mary closely. 'You sure there's nothing wrong? I mean you haven't gone and left David or anything?' Despite her anxious expression, she could hardly restrain a laugh. She had never felt so wonderful, not since before she married Ian, she decided, forgetting the delights of the early years when she had eagerly followed his haversack up mountains and across deserts. But Mary looked so worn, so plain, so old.

Mary smiled back. She knew the proselytising fervour of the newly fled from others of her friends. It didn't last. 'No. I haven't left David and I don't intend to.'

Helen's spirits were only dampened for a second. 'Now I'm trying to get somewhere to live in London and then I must find a job. I can't tell you what it feels like. As if I had escaped from prison.'

'And what about Ian?'

'Ian?' Helen's voice echoed his name as if he were the last person to be considered.

'Ian. Oh, Ian. Well, he's just Ian isn't he. He'll work away sorting out HMG's affairs in the OPEC nations. Nothing I could do would affect Ian.'

'I see.' Mary raised her glass, 'Here's to your new life, then. May it bring you happiness ever after.'

'Thanks.' Helen picked up her glass. 'And, I'm so glad everything's fine with you.'

'I had lunch with Helen today.' Mary handed David a plate of Toulouse sausages and mashed potatoes.

'Why did you do that?'

'She asked me.'

'Why did she do that?' Between each question David bit off a lump of sausage, decorated it with a square of mash and put it all carefully into his mouth.

'Because she wanted to apologise.' Mary wondered if she could learn to hate David as Helen said she had Ian.

'I should hope so too. She behaved despicably.' David entertained briefly an image of Helen writhing tearfully on the carpet. The earlier writhing, in which he took part, happily did not present itself.

'She used the very same words.' Mary pushed her plate away: '"Despicable".' She could not eat, even though she could feel herself becoming withered and dessicated like an old leaf. She poured herself a glass of wine. Her body was useless, ageing, unattractive, an unwanted amalgam of flesh and bone and skin. She felt as David had described her that day he discovered about Richard. 'She's left Ian.'

'What! Really.' David looked shocked. 'Why should she do anything so ridiculous.'

'She says she doesn't love him.'

'Love!' David also pushed his plate away.

'She says she hates him. He is pretty awful.' Mary's voice was impartial. 'So stupid and bossy.'

'Now you're being ridiculous. You don't leave your husband because he's bossy. They've got two young children.'

'Not so young. They're at boarding school. She says she'll see more of them if she doesn't go to Jeddah.'

'She's just bored and self-centred, that's all there is to it.' David rose to his feet and crashed their two plates together irritably.

'Don't get cross with me. I'm just telling you what she said. I agree with you. I've seen other friends like her. The euphoria doesn't last.'

'Then why do they do it?' David slammed the cheese onto the table.

'I suppose they find the situation insupportable. Any change seems for the better.' Mary considered putting her elbows on the table and holding up her face. 'Actually, they usually fall in love.'

'Love!' Again David screeched furiously. 'All it is, is an excuse for juvenile fantasising leading to irresponsibility, cruelty and betrayal. Talk to me of courage, honesty, loyalty, duty, self-sacrifice . . . '

'Oh, David,' Mary interrupted him wearily. 'Don't go on. Please. You loved me once. I think. Then you knew what it meant. Don't go on. Please.'

'What? What do you mean?' Self-righteous anger halted in mid-flow, David floundered. For a moment he saw Mary's pinched unhappy face but it was impossible he should listen to what she was trying to say, not now over a stale lump of cheddar cheese. Perhaps later. Perhaps when they were in bed. 'I've got some work to do.'

'Yes. I'll clear up.'

At last the big fraud case which David had been working on for so many weeks was coming to court. It was a difficult case, involving eleven other lawyers and so many boxes of papers that a man was especially designated to heave them about the place and all the mornings thereafter.

The first morning David walked through the doors of the Old Bailey he felt exhilaration caused by nervous anticipation of a great challenge. Everything else in his life fell away from him so that if someone had asked him what he had eaten for breakfast or questioned him about his wife, or daughter, his bank balance or his car, he would have looked at them blankly. He was pure and concentrated, immune from everything outside his clients, Meyrell, Meyrell, Roebuck and Stevens v. the Crown.

Mary's assistant had just announced she was going to have a baby. She accepted Mary's congratulations with untypical reserve, saying that she had planned to wait another few years until her career was better established.

'And is your husband pleased?' asked Mary hopefully.

'Actually he's not my husband but he is pleased.' Her face lost a little of its temperate blandness. 'On the other hand, he's not the one who has the baby.'

'That's true,' agreed Mary, trying not to let her continuous lassitude sink to the level of the girl's. Yet it was strange, this lack of enthusiasm for her own affairs when she showed so much energy in prying out others. 'I'm sure you'll be thrilled when you get used to the idea.' She pulled over the proof of the report they had been working on. 'And now, have you checked this over yet?'

'Yes,' said her assistant, chewing her finger. 'It's a disaster. Two or three times every page the letter "n" has been printed onto the end of the word.'

'I see.' Mary hoped her voice sounded brisk and efficient rather than filled with the repressed fury she actually felt. 'We'll send it back to the printer with a flea in his ear.' She paused and surveyed the girl's vacuous face. Why should she have a lover and be on the way to having a baby? 'However, if you don't mind a bit of advice,' she could hear her voice, clipped and irritable like an old spinster's, 'don't use the word "disastrous" without a proper appreciation of its meaning. Printing errors can never be disastrous. Never, never, never!'

'If you say so,' replied her assistant, looking much less surprised than was natural. 'I just thought you'd be upset when you'd put so much work into it.'

'I am upset. But it is not disastrous!' What was she saying? Was she going mad?

'Yes. I see that. I'm sorry.'

Why was the girl placating her? Did she look as emotional as she felt? And why did she feel emotional? Because Richard had pointed out that it was she who, twenty-two years ago, had ended their affair? 'What?'

'I said, shall I get it back to the printers now?'

'No. No. I'd better check it through for other errors first. I'll tell you what, you wouldn't be an angel and find me a coffee?'

'Sure.'

Alone at last, Mary immediately pushed away the report. What did she care about local listening habits? Or a plethora of 'n's? What she wanted was a brilliant, in-depth, investigative report on herself, Mary Tempest, rising forty years old, married, with two daughters, a BBC bureaucrat, mourning the loss of her ex-lover. How trivial! How vulgar! How pathetic! No wonder Shakespeare wrote of royal kings and queens. No wonder Tolstoy gave up examining Anna Karenina for examining his conscience. No wonder men despise women. When you came down to it, women were only good for producing children, that was the one act they could perform without being subservient to a man and, even then, his shadow hung over them.

Twenty-two years ago I had the child of a man I thought I loved and I gave the child away and dismissed the man. What does that make me? Why did I do it? All for love. There was a clue there somewhere. I wanted to hang onto the love, preserve it in the desperate way I understood it. I didn't want it to change into something more ordinary. I kept it locked up. I locked part of myself up in it too. When I married David I didn't want to love him in that way. I wouldn't let that happen. What does that make me?

'Your coffee.' Mary's assistant, the reluctant mother, stood over her, cardboard cup quivering.

Mary hoped she had not been knocking her head on the desk or any other lunatic manifestations of her inner condition. 'Thank you so much,' she said with calm dignity, adding to make the performance more convincing, 'you take another copy and mark it up.'

'I have already.'

'Ah, well then.'

She forced herself to smile at the girl and, doing so, saw that her face was tinged with a fearful green. 'You'll be glad about the

181

baby soon,' she said. 'I'll help you sort out the proper maternity leave.'

David and Mary lay in bed. David wanted to sleep because he wanted to be fresh for the morning's work but the day had gone so well, he felt so pleased with himself, so ebullient, that he couldn't make himself sink into sleep.

Mary lay beside him, already half asleep, although it was more like a coma of confusion and despair. Her brain never seemed to become entirely still anymore. She could feel it now, gently seething like a sea which has only temporarily descended from crashing heights.

David turned to Mary and touched her shoulder and her neck. He knew, of course, that they were not on touching terms at the moment, but his self-satisfaction made the barriers seem unimportant, or, at least, surmountable. He wanted to touch her body, he liked touching her body, she was his wife and he loved her.

Mary felt David's hand as if through a thick curtain of impossibility. Why would he want to touch her? And yet she liked the feel of his gently caressing fingers. She always had. And she too began to forget why they shouldn't stroke each other and find warmth and comfort in making love. It was such a relief, not to have to speak or analyse or explain or listen or understand.

Silently, they turned to each other and silently clasped.

The sky was blue, a clear brilliant colour that startled Mary into happiness. This was the first time she had ever visited Lucy at Bristol. It was partly an excuse to leave London, the office and David but she wanted to see Lucy too. Only now, under the great dome of blue, she saw that her restless departure was in tune with nature for spring was coming, the air filled with half-forgotten scents, the sun giving warmth as well as light. She walked to the highest part of the city where the Clifton Suspension Bridge cut the sky in half like a rainbow. She saw the crinkled water far below, its depths still in the dark grip of winter but the ridges making tinsel reflections of the sun.

Her report was done, David was totally involved with his case, which would last at least another two months, she would stay where she was for a few days, and she would not feel a need to force herself frequently on Lucy. If she needed company, she would call in on the BBC radio headquarters in Bristol. Her colleagues would look after her and tell her what to see and do. This feeling of freedom in a strange city reminded her of her first year at Sussex University. Although most of the buildings were built new, on carpets of green outside the town, her memories were of solitary walks through the streets, along the sea-front, lying on the pebbly beach after night had fallen and all other visitors departed.

She supposed she had been still unbalanced, even over a year after the baby had been born and taken away. Certainly her parents had thought so, visiting her often and each time spending an hour with her moral tutor. Perhaps they thought her silence and unsociability meant that she was suicidal. But she felt more as if she had died already and was trying to start living again. She had joined the School of English and American Studies against the advice of her parents who felt she should be in the School of Social Studies, studying economics or sociology or politics or even statistics, subjects to give her backbone.

But her parents' analysis was not accurate for what she needed was not a corrective to her feelings but an increase in her sense of self. Her love for Richard and its sudden ending had decreased her self-regard to a very low level. She was not wallowing in self-pity as her parents suspected but living in a kind of vacuum, a negation of self. When she read Keats, Donne, or Thomas Hardy she was looking to re-create herself.

After a year at college, she was seldom alone. Rather than returning home for the vacations, she went on university skiing trips, university lecturing tours, stayed with friends, the further away the better. Her father had never confessed that he had written warning off Richard but perhaps she guessed. Why else had she stayed away from home so much?

David appeared in her third year. He had already been working in London for several years but his mother, who was a widow, lived in a small house near the university campus. They met at a concert of Early Renaissance music which Mary had helped organise. Afterwards she went back with David and his mother for coffee. Their house was a modern bungalow dominated by coniferous scrubs and a group of large pampas grasses. Mrs Tempest had been widowed for ten years and watching David with her was more like watching a husband with his wife than a son with his mother. He was courteous, helpful and loving. He touched her often, putting his arm round her shoulders and sometimes holding her hand.

When Mary realised he was falling in love with her, it was this comforting, physical presence she coveted most. Up till then, the touch of a man had either come from Richard where passion was intense and filled with anguish or, since then, with men her age who approached her, as she approached them, with a guarded pleasure in sensation. But with David, she sensed the possibility of a third alternative. He loved her and when they lay together, his warm heavy body flattening hers, she felt she loved him.

She left Sussex before she finished her degree. She could read *Ode to Immortality* more easily while wandering round the Kensal Rise Cemetary, which she did while she waited for David to ask her to marry him.

Elizabeth studied the sheet of folded card. It was her wedding announcement, cream-coloured with serrated edges, the lettering in silver, festive but not flamboyant. She and Bob were working people, at the start of their careers. She opened the card meditatively and then shut it again. It was equally appropriate as an announcement as an invitation. Taking up her pen, she wrote 'Mr & Mrs Richard Beck' along the top. Then, picking up another card, she wrote 'Mr & Mrs David Tempest' and, after a moment's thought, using her best loops and frills, added 'Ms Lucy Tempest'.

Mary and Lucy sat in Lucy's room. Lucy was flattered by her mother's visit. It seemed to her that she had changed since their talk about Elizabeth, become more approachable. It made her want to confide in her in a way she hadn't since she was a young girl. But as it happened she had nothing very pressing to confide. Jo did not seem so overwhelming against a backdrop of other students. Besides, she had suddenly noticed that, for all his avowed disaffection from society, he had begun working with just the same ambitious industry as those who believed in such things as 'career structures'. It was ages since she'd seen his cricketing bag and, most telling of all, he had almost entirely given up insulting her. There was the question of jealousy, of course, but she seemed to be suffering less from that than before. Perhaps she was falling out of love with him. The very idea gave her a terrifying sense of vertigo. That would be worse than him falling out of love with her.

'We'll have a plate of pasta and then go to the City Art Gallery,' she said, surprising even herself with an air of decisiveness.

'What about your work?' Mary's initial look of obedience was only slightly tempered with maternal solicitude.

'Oh, I'm well up to date. You should read *Pearl*; it's a wonderful story of loss and regeneration.'

Faced with a second evening on his own, David gave up his searches among the freezer, and went to fetch fish and chips. The queue stretched along the pavement and inspired a feeling of grievance against Mary until, exquisite lemon sole securely boxed, he admitted to himself that the prospect of solitude filled him with satisfaction, allowing his thoughts to flow more freely, his arguments to be better sustained, his memory unalloyed. He had excelled today, dazzling the court with his command and concentration.

Returning to the kitchen, which since the morning had been washed and tidied by the cleaning woman, David allowed himself the luxury of an unacceptable question. Why had he got married? Shocked by such disloyal daring, he immediately supplied answers. Mary and Lucy. But there his mind, stoked by golden chips and slithers of the whitest fish in the crispest batter, rebelled again. Lucy might be his to call reason enough, but when had Mary ever been?

He should have known that first evening when he'd watched her listening to the concert. He hadn't liked the music, going only to please his mother which is why he had stared so hard at the girl in the front row. Although she was pale-faced with lank hair, a gym slip and long boots, just like all the other girl students, there had been something that caught his attention. He could only see her profile when she turned her head but it inspired words like 'vulnerable', 'solitary', images of Pre-Raphaelite heroines with pub-girl sexiness romanticised by medieval legend. What foolishness!

David took another large mouthful of fish with the self-congratulatory glow of a man who knew that being able to buy well was just as important as being able to cook well. For 'vulnerable' and 'solitary', he should have substituted 'secret'. Alias Richard Beck – a particularly irritating secret with his double-syllable Christian name caught short by the silly surname. But there he was, still was, Mary's verray parfit gentil knight. No doubt she'd been dreaming of Mr Beck when he'd watched her at the concert. She was partie prise, accepting him only as clever teddy bear to brighten her bank balance and warm her bed. Well, the truth was out now!

Picking up his knife and fork again, David noted reluctantly that even a fish as wonderful as this lemon sole would all too soon be reduced to a greyish tail and a bonfire of bones. The truth was something about which David spoke and thought a great deal. For months now he'd been trying to untangle the truth in the case of Meyrell, Meyrell, Roebuck and Stevens v. the Crown. Indeed, in his view, he had arrived at it and was now proceeding to convince others of his view. There was the rub. 'In his view.' David was too intelligent and/or sophisticated to believe in the law as identifier and regulator of truth any more than it found good or bad or even, when the chips were down – as they very nearly were – guilty or not guilty. Feeling he'd strayed from the case of Tempest v. Tempest, David gently lifted the very last piece of silken flesh. If Mary had always been otherwise engaged, as seemed likely, where did that leave their marriage, their twenty years in relative harmony? In more than relative harmony.

Wiping his mouth, David left the kitchen and went to find the transcripts of that day's trial.

'Everyone has longings . . . '

Mary was not clear if Lucy was echoing her statement or questioning. They were walking around the top floor of the Bristol Art Gallery. The building dated back to the late nineteenth century and was decorated with mosaic medallions expressing faith in the moral efficacy of art. Below them hung a collection of large Pre-Raphaelite pictures, mostly painted by Burne-Jones. The remark, 'Everyone has longings' was inspired by a swooning woman, wearing a purple robe and garlanded with flowers, who was faced by a slender figure dressed in silver armour.

'The helmet looks exactly like the cap worn by the anemone in my flower fairies book.' Lucy laughed.

Mary decided her 'everyone' had been a question. And yet she believed it. Or perhaps she should be more precise, she should say, 'Every woman has longings.' Or was that being unfair? Were longings part of old Adam's sin? Was her particular longing, in the battered and world-weary form of Richard Beck, a pathetic case of rattling the gates of Eden?

It hadn't felt like that. Far from feeling pathetic, she'd been filled with new life and energy. When she'd gone to Richard, she'd gone as a young woman, hopeful, happy, colourful, confident. It was only when she left him, the colour drained again.

Lucy walked on impatiently. She stopped for hardly a second to look, with quick curiosity, at the paintings, as if the varnish interested her more than anything else. Now she went to the edge of the balustrade for the building was constructed round a great courtyard, and peered down at the ground floor. Wooden partitions, decorated with snippets of geographical information, had been placed about the huge marble hall in an effort, presumably, to emulate the simplification of a modern school. They sat oddly with the Victorian medallions, dome and balustrade.

Mary joined her daughter and for a second they both leant over, side by side, eyes set for distance, like people gazing out to sea. Then Mary took her daughter's hand, clasped her own round it with firm conviction. Embarrassed, Lucy wriggled her fingers and tried not to look at her mother. It was not usual, this desire for closeness which was why she felt uncomfortable. But the clasp was steady as a clamp, unavoidable indeed, so she might as well make the best of it.

'Hand in hand in paradise,' Lucy said smiling into her mother's pale, weary face.

CHAPTER SEVENTEEN

David came home and said to Mary even before he took off his jacket, 'The Beck trial starts next week.' Since he turned immediately and went up to the bedroom, Mary had no need to answer but she found herself saying nevertheless, 'I didn't know.'

She followed him slowly upstairs. She had only just arrived back from work herself and felt the need to remove her shoes and collapse for a moment or two. Such was habit that even though she would have preferred to be on her own, she took herself into close proximity with David, competing first for wardrobe space and then for the bathroom. Eventually David, sitting on the bed and reaching for his slippers, said, 'The chap's admitted he killed the boy but he's pleading manslaughter.'

'How can he do that?' asked Mary, sitting on the other side of the bed.

'It's quite usual. He admits the intention of stealing but pleads diminished responsibility for the murder. In the end it'll be a battle between his psychiatrist and the prosecution's.'

'I see. You mean they want him to be convicted of murder?'

'They?' David looked at Mary for the first time. He thought she looked tired; the sunny spring evening gave shadows to her face rather than warmth.

Mary saw David's expression, and stood up. She wasn't ready for his sympathy. 'By they, I meant . . . ' She faltered. Of course she had meant Richard and his family but that was ridiculous. Why should they care if some underprivileged youth was convicted of manslaughter or murder? It wouldn't bring their son back.

'They,' continued David, also standing, 'are the prosecution. A friend of mine is the QC as it happens. A top chap who always gets his man. As a matter of fact, it's his last case before he becomes a

188

judge. It was he who told me about it.' David started for the door. 'Let's have a drink.'

'Yes,' agreed Mary gratefully. 'We could have it in the garden. It's so warm for April.'

The garden was small but pretty with wisteria, clematis and forsythia all about to bloom along the dark brick walls. David carried out two fold-up chairs with his usual deliberation. They were chairs which had come from his mother's house after her death. They had sat on them when he went to visit her during the summer. Mary had found them several times, he reading *The Economist*, Mrs Tempest cross-stitching a cushion. It had been a scene of great tranquillity.

'It's always exciting,' she said with a kind of unexplained nervousness, 'the first day of the year one can sit outside.'

'Yes,' agreed David. 'When my case finishes we must try and get away.'

'What?' began Mary, distinctly nervous now. They had 'got away' for a month to Somerset only three months ago and look at the disastrous results! How could he suggest such a thing without trembling and seeing bolts from heaven poised to descend. It was only by the intercession of St Stabilitas, the Patron Saint of Marriage, they were sitting like this, side by side.

'Not that our last attempt could be counted a triumphant success.' David smiled and reached a hand to Mary. Again he was surprised by her wan face. What was it that made her look so exhausted? Surely she could see he had forgiven her?

Mary drank her wine silently. A blackbird, hidden in the creeper above her head, whistled repetitively. 'They make such a noise,' she said.

'What?'

'Nothing.'

David thought over the nice things that his friend, the QC soon to be a judge, had said about him that morning. Of course he owed him goodwill since David had passed him the Beck case about which he'd originally been approached. If the Queen versus Meyrell, Meyrell, Roebuck and Stevens hadn't extended itself to three months, he wondered if he would have accepted the case. He supposed not since it would have involved interviews with this Richard Beck. It was an odd coincidence, though not so extraordinary as Mary might have presumed given the small circle of top barristers. He seldom took murder cases now, finding they needed a higher level of emotional involvement and a lower level of intelligence.

'I might have been the QC in the Beck trial,' he said to Mary.

'What?'

'The job came in to my clerk but of course I was otherwise engaged.'

'I see.' Mary leant back in her chair. The sun had gone now and the air was cool. As David had suspected, the coincidence struck her as far-fetched and even macabre. Without too careful an analysis, it made her feel implicated in the death of Richard's son. 'I'm glad you're not doing it,' she said.

For the second time Richard Beck telephoned Mary in her office. 'I'm sorry to bother you,' he began, as if they were strangers.

'Can I help?' Mary reminded herself that she was an adult, sitting at her executive desk with a secretary outside. Men found support in things like that.

'Probably not.' His voice was less frail than when they had met but despite his hesitation, there were no echoes of deeper feelings. Not towards her at least. 'The trial of my son's murderer starts next week.'

'I know.'

'Ah, I see.'

He seemed surprised so Mary explained.

'My husband. He's got a case in the Old Bailey at the moment.' She didn't tell him he might have fought his case. That was irrelevant.

'In that case you can guess what I'm going to ask you.'

Mary could not guess.

Richard, listening to her silence, looked again at the invitation in his hand. Why did it seem so important that one of them should go to Elizabeth's wedding?

'I'm sure you had an invitation to Elizabeth's wedding.'

Mary's secretary came into the room and placed a pile of newly typed letters in front of her. The top letter began 'Dear Mr. Langdon-Utterly'. Could that really be right?

'Yes, she did send me an invitation. But of course I shan't go.'

'What?'

'She behaved so dreadfully when she was over here, first trying to kill my husband and then horribly disturbing my daughter.' What a relief there was in putting these bitter accusations into words. 'Really, I think the girl's half deranged, coming over here like that, forcing herself on us. She shouldn't be encouraged. Definitely not.'

'But, Mary . . . '

At least he called her 'Mary', although her anger seemed to have stunned him for a second. Well, she wasn't going to take any of it back.

'But, Mary, I saw her. Cherry and I visited her in New York. You know, I got the address from you. She's a nice girl. Hardworking, sensitive. Straightforward. She just wanted to see her real mother . . .'

'I'm not her real mother!' Mary snapped off his defence furiously. 'I gave birth to her but that doesn't make me her real mother.' She felt near tears, hysterical. 'Mr Langdon-Utterly' danced in front of her eyes. 'Her real mother is the one who looked after her, brought her up, loved her! I can't help it if she's not altogether satisfactory. She's the one who should be at the wedding, not me.'

'She will be there but . . .'

'Then why do you want me to go? Can't you understand she's nothing to do with me!' Her anger would have liked to add 'just as you're nothing to do with me' but, the opposite was true. 'I hate her! Don't you see! I hate her! She was the one who separated us all those years ago and now she's doing it again! No! I know that's not true. We were never together this time! But just understand, I won't see her, I don't want anything to do with her. Don't ask me. Ask me about me, if you want anything. Not her!' Half realising she was talking nonsense, Mary still could not stop herself. 'She's not important. Not between you and me. Oh, Richard!' The word came out like a child's wail, concentrating all the reproaches she had never made more than twenty years ago.

Richard heard it all from a far distance. Everything, except the consolation he and Cherry had been able to give each other, had felt like that since Nicky's death. He looked at the wedding invitation again. The silver lettering and serrated edging seemed pathetically hopeful. 'I'm sorry,' he said.

He was sorry. Mary stared with hatred at Langdon-Utterly. She had behaved badly, worse than badly, to no effect. Was that why she had not screamed all those years ago, because she knew it would have no effect. She supposed now he would not even respect her. 'I'm sorry.' She could apologise but she still would not go to the wedding. What she wanted, she realised suddenly, was a final conversation with him, in which they could part with dignity. But between them, inexorable, stood the living and the dead, Elizabeth and Nicky. This inner pronouncement of the dead boy's name brought Mary back to her sense of the present reality. 'You must be longing for the trial to be over.'

'Yes. Of course. It will be terrible. Except that while it's on, he's not quite dead yet. I'm afraid the worst thing of all will be afterwards when I have to accept that he's gone absolutely. Pain is better than nothing.'

It was only after Richard had put down the telephone that Mary thought of how she wanted to respond to his final statement. Letting go is the hardest thing of all.

The unusually warm weather continued. London had a festive and careless air. People sat drinking on parapets. Even in the city the dark hues of acceptable suiting were leavened by emergent pink limbs and revealed shirt-sleeves. There was surprise on the streets, Mary thought as she walked from St Paul's underground station towards the Old Bailey, surprise in the faces of the passersby, that they should feel so free and easy this early in the year. Even she, bewildered as she was by her present action, felt a kind of cheerfulness, as she passed Ave Maria Lane and the Bastille restaurant, which could only be attributed to the weather.

Nevertheless her pace slowed as she neared the great theatre of justice. She had visited it before whenever David had been fighting a case he thought would interest her. When they first married she had come regularly, at first fascinated and then repelled by seeing other people's tragedies expounded in public. She had recognised this reaction as emotional, idiotic and irrelevant. Later the IRA bombing of the building, which had killed one innocent man and injured many more, darkened her image still further, making it a citadel both threatening and threatened. 'Domine Dirige Nos' was written under the coat of arms.

Yet she knew that David who understood the law so much better than she, saw it in a different light. To him the Old Bailey was no more threatening or threatened than Broadcasting House. Even she could see the marble and Biblical frescoes had much more in common with the Bristol Museum of Art. For him they were background not for drama but the pursuit of a career. It was an arena, in which he, gladiatorial with his gown and brief, could excel.

David, waiting to start the morning session, was chatting to his junior outside Court 13. Now into the third month of his case, he had a tranquil unrushed air. Around him other barristers, less fortunate in their length of stay, adjusted their wigs nervously or studied their notes. Some, like actors learning their lines, could be seen to be mouthing a speech of which they were not quite certain. The whole long hall had a backstage atmosphere, except that the variety of protagonists was so much greater, including lawyers, officers of the court, victims, witnesses, who were often policemen, and even, if they were on bail, the accused.

A tall barrister, gown flying, racing the piles of documents carried by his juniors behind him, came hurrying through the crowd. David moved in his path. The barrister stopped abruptly almost causing his attendants to cannon into him. 'First morning nerves,' said David, smiling. 'Surely not?'

'Don't you be so sure.' The barrister also smiled. 'My psychiatrist's got a stutter. Can you believe it. You'd think the DPP would save him for football violence.'

'Physician cure thyself. Well, good luck.'

'I haven't told you the worst.' The barrister leant closer and whispered, 'The accused has the face of a Botticelli angel and lives with his partially paralysed mother.'

'Phew!' David reeled back in mock alarm. 'No wonder you were running. I shall go back to my eight and a half million under the carpet with a feeling of there but for the grace of God . . . '

The two men parted, cheered by their meeting, conscious of the camaraderie of the lists.

'That was Duke, wasn't it?' asked David's junior just before the doors opened and they entered the court.

'Yes,' David still smiled.

'Doing the murder case in Court 1? Young boy, wasn't it. In cold blood?'

'There's no such thing as cold blood.'

Mary entered the outer door of the Old Bailey with a nervous determination. At least there were not many people around for she had purposefully chosen the moment soon after the morning session had started when most people had gone to their designated places. Downstairs there were only the police in blue shirts and a few harassed-looking visitors. She knew it would be different upstairs where relatives came as a support but either at the last minute, or, as a matter of policy, decided not to go into court. She had always found it odd how these opposing sides who should have been screaming at each other with rage managed to co-exist peaceably in a not very large area. It was a tribute, she supposed, to the civilising effect of British justice. Perhaps that's why she had come herself. David and Richard Beck were under the same roof. A wide and expanded roof, certainly, from Court 13 in the new wing to Court 1 in the original building was a street-length walk – but still the same roof.

Mary went up in a lift.

Elizabeth looked at the cream and blue silk dress. She laid it out on her bed and stroked the skirt into smooth waves. When her American parents had offered fifteen hundred dollars she had told Bob, 'Of course we could put it in savings.'

But he had seen through her careful expression and responded without hesitation, 'It's for your wedding.'

'For our wedding.'

'For your dress, your shoes, the party. Our friends will want to celebrate.'

Bob wanted her to be happy, that's what it was. He loved her. Elizabeth picked up the dress and held it along her body. It was the most beautiful dress she had ever seen.

She had felt a duty to add, for the record as it were, 'I guess the money is their apology for not coming in person.'

But neither of them dwelt on that. It was not important now for they were looking forward wholeheartedly to the future.

Turning her head to the window, Elizabeth saw the sky, postcard blue, and thought how glad she was both to be married at the start of summer and to have rented an air-conditioned hotel room. It was a propitious conjunction of the romantic and the practical in her nature.

Mary sat on a long leather bench outside Court 1. She realised as she sat looking at the doors that to go through them into the small room, where the tragedy of Richard's son's murder was being examined in all its ugly detail, would be a gross and unforgivable act. This certainty was, perhaps paradoxically, since that was her object in coming, a relief. For it was as if she had had to make the journey in order to discover the truth, now so obvious, that Nicky Beck's death had nothing whatever to do with her. Yet, even having decided this with no possibility of changing her mind, she continued to sit on the bench. Her body, tired and ageing as it was, seemed tied to this position where she was within the aura of the trial. She knew she ran the risk of Richard or his wife or their other son coming out and seeing her but as yet could do nothing more about it.

However, after about half an hour, she did shift her position, recrossing her legs on the other side and inclining her head so that she no longer directly faced the door.

Inside the court, the psychiatrist for the defence was giving evidence. He seemed in a hurry, clipping his words as he read his own report and answering queries from Duke, the prosecuting QC, with an irritable air. No one, his manner indicated, could possibly disagree with his findings which found this youth, this beautiful pale-faced youth who stood in the dock, mentally severely subnormal and psychologically unstable. According to the psychiatrist's findings the boy acted purely defensively, but out of the same kind of terror that makes a cornered rat jump at a man's throat.

Duke frowned and took a paper from his junior. 'Although the accused is presently unemployed that has not always been the case. The court might like to know that the accused, since leaving school four years ago, has held four jobs, one for a firm of packers lasting two years. Would Dr Cornell's rat be capable of that?'

'As I understand it the accused has been unemployed for the last two years and living in extremely close quarters with his aged and bedridden mother. This could produce dangerous pressures on an unstable personality.'

Duke's junior passed a note to his master. 'What he means is he would have preferred to murder his mother.' Duke nodded.

Again the judge interposed, 'Do I understand it is impossible for the mother to attend the court?'

'Quite impossible, I'm afraid, my lord,' replied Duke firmly. The last thing he needed was a pathetic old lady boasting of her son's self-sacrificing kindness.

'A pity.' The judge who was not particularly old and whose youngest son was almost exactly the age of the accused, sighed audibly. It is the nature of the law, he thought not for the first time, that you can make nothing better for the victim but only make things worse for the villain. For villain he was, despite his soft hair and his little pink mouth, and no amount of excuses by this clever psychiatrist would make him anything else. Which did not mean that he would necessarily be convicted of murder, for juries, unlike judges, allowed themselves to be swayed by the power of the living. The victim was only a photograph. A harrowing photograph, certainly, but still only a photograph.

The judge, conscious that he was not properly attending to the continuing dialogue between the doctor and counsel, nevertheless turned his attention to the victim's family. Father, mother and son. Remaining son. They made an island of suffering in the court, looking only towards the witness box and towards each other. The mother was touching her son's hand, as close to holding it as acceptable, and the father supported his wife's shoulder. His was the sort of face the judge knew well; it might have been one of his less clever friends. In fact it was extremely like his wife's brother's face. Not very interesting, perhaps, but probably capable of bearing such a tragedy. He would have to give evidence, poor chap. Well, children are one part pleasure and two parts pain, as he said to his wife that very morning while discussing their poor Amy's impending divorce.

Richard returned to his place after giving evidence. As he went through the facts which he could now repeat without full consciousness of their meaning, he had an uneasy sense of some question that had to be answered. This trial was held to discover whether the young man, so innocent-looking and, in his youthful blondness, not unlike Nicky, was guilty of murder. But to him that hardly seemed the point. Almost certainly he would be convicted of manslaughter – but the point was something else. It was to do with loss. It was to do with love. He had lost a son and only then discovered he had never had him to lose. He had not loved him properly, nor anyone else. All his life he had spread love about, prided himself on it as if it were a kind of generosity, like handing out boxes of chocolates. He had loved his first wife in that casual way and lost her, he had loved Mary in that way and lost her. He had taught the eighteen-year-old Mary to love him in that way and she had given away their daughter.

Richard looked up to the boy in the dock. Yes. Manslaughter. He would be glad if his son's murderer were allowed to contemplate some sort of future. There can be no proper justice in this world.

David had not spoken for an hour. It was always a bad sign when he began to imagine a glass of wine before midday. The problem was that he now had solved most of the problems in the case, at least to his own satisfaction, which felt rather like looking at *The Times* crossword puzzle with all the answers filled in.

Mary stood up abruptly so that her handbag which had been resting on her knee fell noisily onto the marble floor. She looked down but made no motion to pick it up. A policeman, emerging from a wall, gave it to her with a wink, 'You don't want to lose this – not with the sort of people you find round here.'

Mary looked at him, not understanding, but then, as he was about to leave, touched his arm, 'Do you know the time please?'

'Twelve thirty-five.'

'And they break at one?'

'Usually at one. Not later. But sometimes before.'

'Thank you.'

The policeman, on the point of leaving, paused as this woman who had seemed perfectly ordinary up till then – anyone could let their handbag fall – began to twist first one way and then the other, take a step in one direction, turn and take a step in another, stand still, poised, head high, and then lower her head and seem to sink as if she would sit down again. It was a strange sight, reminding the policeman of his small daughter's first attempts at a pirouette. A great many disturbed people passed through this hall, of course, but she hadn't struck him like that.

'Can I help you?'

'Help?'

'Direct you anywhere. It's such a big confusing place.'

The policeman was heavily bearded but the visible skin was smooth and youthful. His eyes, although small, were uncritical. 'Yes,' said Mary, 'I'm a visitor, you see. And I can't decide whether to go in here, to Court 1, or go along to Court 13.'

The policeman did not consider for long. 'It depends whether you like murders.'

'Oh, no!' cried Mary on a kind of reflex.

'Well, then, you can't possibly want to go in there. I don't know what's on in Court 13.' He looked at his watch. 'They'll both be out in a couple of minutes anyway. Why don't you have a spot of lunch instead?'

As he finished speaking there was a sudden noise and the doors behind them burst open, pouring out clerks of the court, ushers and jury first, followed soon after by journalists and visitors.

Propelled by panic, Mary started ahead of the crowd. It would be too dreadful if Richard saw her here like some horrible ghoul, some guillotine-obsessed tricoteuse. Trying not to run, because if she ran she would slip and then she would fall and the crowd would swallow her and maybe disgorge her at his feet, she walked extremely fast towards the stairs. He would take his family in the lifts.

She had reached the top of the stairs, at a point where Court 1's contents were diluted by emergants from the other courts, when she felt a hand clutch her shoulder.

'Darling! I didn't know you were coming!' David looked at his wife with great pleasure. He couldn't imagine a nicer surprise. It was so long since she had last heard him speak in court.

Mary felt tears in her eyes. In the end she had not been able to choose. Once again she had been chosen.

Mary looked at David's face which was filled with happiness and love, occasioned entirely by her presence. She wanted to say something equal to his expression but could think of no words. Instead she leant forward to kiss him but as she did so a face appeared over his shoulder. It was some distance away but directly behind David so that the effect was as if the two heads were superimposed. One nearly on top of the other, something like two photographs on the same frame. Mary, in leaning forward to kiss her husband, found herself apparently in close proximity to the cheek of another man.

Her lips, too close for David to see, mouthed 'Richard' and they pursed as if to kiss, but the flesh they met belonged, of course, to the man whose whole body curved round her now. And the head behind her, in another shift of focus, had become merely the top of a far-away figure, standing, indeed not alone, but in a group of other figures, including a woman with light fluffy hair, a girl, a boy and two barristers. One of these gowned barristers, Mary noticed, all in the split second it took to deliver her kiss, swung his wig round and round his finger as if it were a toy.

'Let's go now!' Mary took her husband's arm in a forceful gesture. Which surprised him less than normal because it was in tune with his own feelings.

'Of course, we'll go. I hear there's a tremendous day outside.'

Richard squeezed Cherry's hand. His other hand was held tightly by Nicky's girlfriend. The girl, who he had never liked and who had come between him and his son, now clung on grimly. He supported them both with his height and masculinity, although his body felt like glass. When he saw over their heads a woman in Mary's shape, his eyes sent no message of recognition to his brain.

The guest list with its neat ticks and crosses lay near enough on Elizabeth's bedside table so that she could touch it while still lying down. It was hard to believe that all these people were to come to her wedding. It was like a happy ending, like a fairy-tale. Some of them, certainly, were people she had little time for in real life but tomorrow they would be transformed into perfect guests just as she, with the help of her silk cream and blue dress, would be transformed into the perfect bride. It struck her that one of the reasons she hadn't wanted to be married in white was it reminded her of hospital. Elizabeth brought her arm back into the bed and wound it round herself.

'Go to sleep,' mumbled Bob at her side.

'Go to sleep yourself,' Elizabeth prodded him affectionately. She had considered staying with a friend this last unmarried night but she would have been too nervous without Bob. In her mind she had compromised on a good-friends-but-nothing-more-night which had worked out fine since he had shown no desire for sex. Oh how could she ever sleep! Perhaps if she could just give him a hug.

The bright day had turned warmer. The heavy stone of the Old Bailey glowed like billowing honeycomb. Around it swarmed the lunchtime escapees, some shading their eyes from the unexpected glare. A Whitbread cart pulled by four white shire horses passed by.

Mary saw dust and dandruff dance on David's black gown. 'You've forgotten to take off your gown!' she exclaimed, but kindly, for he had only forgotten because he was concentrating on her.

David swirled the black cloth off his shoulders. 'Ah, ha! Matador!' he cried.

To her surprise, Mary found she was smiling. David's hair was ruffled, his usually flat, pale face animated into more distinct features. She remembered this boyishness had been one of the things she liked most about him when they'd first met. It was the reverse side of the good responsible son, the silly little mother's boy. But for that reason, seeing it as part of his close relationship with his mother and nothing to do with her, it had also irritated her. Half unconsciously, she had made fun of him when he played or pounced – pinching her suddenly had been one of his favourite pastimes – until that side of his character had almost disappeared.

Yet now she saw it, on this spring lunchtime, reappearing with youthful energy, her spirits lifted. How perverse!

Other barristers passed them, their faces as pale as the stripe in their suits. Some nodded or waved at David but he, gown trailing over his shoulder, hardly noticed. Mary's attention was caught by an advertisement painted on the side of a passing taxi, 'Where do you think you're going, sunshine?' She turned to David and caught hold of his arm so that he came to a stop and faced her enquiringly.

CHAPTER EIGHTEEN

The heat was tremendous, a positive force of warmth that made Mary's limbs heavy in a ridiculous way. They were quite out of tune, too, with her head which felt light and airy and filled with energy. She could go anywhere, do anything, if her legs would carry her.

Emerging from Kennedy Airport, small suitcase in hand, she joined the queue for yellow taxis. The sky was striped, blue and yellow and navy. Blue for the day, brightest and best, yellow for the sun, receding now but leaving this unlikely heat, and navy for the night, pushing up from the horizon.

'Fifty-Six Street,' she said to the taxi driver, although he hardly seemed to care, 'the Hotel Metropolitan.'

Elizabeth's face was flushed with excitement. She was, just as she'd imagined, surrounded by loving friends who were making her the centre of attention. Bob, of course, was getting much the same treatment but, somehow, despite the beating of feminist wings for so many years, there was still something special about being a bride. She liked the pink champagne Bob had chosen and his suit and his best man who had flirted with her all through the ceremony. She knew the world was a serious place and she was a serious girl with years of study still ahead and then years and years of work but just today she felt as frivolous as the ruched cerise and gold curtains which adorned the windows of the Marie Antoinette Salon – for hire, by the day or by the hour. Catching Bob's eye over three over-lapping shoulders, she waved her hand, complete with its glitter of empty champagne glass.

'I hear you went to England?' It was the best man again, hardly serious.

'Oh, yes! It was desperate. I went to find my mother, my natural mother. At first she hated me and then when she started to come round and behave in, at least, a civilised manner, then her daughter got really mad. I can tell you it was a nightmare trip.'

'Did you expect better? What made you go?'

'Simple curiosity, I suppose, although I called it finding myself. So what did I get? A biff in the eye!' Elizabeth's voice was shrill. 'She's a cold woman turned right in on herself and he, her husband that is, is a terrible stuffed shirt. But I'll tell you something neat.' She must be drunk to be talking about England to this bridal Romeo. 'My English father came here on purpose to see me and he's terrific.'

'You mean you have a father as well?'

Elizabeth was pleased by his eye-stretching reaction. 'He's very good-looking and has a really lovely wife. They would have been here today except they're in court. Their son was killed, you see . . . ' Elizabeth stopped suddenly. Even in her anaesthetised state she could see that the murder of a boy was hardly appropriate smalltalk. Nevertheless she found herself laughing again as she said, 'To sum up, I went looking for a mother and found a father.'

Lucy buttoned up her shirt with a dazed expression on her face which was not due to the power of Jo's love-making.

'You mean you want me to go home with you?'

'Want? I wouldn't put it as strongly as that.' Jo, who was still in bed, turned his excellent profile sideways to the pillow.

But Lucy who'd recently identified a somewhat bulbous tip to his nose, wasn't to be put off. 'You said "want".' She jumped onto the bed and tickled him round his waist. 'You WANT me to go home with you, that's what you said.' Her voice was conquering, full of joy. But as she sat back on her haunches to survey her prey, she was forced to deal with a twinge of doubt. Would he be so Dostoevskian with the addition of parents?

Bob looked at Elizabeth glowing with life and joy and pink champagne and then looked at this Englishwoman arrived at the door. She too glowed, not a word he was generally over-keen on using. The truth was that they both glowed in the same frantic way.

'So you're Elizabeth's mother,' he said, playing for time in case she was planning to burst across the room and snatch Elizabeth from among the guests, which didn't seem fair or appropriate. Where, if it came to that, was the cold woman so repeatedly described by Elizabeth?

'I've only just arrived. I hope you don't mind.'

She seemed to be calming slightly. Bob dared to smile – really her tension was terrifying, although, mysteriously, her regular features retained a kind of blandness. 'It is a surprise. But you're welcome.' Suddenly he noticed she was standing at the sort of angle from which people usually fell over. 'Here. You'd better sit down.'

Mary sat, stiffly upright. 'I'm sorry. It's after midnight for me.'

'Are you sure you need to see her today?' Tomorrow they would be gone.

Mary didn't answer. She had travelled across the Atlantic, she had arrived at Elizabeth's wedding party, she had found her husband who, under peculiar circumstances, seemed sympathetic. But now her strength had left her. She could do no more than sit on this uncomfortable little gold chair and wait for Elizabeth. Perhaps she would never come.

'What?' Bob looked down anxiously at this stranger, this long-lost mother, this mother-in-law, who'd begun to mutter under her breath. Elizabeth had never suggested she was deranged. Or had she? There had been mention of screaming and shouting but in reference, he felt sure, to the daughter. 'I'll tell you what, I'll get you a glass of champagne. Pink,' he added persuasively as she made no response.

The room was so very crowded that from the little space by the door where Mary sat she could only see a whirl of backs. They were alien backs, with alien hair, alien clothes, alien voices and alien smells. I'm in America, she told herself disbelievingly.

'It's over!'

Where had Cherry found this new briskness? Richard watched unbelievingly as Cherry made them sandwiches and cups of coffee.

'I'll have a scotch actually.'

'You're right. I'll have one too.'

The ice cracked against the glass. They looked at each other. 'I always said he was mad.' Richard was not surprised by the strength of his own voice. It was as if this sentencing, this deliberate course of public justice in which they had played their part, had, against all his expectations, produced a right out of what had been altogether wrong.

He found himself knocking his glass against Cherry's as if in celebration. Her eyes were bright as he imagined his must be. It was hope, he supposed, something hopeful about their drinking scotch together in the kitchen.

David reached for his watch on the bedside table. Twenty past twelve. She'd be there now. It was strange that he didn't feel the usual pleasurable sense of freedom in her absence. Not that he didn't welcome her back, of course, anytime she went away which wasn't often. But tonight he felt uneasy, incapable of settling to sleep. Perhaps it was because she had gone so suddenly. Or perhaps because she had gone so far away, which was a ridiculous idea since absence is complete whatever the intervening space, whether two miles or two thousand. Or even two yards given an absentee state of mind. This was impossible, he'd never sleep. In which case he might as well read or play music or stand on his head. Feeling slightly hysterical in his unaccustomed inability to sleep – David seldom lost the key to unconsciousness – he removed himself from the scene of defeat and hurried to the kitchen where he made himself a large honey sandwich.

Elizabeth moved towards her husband. He had waved to her but there were so many people on the way. She had never felt so happy. When she was old and looked back on her life, she would see that this was where it all truly began.

'Oh darling, Bob!' She'd found him at last, run into his arms. She knew she was drunk because she was feeling a little dizzy and her eyes weren't focusing well but that didn't invalidate her real deep-seated emotion. Deep-seated emotions, she thought the words to herself and could hardly restrain herself from more laughter.

'There's another guest arrived,' Bob's serious voice only increased her exhilaration. She was glad he had a deep masculine tone. Deep masculine tone, she repeated these words to herself, too, with a satisfied expression.

'You should greet her,' said Bob.

'So late!' cried Elizabeth. 'All the speeches over and we'll be going soon.'

'She's been sitting down by the door,' Bob turned Elizabeth round and pointed her in the right direction.

'There's no one sitting there. There is a chair.' Elizabeth put her hand to her head. The dizziness was beginning to go to her stomach.

'She was there a moment ago.' Bob let go of Elizabeth who slipped sideways. She righted herself with the conscious effort of someone who feels herself on rolling seas.

'I think I'll go visit the Ladies Room.'

'She was here.'

'Perhaps she went to find herself a drink.'

Mary had lost her nerve. She peered at her reflection in the glazed mirror. She was comforted by its pinkness which gave her skin a warmth which couldn't be real. The whole room was bathed in an artificial glow, washing down from shell lights above each little dressing-table and mirror. In some ways it was like being inside a shell with the harsh light of the world muted through its skin.

Sitting on a velvet-covered stool, Mary opened her handbag and prepared for a long relaxing stay.

Elizabeth rolled gently towards the Ladies Room. She didn't know whether she was going to be sick or faint but when the corridor lights began to dim she realised it would be the latter.

Mary looked round in unwelcome surprise as the door to her nice pink womb burst open. She had foolishly not prepared herself for the advent of a stranger. But it was not a stranger. Elizabeth crashed through the door, squealed protestingly and crumpled gently to the floor.

Elizabeth opened her eyes. She was surrounded by whirling pink lights and the face of a strange woman repeated in front of her, on either side of her and in fact all around her, over and over again. She closed her eyes. But that wasn't very satisfactory either, causing a whole firework display to explode. Better brave the repeating woman.

'Who are you?'

The face, all hundreds of it, smiled. 'I'm Mary Tempest. Are you all right?'

'Yes. But I wish my head would stop whirling round.' So her mother had come to see her married. If only she could welcome her appropriately but it was no use. Much easier to let her put a cold flannel to her head and wait till she could see straight. 'Why are there so many of you?'

'It's the mirrors.'

So that was solved at least and in fact the action was slowing now so that she could see the pretty powder room.

'Do you often faint? I had a terrible job dragging you off the floor.'

'When I'm tired or excited or drink too much. This time it was all three.'

'It looked like a terrific party.'

'I'm so happy.'

'Thank you for inviting me.'

'I meant it truly.'

'That's why I came.'

'I'm glad.'

Now that she was well again, they had become stiff with each other like strangers. But it didn't matter. Her mother had come to her wedding and just down the corridor, Bob waited for her. 'Bob will be wondering.'

'Oh, yes. You must hurry back.'

'You too.'

'Shall I?'

'Of course you must come! You'll be the star attraction, after me, that is, and Bob. Everyone will want to meet you. Quick. Quick. Before too many people leave . . . '

Fully restored to her previous state of euphoria, Elizabeth thrust her arm through her mother's and propelled her forth from Ladies Room to festive salon.

David thought it must be about five in the morning since some light was just showing through the curtains.

206

'She was out cold, possibly dead, at my feet.' Mary's voice sounded wide awake.

'So what did you do?'

'Picked her up. Which wasn't as easy as it sounds. In fact I sort of dragged her.'

'Like a sack of coal.'

'Apparently she often faints.'

'She didn't when she was with us.'

'She had drunk a lot. Actually she was paralytic. A strange thing . . .'

As she paused David settled himself more comfortably and registered with a sense of relief that he had not slept because he was waiting for this telephone call.

'It is strange and a bit idiotic but I find this Elizabeth I've discovered in New York bears no relationship to the one who came to us in Somerset.'

'The would-be murderer, you mean.'

'Oh, David!' But she didn't mind him joking. It gave her a sensation of his closeness particularly agreeable given her isolation in the middle of a hotel in the middle of Manhattan. 'I heaved her into a chair and then she came round. Guess what she said?'

'Mother!'

'She said, "Who are you?" She didn't recognise me.'

'Aha. So you said "Mother!"'

'No, of course I didn't. I made a cold compress and held it on to her forehead while she put her head between her knees. She recovered remarkably quickly.'

'She's young,'

'Then we went back to the party in case Bob was worried.'

'Bob?'

'Her husband Bob. Eventually they left for Mexico. I might not come back.'

'Mary?'

'The beaches in the South are long and hot and sandy and the sky is always blue.'

Jo's mother stood at the sink. She was remarkably like her son, with the same noble profile and black hair, although its purplish glint was not altogether convincing.

'I'll dry,' offered Lucy, taking up a tea towel printed with the smiling face of Princess Diana.

'You mustn't spoil Mother.' Jo lounged at the door to the kitchen but his lounging was watchful rather than careless.

'No. You go off, both of you.' She was friendly and sensible, Jo's mother, nothing to be ashamed of.

Lucy sighed. She had always thought that falling out of love would be more painful than falling in love and now she was being proved right. So lowering, so debilitating. Like a death. She held the dishcloth towards Jo.

'No one tires of royalty.'

'That's because they keep their distance!'

Jo's mother twitched away the cloth in an almost flirtatious gesture and, screwing the pretty face into a puffy ball, she wiped it firmly across the draining-board.

Elizabeth and Bob were trying to explain to a foreign and unsympathetic concierge the problem with their hotel bedroom.

'We did specify a double bed.'

'You have double beds.'

'No. We have two beds, yes. But we want one bed.'

'But you say double bed.'

'One bed for two.'

'I not understand. You two are one?'

Elizabeth gripped Bob's elbow. He looked so hot and uncomfortable. 'Give up, dear. He'll never get it. He doesn't want to get it.'

'But it's our honeymoon!' It was a wail, a howl of distress. So unlike Bob, so sweetly unlike him.

The worse-than-uncaring concierge, who had turned away, spun round, a look of joyous understanding illuminating his face. 'Ah, honeymoon! You should say. Now I give you special bed with waves and mirrors,' here he chuckled encouragingly, 'and silk covers and low lighting and sea view so you can stay forever. Honeymooners we love here. In the dining-room there will be a spotlight especially for you and the band will play "Honeymooners at last return." You know the song? And everyone smile and be happy. As I now am very happy!'

Elizabeth and Bob, unwilling to see each other's expression, stared like frightened rabbits at his broad and lascivious smile.

Richard and Cherry sat in deck-chairs in their garden. Daniel, their son, lay half asleep on the grass. The only sound was a persistent blackbird protecting its young and the financial pages of the *Telegraph* manipulated expertly under Richard's fingers.

Mary lay flat on her stomach, her head sideways to the sand. Since the impossible sun shone from the other direction she could open her eyes for a second or two and see the multi-coloured grains and beyond that, far beyond but not as far as the sky which towered in a blue avalanche all round her, the sea. And in the sea David swam. Soon, she too would head for the water and a cool dousing before lunch. But now she lay prone, blotted out, smashed down, rolled over, as if the millions of sun's rays had merged together to form a giant iron which flattened her every twitch and crinkle, her every flaw and wrinkle.

David dipped up and down in the green waves. The water slid off his head and then his shoulders. In the morning he swam, renewing desk-bound muscles with holiday energy, but the waves were entering their thrusting afternoon cycle and he preferred to bob up and down like a child. Mary should join him in the water before it became too rough. Shading his eyes, he looked inland. But she was so languorously close to her sandy ironing-board that she had made herself invisible. He could only see her scarlet and white wrap which was attached to the parasol and beginning to twitch in the breeze.

Mary felt the hair on her head move as a coolness blew upwards from her heels. Time to move. Soon the dissolution of her limbs would be teased by the will of the wind and even the sun's strength would be shredded and made ineffectual.

'You're a coward.' David watched Mary stir the froth of the sea with her toes.

'I like being hot. I like sweat rolling out of every pore. I like my brain turning into a syrup. I like being blinded, deafened and rendered insensible by the sun.'

'You're crazy.' David looked at his wife and laughed indulgently. It was so long since they had taken a hot holiday.

'I'm going to slightly splash myself,' said Mary decisively.

Again David watched his wife with the kind of pleasure a parent gets from a loved child. She seemed so certain and yet also unconscious or uncaring of the impression she made. He remembered that was what he'd first admired about her. He had imagined himself laying his life at her feet and her staring over his body with cool detachment. His mother, with whom he had been so close, had given him the hint that women were special, not all women, but the women he loved and certainly the woman he married.

'I intend to make a thorough pig of myself at lunch,' he boasted.

The evening sky was nearly the same colour as the sea, only the merest gleam along the horizon marked the separation. Like Shakespeare's girdle round the earth, thought Mary, who walked hand in hand with David along the sand. There were no waves now and therefore no noise, except the soft flurry of their feet.

'One more day,' said David. He stopped and stared at the sea.

'You'll be glad to be back.'

It wasn't a question but David seemed to ponder it, eventually resolving it with a question himself. 'Will you be glad?'

'No. Not really.'

'Why not?'

'I like it here.'

'Why do you like it here?'

'I don't know.'

'Do you like being with me?'

'Yes.'

'But that's not it?'

'No.' Mary tried to think. 'I like doing nothing, being nowhere. I like the feeling of not existing. I get that a little here.'

'Why do you like not existing?'

'It's a relief. A relief from myself. You get it from work. A lot of men get the feeling from work, I think.' Mary stopped. It was so dark now that she could hardly see his face. She was tempted to continue with her thoughts out loud. She was thinking, The only time I completely lost the burden of myself and became happy was making love with Richard Beck, but she forced the idea to flip over like a red herring and disappear. She remained silent, and concentrated on the kindly warmth coming from David's hand. Even while she had been half dreaming in the dusk, they had been linked in this way, as naturally as two children. What was it Lucy had said?

'The Garden of Eden,' Mary murmured to herself.

'What?'

'Adam and Eve walked hand in hand in the Garden of Eden. They were completely happy, passionately in love, comfortably in love.'

'I don't understand.'

'But the serpent came along and they were tempted and they succumbed and they were ashamed and they needed their hands to hold on their fig leaves. And then, worse still, they were chucked out. So they weren't happy anymore.' Mary let go of David's hand and walked to the very edge of the sea.

David followed her good-temperedly. 'And ever since we've been trying to get back in. That's what you mean, don't you?'

'But of course it's impossible. We can't find their sort of love now.'

'Absolutely not.' David spoke light-heartedly for he was glad to have read her thoughts. 'But it doesn't stop people trying.' He thought of Veronica with the slight ache of sexual nostalgia.

'How far away is that star?' Mary looked up to where the first star had just appeared low over the horizon.

'Only British Rail porters can answer questions like that. Adam and Eve, though doubtless an exemplary couple in all ways but one, didn't have to stand up in court, nor face difficult and unknown stepdaughters.'

'No.' Mary kept her eyes fixed on the star. 'Nor even not very difficult daughters. All in all, it's quite a challenge to imagine what Adam and Eve did with their time. Perhaps they suffered from acute boredom.' Suddenly smiling, she whisked round to David and gripped his arm. 'Remind me now and again, particularly if you see me sucking cream behind fridge doors, that paradise is as far away as the first star of the evening.'

'If it exists at all.' David put his free arm round Mary's waist.

'Oh, yes. It exists.' Mary pulled back a little, although without leaving the encircling arm. 'That's the whole point. That's what lies beyond. Just out of reach. Our mistake is believing we can ever reach it through any kind of human love.'

'You've always been a romantic. Now close your eyes and see what a little ordinary human love does for you.'

Obediently, Mary brought her face closer to David's but still she couldn't resist murmuring, 'Romantic yearnings, immortal longings . . .'

'Shut up.'

He was right. In the end words were not much use either.

FOR THE BEST IN PAPERBACKS, LOOK FOR THE

In every corner of the world, on every subject under the sun, Penguin represents quality and variety – the very best in publishing today.

For complete information about books available from Penguin – including Pelicans, Puffins, Peregrines and Penguin Classics – and how to order them, write to us at the appropriate address below. Please note that for copyright reasons the selection of books varies from country to country.

In the United Kingdom: Please write to *Dept E.P., Penguin Books Ltd, Harmondsworth, Middlesex, UB7 0DA*

In the United States: Please write to *Dept BA, Penguin, 299 Murray Hill Parkway, East Rutherford, New Jersey 07073*

In Canada: Please write to *Penguin Books Canada Ltd, 2801 John Street, Markham, Ontario L3R 1B4*

In Australia: Please write to the *Marketing Department, Penguin Books Australia Ltd, P.O. Box 257, Ringwood, Victoria 3134*

In New Zealand: Please write to the *Marketing Department, Penguin Books (NZ) Ltd, Private Bag, Takapuna, Auckland 9*

In India: Please write to *Penguin Overseas Ltd, 706 Eros Apartments, 56 Nehru Place, New Delhi, 110019*

In Holland: Please write to *Penguin Books Nederland B.V., Postbus 195, NL–1380AD Weesp, Netherlands*

In Germany: Please write to *Penguin Books Ltd, Friedrichstrasse 10–12, D–6000 Frankfurt Main 1, Federal Republic of Germany*

In Spain: Please write to *Longman Penguin España, Calle San Nicolas 15, E–28013 Madrid, Spain*

In France: Please write to *Penguin Books Ltd, 39 Rue de Montmorency, F-75003, Paris, France*

In Japan: Please write to *Longman Penguin Japan Co Ltd, Yamaguchi Building, 2–12–9 Kanda Jimbocho, Chiyoda-Ku, Tokyo 101, Japan*

A CHOICE OF PENGUIN FICTION

Stanley and the Women Kingsley Amis

Just when Stanley Duke thinks it safe to sink into middle age, his son goes insane – and Stanley finds himself beset on all sides by women, each of whom seems to have an intimate acquaintance with madness. 'Very good, very powerful . . . beautifully written' – Anthony Burgess in the *Observer*

The Girls of Slender Means Muriel Spark

A world and a war are winding up with a bang, and in what is left of London, all the nice people are poor – and about to discover how different the new world will be. 'Britain's finest post-war novelist' – *The Times*

Him with His Foot in His Mouth Saul Bellow

A collection of first-class short stories. 'If there is a better living writer of fiction, I'd very much like to know who he or she is' – *The Times*

Mother's Helper Maureen Freely

A superbly biting and breathtakingly fluent attack on certain libertarian views, blending laughter, delight, rage and amazement, this is a novel you won't forget. 'A winner' – *The Times Literary Supplement*

Decline and Fall Evelyn Waugh

A comic yet curiously touching account of an innocent plunged into the sham, brittle world of high society. Evelyn Waugh's first novel brought him immediate public acclaim and is still a classic of its kind.

Stars and Bars William Boyd

Well-dressed, quite handsome, unfailingly polite and charming, who would guess that Henderson Dores, the innocent Englishman abroad in wicked America, has a guilty secret? 'Without doubt his best book so far . . . made me laugh out loud' – *The Times*

A CHOICE OF PENGUIN FICTION

The Dearest and the Best   Leslie Thomas

In the spring of 1940 the spectre of war turned into grim reality – and for all the inhabitants of the historic villages of the New Forest it was the beginning of the most bizarre, funny and tragic episode of their lives. 'Excellent' – *Sunday Times*

Only Children   Alison Lurie

When the Hubbards and the Zimmerns go to visit Anna on her idyllic farm, it becomes increasingly difficult to tell which are the adults, and which the children. 'It demands to be read' – *Financial Times* 'There quite simply is no better living writer' – John Braine

My Family and Other Animals   Gerald Durrell

Gerald Durrell's wonderfully comic account of his childhood years on Corfu and his development as a naturalist and zoologist is a true delight. Soaked in Greek sunshine, it is a 'bewitching book' – *Sunday Times*

Getting it Right   Elizabeth Jane Howard

A hairdresser in the West End, Gavin is sensitive, shy, into the arts, prone to spots and, at thirty-one, a virgin. He's a classic late developer – and maybe it's getting too late to develop at all? 'Crammed with incidental pleasures . . . sometimes sad but more frequently hilarious . . . *Getting it Right* gets it, comically, right' – Paul Bailey in the *London Standard*

The Vivisector   Patrick White

In this prodigious novel about the life and death of a great painter, Patrick White, winner of the Nobel Prize for Literature, illuminates creative experience with unique truthfulness. 'One of the most interesting and absorbing novelists writing English today' – Angus Wilson in the *Observer*

The Echoing Grove   Rosamund Lehmann

'No English writer has told of the pains of women in love more truly or more movingly than Rosamund Lehmann' – Marghanita Laski. 'She uses words with the enjoyment and mastery with which Renoir used paint' – Rebecca West in the *Sunday Times* 'A magnificent achievement' – John Connell in the *Evening News*

BY THE SAME AUTHOR

Occasion of Sin

Rachel Billington's tender and passionate novel encapsulates the life of contemporary woman . . .

'Brilliantly charted, set down with freshness, conviction and psychological truth' – *Daily Telegraph*

'Marvellous . . . How could you resist such a novel' – *Punch*

'Irony, tenderness and wit . . . a considerable imaginative achievement' – *Financial Times*

A Woman's Age

'Through four generations, from the glittering Edwardian age to our own make-shift times . . . Rachel Billington is first rate' – *Daily Telegraph*

'It kept me utterly content through two long evenings and what greater recommendation can there be?' – Margaret Forster

'An infinite variety of human knots fasten down this large family saga that spans four generations . . . Billington handles it with assurance, ease, warmth and wit' – *Newsweek*

The Garish Day

Men envy him, women desire him, rich, handsome and talented, Henry is destined for success . . .

Spanning four decades of history and as many continents, alive with finely created characters and dramatic incidents, this subtle and richly textured novel of personal and world crisis is Rachel Billington in superb form.

'Rachel Billington's marvellously readable novel . . . is a real treat. Telling insight and poker-faced humour' – *Daily Mail*